Dark Veng
Autho
Bongani M
   Characters by
Bongani Mpanza
   Creative concept
Bongani Mpanza

Dark Vengeance

Bongani Mpanza

Published by Bongani Mpanza, 2024.

This is a work of fiction. Similarities to real people, places, or events are entirely coincidental.

DARK VENGEANCE

First edition. June 11, 2024.

Copyright © 2024 Bongani Mpanza.

ISBN: 979-8227899941

Written by Bongani Mpanza.

Table of Contents

Dark Vengeance 1
Chapter 1 6
Chapter 2 12
Chapter 3 23
Chapter 4 32
Chapter 5 40
Chapter 6 48
Chapter 7 61
Chapter 8 77
Chapter 9 91
Chapter 10 110
Chapter 11 130
Chapter 12 147
Chapter 13 163
Chapter 14 179
Chapter 15 196
Chapter 16 204

Thanks And Dedications

First of all I would to start by saying this is without probably one of my favorite works considering the amount of emotions I have had to pour in to it at a time when I was going through a loss of a loved one. I believe I was able to transform some of the emotions I was feeling at the time into positive energy that would allow me to bring these characters to life.

A huge dedication to my late sister Nomusa Mpanza who would be so proud of me for overcoming my fears and doubts and fully embracing my passion for writing.

I also dedicate this book to every man who is standing up and taking the responsibility to lead their families and communities. Also to the women, the queens who against all odds play a huge role in nurturing communities that will ultimately become great nations.

Special Thanks to:

My siblings for always being supportive of my work, you guys are a special bunch. I love you.

To al my friends and relatives who are my biggest fans, till the next one guys.

Other work

The Taxi Boss
A government black ops agent must infiltrate the dangerous taxi industry in order to stop an arms deal and a possible terror attack

Triangle
Friends must find a way back to each other when secrets threaten to tear them apart

The Dark World
A family man's life is turned upside down when a mysterious man shows up at his office with a business offer.

Blurred Lines
Love must find a way when a couple in a interracial relationship face opposition from family and friends

Alpha
A young business woman must prove herself to colleagues and even family members that she is worthy to sit on the throne of a family business empire.

Nominated
A young woman dealing with loss finds comfort in one thing she loves than anything- music

Triangle 2: Old Habits Die Hard
Friends are back and once again they must each deal with skeletons of the past that link them together.

Upcoming work

Awkward
Two strangers meet at the airport and immediately strike a chemistry, little did they know they are more connected they thought.

Timeless
High school sweethearts who lose contact find each other again 20 years later. They discover that a lot has changed in their lives but can they rekindle their chemistry?

Wet24

After 24 hours of devastating floods, families in the communities must try and rebuild their houses again but also try to revive the concept of Ubuntu

Ghost town

After a virus wipes out the city; turning it into a ghost town; woman and her child must try to survive by fighting whatever and whoever is out there.

Dark Vengeance
Premise

A man who comes back home after 12 years since he disappeared learns of a traumatic experience that his sister went through and now he is back to inflict vengeance to those responsible while taking on a drug lord whose daughter he's fallen in love with.

Dark Vengeance

Chapter 1

Prodigal Son

"Uhmm...I don't know if this is a joyous or sad occasion mfanawami(my son)...it's bitter-sweet I guess..." Dora Gumede says with a low voice, wearing a sad face as she sits in a lounge with his son Ntokozo on a Sunday afternoon. "Yeah I know mama, uhmm...I'm struggling myself how to describe this very moment..."Ntokozo says but he doesn't finish as Dora cuts in, "But you have been gone for 12 years Ntokozo...12 years." she says with a shaking voice as tears threaten to flood her cheeks. "You didn't even come back when your father passed on 2 years ago. What about your sister Lungile? Do you know what she has been through all these years you weren't here?"

This question suddenly makes Ntokozo feel so bad as he struggles to look at his sad mother in the eyes. The mood in the room has suddenly become heavy as both mother and son don;t seem tp know what to say to each other next.

Dora Gumede is a recently widowed 63 year-old woman living in the suburbs of Umlazi section BB, in this rather huge mention with her dauther Lungile who has a 12 year-old daughter. The Gumedes are a well known family in this community as Dora's late husband Bongani was a businessman who often gave locals opportunities to make something of themselves. He was also well respected throughout the City of Durban and the surroundings because his businesses which included patrol guarages and supermarkets were spread across the City. He was also thought to be well politically-connected judging from guests who'd usually attend events that he hosted.

Dora now runs her late husband's businesses but has every intention of handing over the reigns to her daughter Lungile when she retires at the age of 65. She has been described by many as very elagent even in her 60s now because of her taste and style in almost everything. While she may not be much into politics like her late husband, she is well respected by her business peers in the City. Lungile also works in the family business and she doesn't seem to have time for anything else besides being in the office which is in this house's basement. She is in a not so clear relationship with Thulani, owing to her distrust of men after having gone through worst relationship experiences over the years. Her daughter Mbali, who is 12 years old, is her treasure and she would go to hell and back for her.

Ntokozo, a 37 year-old first born of Dora and Bongani Gumede left home about 12 years ago when he was just 25, much to his family's confusion. He is not a person who talks too much, which only makes his life even more mysterious. No one knows anything about him or his life in the last 12 years and he is good at keeping a straight face, so he is hard to read. The neighbourhood has changed so much from the time he left he doubts he will even recognize some of the people who live in the area.

"Your sister has been through a lot the past few years and you weren't there to protect her Ntokozo...how do you think I should feel, huh?" a sad-looking Dora asks as she wipes her tears. "How do you think Lungile will feel, seeing you for the first time after 12 years Ntokozo? Don't you think that will open the old wounds that were actually beginning to heal? You left without saying goodbye or why you were leaving. The only person who was on your corner...who tried to justify what you did was your father, and you didn't attend his funeral. How do you really expect me and your sister to feel when you just show up like this Ntokozo? And your niece? You have never met her and she is almost a teenager now" Ntokozo just doesn't know how to respond to this as he looks down as though he is thinking about something. "What happened to

Lungile mama?" he asks as he looks embarrassed and ashamed by his question but his mother cuts in sharply, "No, no, no Ntokozo...you don't get to ask that question now, okay? Where were you then? What difference does it make now to know, huh?" she asks as she raises her voice but Ntokozo lifts his head and looks at his mother. When Dora sees that her son won't let this go she takes a deep sigh and thinks for a second before saying, "Your sister went through trauma of rape..." with a low voice as she looks down in sadness which almost sends Ntokozo tmbling the floor in shock. This is not what he was expecting his mother would say. He would have handled anything else like failing a module or losing a job or anything like that, but this? This is too much for him as feeling of guilt suddenly falls on him like a huge brick. *Jesus, did I allow that to happen to my little sister?* he asks himself as his eyes turn red with rage and his palms become sweaty.

When his mother notices that she shakes her head in sadness and says, "Yeah uhmm...the first incident happened when she and her friends celebrated writing the last paper of the matric exams..." but Ntokozo quickly cuts in, "the first? You mean there's been more than one?" he asks as his eyes pop out in shock. There's visible rage beginning to build inside him as his eyes turn red.

A relunctant Dora looks at his son and sees a look that is scaring her, but she takes a deep sigh before saying, "Uhmm yeah, it actually happened a few times...I don't know, it's like the first incident became a curse." She starts to looking all sad as she drops her head, which makes Ntokozo feel just as bad seeing his mother like that.

When he attempts to say something, Dora interjects, "The first incidence led to her falling pregnant..." she says with a low voice as she lifts her head to look at Ntokozo. "That boy who was her schoolmate dissappeared and Lungile never saw him again, so she is raising the child alone.

"The second incident happened when she was in tertiary and again it was a a fellow student with rich parents. The court said there was no suffecient evidence to find the boy guilty but we all know that money had somethinmg to do with that. The last incident happened few months before your father passed away and I really believe that this was one the reasons that added to your father's stress resulting in his heart attack. It was becoming increasingly hard for him to watch his daughter suffer like this because Lungile went through depression because it was now the 3rd rape incident. She started hating herself because she thought she probably was the problem or the cause of all this.

"Psyologists didn't help that much. It's only now that she is getting better and trying to be strong for her daughter but she is still a long way off from being okay because she has no closure. It really pains me to see my daughter like this so I decided that in 2 year's time I will hand over the reigns to her, to run the family busines. Maybe that will help her fous on something else because she will be building inheritance for her daughter."

Listening to his mother relaying the painful experiences that his sister had to go through, Ntokozo is suddenly filled with guilt and shame as he looks away from Dora. His mind is racing as though he is thinking about something. "But mama, I don't understand...dad was a well connected individual, how did all these people get away with this disgsting crime? How?" he asks as he raises his eyebrow but that seems to irritate his mother who interjects, "Hey, hey, hey...you don't get to ask that question okay?" she says as she raises her voice a little bit. "You yourself weren't here to protect your sister, alright? So nothing gives you the right to act like you care"

That last part seems to have cut really deep into Ntokozo's heart as he struggles to respond to that. But this tense moment is interrupted by someone coming through the door. It's little sister Lungile who almost drops her bag as she sees who is sitting in the lounge couch. Well, if Ntokozo thought he was going to catch a break from his mom he was wrong, as tension starts to build to a new whole level.

Well, Ntokozo can't say he didn't expect this from his sister as he stands up to welcome his Lungile with a hug but its a bad call as he is greeted with a hot clap across the face. "What the hell are you doing here, you bastard?" Lungile asks as her eyes immediately turn red with rage but Dora quickly stands up to go stand between the two siblings, "Whoa, whoa, whoa bantabami yimani(my children, hold on) let's not do this right now okay?" she pleads as panic is written in her face but Lungile quickly interjects, "No mama why should we wait huh?" she shouts as she breathes heavily while she looks at heer brother in the eyes.

Ntokozo must have expected all this anger from her sister after hearing what she had to go through in his absence. "Its okay mama, I deserve that..." he says as he holds her sore cheek. "No, you desreve more than that, so why don't you go back to the dead and stay there because you are not wanted here Ntozko, okay? Just get the hell out" the furious Lungile shouts as she points at the door.

"Lungile mntanami(my child), please can we talk about this?" Dora says with a begging voice and a sad face but her daughter cuts in sharply, "No mama, there's nothing to talk about okay?" she shouts while looking at his brother. "This one is not welcomed here. We are doing just fine without him so he should just go back to where he came from...we don't need him here mama."

"Uhmm...she is right mama, I shouldn't be here..." Ntokozo says with a low and sad voice but his siser quickly interjects, "You are damn right, you shouldn't have...how dare you show your face here after all these years and expect us to be okay with it..." she shouts but Ntzokozo cuts in, "I'm not expecting you guys to be okay with..." he says but doesn't finish as his mother also cuts in, "Wait bantabami(my children)...can we just take a second to breathe here okay? Can we talk about this like adults? I beg you guys..." she says as her eyes begin to be teary but Lungile once again jumps in, "Time for talk was 12 years ago mama okay?" she says as she breathes heavily. "Now if you want to stay here with your son fine but I'm leaving then..."

"Oh baby, come on...please don't say something like that okay? I beg you darling..." Dora says with a beging voice as she wipes a tear but Lungile ignores as she storms out of the loung heading upstairs to her room. But she then turns and says, "You...you better not be here when I come back, you hear me? I'm going out to see my friends and you better be gone by the time I'm back..." she quickly climbs the stairs leaving her shocked mother and brother in the lounge lost for words.

Chapter 2

A known stranger

After yesterday's afternoon drama Ntokozo doesn't seem to know what to do with himself as he sits in the lounge on a Monday morning watching news. When his sister asked hm to leave yesterday he was ready to do just that but Dora begged him to stay and not leave. She promised to speak to Lungile about this so that they sit down as a family and talk things through. The last thing Ntokozo wanted was causing tensions between his mother and his sister but there's no turning back now as they will have to face each other at some point.

Luckily for Ntokozo, his room has never been used by anyone since he left home 12 years ago and it brings so many memories for him when he looks at the pictures on the walls. It feels just like yesterday when he sat in that bed and listened to music on his headphones. He remembers many conversations he has had in that very room upstairs with her parents, and even his little sister and it brings a little smile on his face.

As he sits in the lounge looking at all the pictures on the walls he realises that nothing much has really changed in this house. There are pictures of him and Lungile; some pictures of his parents and some pictures are of the four of them in happy times and it warms his heart. But part of him is also sad as he realises that he has been gone for such a long time that he has missed a lot. Another part of him feels so guilty for having abandoned his family without giving any explanation, especially is little since who has had to go through a lot in the past few years. He doesn't know how to explain everything to her and his mother.

While sitting there and watching TV he sees his sister Lungile coming down the stairs. She is dressed for work with blue jeans, white shirt and high heels. She looks a little hungover though as she wears sun glasses. *'She must have come back late last night because I didn't hear her coming in',* he thinks to himself as he stands up to walk away because he thought, *'perhaps it's better if I got out of her way because the last thing I want is fight with her'*

"Oh no please...you don't have to leave on my account, I'm off to work anyways..." Lungile says with a straight face. "Uhmm...look I think it'se better that I give you space and uhmm...I'm sorry that uhmm...I know that you said I should leave but mama thought that..." a nervous looking Ntokozo says as he looks down but his sister cuts in, "Look, this is your home too, I can't expect you to sleep on the streets when you have a home. Yesterday I was angry and frustrated." she says with low voice as she also looks down but Ntokozo interjects, "Yes I know sisi and I just want to say I'm sorry for not..." he says but he doesn't finish as his sister cuts in, "Oh no...we are not at apologies yet Ntokozo okay?" she shouts as she motions with her hand. "I don't even know what you are apologizing for so don't act like you and I are suddenly best buddies, as if things are okay between us..."

"Look, mama told me about what happened to you okay?" Ntokozo says with a calm voice. "I know that it must have been..." he doesn't finish as his furious and emotional sister cuts in, "That's the thing okay? You don't know sh*t..." she shouts. "You have no idea what I have been through okay, so stop pretending that you know or you care..."

Ntokozo is suddenly filled with guilt as he looks down in shame, "Uhmm yes...you are right, I don't know okay?" he says politely as he takes a deep sigh. "But mama told me about what happened to you sisi...what happened to those men, that...you uhmm...you know..." he stutters as he looks embarrassed but an irritated Lungile cuts in, "Why does it matter Ntokozo, huh?" she shouts. "You weren't here to protect me against those monsters when I needed you the most.

Knowing what happened to them or where they are...what good will that do now? So suddenly you are tough guy when you ran away from home and went God knows where?"
This leads to a little awkward silence as Ntokozo doesn't want to escalate the situation any further. He needs to think carefully about what to say next because it may just trigure his sister. "Look sisi...I wish I could explain some of the things to you but..." he says as he lifts his head to look at Lungile who cuts in, "But what Ntokozo? Huh? What is that you can't talk about? Do you know that mom and I actually thought you were dead?" she shouts. "We never understood why you just took off like that without saying a word to us and now you come back and what...we must just accept?" Ntokozo takes a second to think but, as he is about to say something his sister interjects, "Look, I got to go to work okay?" she says as she throws her hands in the air and storming out of the house in a rage.

***

Later on in the day as Ntokozo sits in the lounge balcony over-looking the street where people are walking up and down and little kids playing football, he notices a farmiliar face. *Geez, is that Sthembiso?* he thinks to himself as he stands up and putting the newpaper he was reading down. He makes a whistle down to the street to a guy who looks up and smile in surprise. Ntokozo quickly goes down and out the gate to greet the guy. "Hey Sthe man...Oh my God...how are you?" he says with a huge smile as he greets the guy with a hug. "Oh my God man...Ntokozo, I almost didn't recognize you man, how long has it been man?" Sthembiso says as he hugs Ntokozo back.
"Uhmm geez I don't know man...it must be 14, 15 years, give or take?" Ntokozo says as they break the hug. Clearly this is the person he is really excited to see, even though he looks a little uncomfortable being in the streets where there is a lot of people

moving up and down. He keeps looking around to see if he can recognize any of them, but he doesn't.
"Hey man...where have you been and when did you come back?" Sthembiso asks as he still looks to be in disbelief. "Arg man, I've been away for a little while man I only got back yesterday afternoon..." Ntokozo says as he pulls away from eye contact but Sthembiso interjects, "Yeah man I remember that I used to come by your house to look for you but your dad would say that you weren't home..." he says with a curious face and continues, "Speaking of which man...I was sorry about your dad man...I actually thought I'd see you then you know...at the funeral, but you weren't there bro..." Suddenly this comment threatens to make this reunion tense a little bit as Ntokozo looks at his highschool friend. "Yeah man, I was overseas when it happened but on the eve of the funeral the weather that side was so bad that they grounded all flights so I couldn't attend. It really devastated me man..." he says as looks down again but Sthembiso, not wanting to bring up old wounds tabs Ntokozo on the shoulder and says, "It's okay man...I hope your mom told you it was a beautiful send off for the old man. Remember he was really loved by the community. The Gumede's are very famous here and I'm sure all the girls will be happy to know that Ntokozo Gumede is back, hahaha..."
Ntokozo blushes but wants to dismiss this joke from his longtime friend by saying, "speaking of which man...Uhmm...how was my sister's matric dance? You know, I had actually promised to take her but out of the blue a job offer came and I couldn't honor that promise." with a low voice as he looks down but it looks like Sthembiso is uncomfortable with the question as he raises an eyebrow at his friend. "Arg man, you know...I'm not sure how that went or if your sister even went to the matric dance after what happened" he says as he also looks down as though he is embarrassed by discussing this.

"What happened?" Ntokozo asks as though he has no idea what his friend is talking about but Sthembiso quickly interjects, "Oh come on man...weren't you even calling home when you were away? Come on bro I'm sure your mom must have told you about what happened to your sister back in highschool. I don't think it's my place talk about it...especially not after 15 years since I last saw you"
This makes Ntokozo think for a second before talking a deep sigh. "Look man...ofcourse she told me but not in so much details..." he says with a low voice. "What do you know? Who is the kid that dared to put his hands on my little sister?" Suddenly his face changes to being serious, in a way that makes Sthembiso raise an eyebrow as he wonders if this is the conversation to have with a friend you haven't seen n a very long time. He thinks for a second as he looks at Ntokozo in the eyes. "Look man, that guy is not a kid anymore. He is probably your sister's age now and is from a very rich family. Lungisani Mbhele was his name I think but I'm not sure where he and his family live now...probably Umhlanga or something. Why do you ask?"
"Nah man...I just need to understand why he got away with this. How come he was never punished for his crime..." Ntokozo says calmly but Sthembiso interjects, "Probably because his family is rich man..." he says as he shrugs his shoulders. "You know how these families always get away with everything...this country is a crime scene."
"Well, I want to re-open the case..." Ntokozo says as he looks around the people who pass by but Sthembiso quickly cuts in, "Really? Is that what your sister want too?" he asks curiously, which makes Ntokozo think for a second before saying, "Uhmm...I still have to talk to her about that man but this can't just be the end of it." He suddenly looks enraged by this but Sthembiso once again interjects, "Don't you think uhmm...this may open old wounds for your sister and your mother bro? Is she not trying to heal from all this man? I

thinking even talking about this with her may just trigger mfwethu(brother)"
Ntokozo listens to his friend attentively but doesn't respond to it but instead shrugs his shoulders. Sthembiso, wanting to change this sensitive subject says, "Come on to my house bro and lets have a beer so that you will tell me all about your travelling and all the bad stuff you have been up to okay? Hahaha..." They walk down the road to Sthembiso's home.

***

Meanwhile, Lungile is having dinner at a restaurent with her boyfriend of one year Thulani Zulu. The two actually met over two years ago after Lungile's rape incident where she had to see a doctor at the hospital. Things really didn't start that well between them, which wasn't surprising because Lungile had just gone through a very traumatic experience and she dispised men at that point. Thulani is the doctor who was attending to her and he is the one who reffered her to a psycologist whose office was based in the same hospital. Over time the two began to talk and eventually became friends. Over the past year they decided to give love a chance as Lungile was slowly learning to trust a man again.
In the beginning Lungile's mother Dora didn't approve of the relationship because she feared for her daughter, understandably so. It was hard for her to watch what Lungile had to go through since she turned 18 and all she wanted to to protect her from me, especially now that her father had passed on. All she wanted was for her daughter to be safe so she didn't want men around her, but after seeing how Thulani makes her daughter happy she began to slowly warm up to him.
35 year-old Thulani is a very quiet man who is very patient and understanding with Lungile's sometimes short temperedness amd easily triggered mind. He knows that it will take a little while for her

to fully trust men after what she has been through. Luckily for Thulani, Lungile's daughter Mbali likes him and sees him as a father figure and someone from whom she can get advice. He is not really a glamorous individual but does everything to make time for Lungile and her daughter as much as he can.

"So uhmm...your mom has changed her mind about dinner tonight? Because I thought I was coming over to your house..." Thulani asks curiously as he sits across his girlfriend Lungile who is not really dressed up for what was meant to be a romanetic dinner. She didn't even go back home to change after work. She's still in her blue jeans and white shirt while Thulani is in a dark blue suit looking all clean. Lungile takes a second to think before saying, "Uhmm...no babe, it's not her. It was my idea that we come here instead of being a home..." with a rather sad voice as she looks at her boyfriend.

"Is everything okay baby?" Thulani asks as he raises an eyebrow. Once again Lungile thinks for a second before saying, "Uhmm...not really babe..." as she takes a deep sigh. "Do you remember my brother I told you about? Yeah so uhmm...he showed up yesterday afternoon unexpectedly, so I just didn't want to ruin our dinner plans. I figured it would be better if we were away from the house you know..."

Oh my God...Wow...so uhmm...did he say where he was? I mean, did you guys speak?" a shocked Thulani asks in disbelief. "Uhmm...we spoke a little this morning when I was going to work but you know uhmm...it really wasn't a good conversation, and no, he hasn't said much of anything about where he's been or doing what. So that atmosphere would have made things awkward so I'm sorry that we had to cancel on those plans babe, but I promise that once everything comes back to normal we will." a downcast Lungile says as she takes a sip of her dry red wine. She looks a little embarrassed by all this.

"Oh no sweetheart you don't have to apologies okay? I understand completely baby okay?" Thulani says as he reaches across the table to take his girlfriend's hand. "So uhmm...did you guys get a chance to talk about, uhmm...you know...what you have been through the past few years? And what did he have to say about that?"
"I think he and mom spoke about it yesterday and he tried to speak about it this morning but it's infuriates me that he thinks he can come back after 12 years and ask me aboiut this as if he cared..." Lungile says as she takes another sip of her glass. Clearly this is making her very upset. "I just walked out of the house because I can't even look at him right now" she says as she looks around the table to see if anyone is listening in on their conversation. "Uhmm...but you know...at some point baby you guys will have to talk okay? And find out the whole truth...to understand why he left the way he did." Thulani says politely as he is trying to be careful about what to say about this whole thing.
"Yeah I know that baby okay? But right now things have been coming okay in the house so him returning is just opening up old wounds and I just can't deal with it at the moment, you know..." Lungile says with a low and sad voice. "Yeah honey, I understand okay? It's gonna be alright, I'm here for you baby all the step of the okay?"
Lungile doesn't say anything but just smiles at her boyfriend for those comforting words. "Okay enough about that okay? Let's just order a meal and then maybe we can go for a later movie, if you are up for it..." Thulani says with a smile, which seems to brighton Lungile's eyes as she smiles at the idea.

***

Back in the Gumede mansion Ntokozo is back from spending a little time with his highschool friend Sthembiso. He is sitting in the lounge with his mother and niece Mbali. While Dora still struggles to believe that her son is really back home part of her is relunctant, perhaps because she still doesn't know what happened to him or why he decided to come back home after 12 years. One thing she knows though is that Ntokozo is her only son and it really hurt her when he left without saying anything and some point she had to concede to the possibility that he could be dead.

"So uhmm...did you talk to your sister?" Dora asks his son as they sit in the dinning room while young Mbali is sitting in the lounge watching TV. Ntokozo thinks for a second before saying, "Uhmm...I wouldn't really call it a talk mama..." with a ow voice as he looks down. "But I don't blame Lungile for being angry with me...I don't blame you for being angry mama. What I did...What I did was wrong...I should have been considerate"

"Look, it's not even about you leaving home Ntokozo...you were 25, old enough to make your own decisions..." Dora says with a low and sad voice. "But it's how you left home that broke our hearts and worse was you not even coming back when your father passed away. That is why we assumed that you may have died as well. So will you ever tell us why why you left, where were you or what have you been doing all these years? I mean, don't you think me and your sister deserve that atleast?" She suddenly becomes very sad as she looks into her sons eyes but Ntokozo is filled with guilt as he looks down in shame.

"Look mama...time for that is coming okay?" he says with a low voice as he lifts his head. "But right now I'd like us to talk about what what happened to Lungile mama and how we can make things right. It's hard for me to accept that all these boys were never arrested for what they did to my sister, it just can't be mama..."

This seems to upset Dora as she throws her hands in the air before saying, "Oh no, not that again Ntokozo...what else must we do huh? What else must we do? I told you that in all three of those cases the police didn't find evidence. Oh no wait uhmm...the last incident

that happened over two years ago the docket dissapeared at the police station. The incident that happened when Lungile was in UKZN the police said there was not enough evidence to make an arrest. The very first incident when she was 18 never was ever followed up by the police. They kept saying they were investigating. So tell me, what do you want us to do Ntokozo?"
"Well, look mama...I think we should re-visit the cases okay? This isn't fair..." Ntokozo says but doesn't finish as his mother cuts, "So you see why you should have been here for your sister? What good will all this do now, huh?" she asks as she looks really upset. It is as though this is opening wounds for her as well, just as it would for her daughter Lungile.
Ntokozo keeps quiet as he thinks about what to say but his mother picks up her phone and scrolls down. "Here, maybe you can try and call this detective...he was the one who was leading the investibation on the last incident two years ago." she says as she gives Ntokozo her phone. Ntokozo takes his mother's phone and looks at the number and the name of the police officer. He decides to save it on his phone before giving his mother her phone back. Suddenly he has this look on his face that suggests he is thinking about something. "But I'm telling you Ntokozo, this is not a good idea..." Dora says as she takes her son's plate together with hers. "Or atleast speak to your sister about this first before re-openning the cases. "She is still struggling to accept that you have come back, how do you think she will feel if you immediately interfere with her life?" She takes the plates to the kitchen while Ntokozo decides to go out to the balcony and closes the glass sliding door behind him.
He looks at his phone as scrolls through the contacts and makes a call.
Man: "Hallo"
Ntokozo: "Hey it's me, can you talk?"
Man: "Yeah sure, what's up man?"

Ntokozo: "Look, I need you to find someone for me very fast..."
Man: "Very easy...who?"
Ntokozo: "I will send you the details in a moment. But man, I need details on him...his where about, his schedules, friends and family and all the works okay?"
Man: "Yeah man that shouldn't be a problem at all, just send me the particulars..."
Ntokozo: "And man...I really need this ASAP, like in a day or two bro...5 days at most"
Man: "Uhmm...that's gonna be tight man considering you want his day to day schedule as well, but I will see what I can do"
Ntokozo: "Thanks man, I will send you his particulars now..."
Call dropped

Chapter 3

Keep your eyes opened

After 5 days since Ntokozo came back home after 12 years of being away things between him and his sister are still very much rocky. Lungile doesn't seem to want to be anywhere near her brother as she leaves early to drop her daughter Mbali off at school and comes back a little late after dinner. She usually works in the house in most days and only goes to sites when there's a need to but clearly she is trying to avoid having to bump to her brother throughout the day. She and Ntokozo have been on the same dinner table at the same time only twice since the prodigal son returned which has obviously made it difficult for the family to discuss Ntokozo's suggestion that the rape cases be re-opened and Dora had warned Ntokozo to not go ahead with it until he has spoken to his sister first.

Dora has worked from home since Ntokozo's return so they have become farmiliar once again and she is getting used to the idea of her son being home. They still haven't spoken about Ntokozo's mysterious dissappearance but Dora doesn't want to push him too hard lest he leaves again, for good this time. She figured she will wait for him to open up about it.

So today is a Friday, which happens to be a holiday so Lungile had a short day at work and decided to have a date with her friends at a resturent in Gateway. Anything that will make her not go home she will take it but the only people she can vent to are her friends if her boyfriend is not around.

"So how is the gorgeous Ntokozo Gumede doing? Hahaha..." Lindiwe Ngcobo asks with a naughty tongue out which leads to laughter from Lungile's other friend Nompumelelo Mbutho as she says, "You know what I really also want to meet him as well my friend, I bet he is very hot...hahaha..." but Lungile rolls her eyes and says, "Anikameni guys(guys please don't start)...I can't stand being in the same room with him, that house has turned into a bore" as she takes a sip of her dry red wine. She is not necesarily offended by her friends because she knows they are just jokimng and trying to cheer her up.

32 year-old Lindiwe has been friends with Lungile since childhood and she knows Ntokozo very well and years later she has become a teacher in one of the schools in the townships. She also lives not far away from Lungile's home in Umlazi BB section. A very talkative individual, unlike the 33 year-old Nompumelelo who met Lungile in University and they have become best friends ever since. She is a lawyer working for a very well-established lawfirm.

"You guys don't know how angry I am at this guy hey...I actually didn't even realise it myself until I walked into him sitting in lounge with mom on Sunday afternoon." Lungile says with an irritated face as she takes another sip of her wine. "Alright friend, but what does he say? Surely if he explained himself to you guys you will have a better understanding about why he left while you were still in school in highschool?" Lindiwe asks as she looks at Nompumelelo who nods in agreement with the question. Lungile thinks for a second before saying, "No actually...he hasn't said much of anything about why he did what he did or whatever"

"But did you ask him? Did you atleast give him a chance to explain himself?" Nompumelelo asks as she raises an eyebrow but Lungile just shrugs without uttering a word. "You see? It's important friend that you really down with him and find out before you and your mom drive yourself mad making assumptions when the person with answers is under the same roof as you guys..." Nompumelelo says as she also takes a sip but Lindiwe interjects, "Speaking of which, where does your mother stand with all this?" she asks curiosuly as she takes a sip of her drink.

"Arg you know how mothers are like..." Lungile says as she looks a little annoyed. "But you guys are right...I can't live like this forever. I need to know why Ntokozo left and why he wasn't there when I needed him the most but part of me is terrified of finding out the truth. I suspect it's something very terrifying guys, I don't know..." She suddenly looks a little worried but Lindiwe interjects, "But babe, it's better the truth than assumptions hey. Assumptions can really drive you crazy because you will always think of the worst case scenario, whereas the truth can hurt but very liberating at the same time" she says as she shrugs her shoulders while taking a sip.

This makes Lungile think for a secoand before sheruging her shoulders as well as though she's got nothing to say to it. "What I want to know is...what does he do now? Has he joined the family business or, does he wake up and go to work somewhere? I don't want a broke guy, hahaha..." Nompumelelo asks as she bursts out laughing just to throw in humor into a thoughtful question. Lungile shakes her head in disbelief as she smiles. "First of all, you two better stay away from my brother okay? Find your own men, Hahaha..." she says with a laughter. "But seriously though, I really don't know hey. I usually leave him in the house when I go to work in the morning and I find him there in the evining, so I don't know what he does. And no...he is not working for the family business...mama and I haven't discussed Ntokozo since he came back. But you know, he is driving a very beautiful car so I'm asuming he has money...as long as it isn't drugs or some proceeds from crime" "Anyway enough about that, so on Tuesday it's Mbali's birthday party right?" Lindiwe asks with some level of excitement. "Oh yes guys and please I expect presents from you hahaha..." Lungile jokes. "Ofcourse friend and...I will get to meet your brother hey, hahaha..." Nompumelelo says which makes Lungile shakes her head as she calls on the waiter for a re-fill.

***

Meanwhile, at the Gumede mansion, Ntokozo seems to be a little bored as he has nothing to do during the day and he doesn't want to ask his mother if he cn help with the business. He has been gone for a very long time 5 days is not a longtime for one to re-intergrate themselves in the family, so he figured he would start with little things like doing house chores and be available for whatever his mother needed.

So after a long day of working the garden he decided to stretch his legs and go to the nearest tuckshop to buy a few things. This gives him time to see people of the area and maybe bumped into a few that he grew up with. Now, as he comes back from the shop he hears a voice calling out from behind him, "Hey Ntokozo..." it says softly.

When he turns around to see who is calling his name, his eyes immediately brighten when he sees the most beautiful woman smilling at him. *'Oh my God...this is probably the most beautiful woman I have ever seen'* he thinks to himself as his eyes pop out. This light-skinned woman wearing a beautiful floral, short summer dress has the most beautiful eyes and smile. Her huge afro that is styled very well makes her look very authentic and grounded.

"Uhmm...hi, how are you?" Ntokozo responds with a smile. "I'm okay thank you...so it's true...you are back to the land of the living?" the beautiful lady asks with a bright smile but Ntokozo quickly interjects, "Oh uhmm...I'm sorry, do we know each other?" he asks with a polite voice as he looks a little embarrassed by that question himself. The lady thinks for a second before saying, "Oh well, I suppose we don't because growing up we were not close but I used used to see you from a distance..."

"Oh really?" Ntokozo says as he tries to recall. "Yeah I'm from Dlakodle street that other side..." the lady says with a smile as she points to the other road paralell to this one. "Oh uhmm...sorry, I'm

Pearl Ngubeni..." she says as she extends her hand, which Ntokozo accepts as they both shake. "Yeah I don't think there's a girl that didn't know Ntokozo Gumede here in these streets, so I was no different hahaha..." Pearl says with a blush.
"Oh wow, so uhmm...so how come I never noticed such a beautiful girl in my neighbourhood?" the clearly smitten Ntokozo says as he holds on to this beautiful lady's hand. "Oh well I don't know really...maybe I wasn't really your type hahaha...or maybe cause were other more beautiful women in this area at the time hahaha..." Pearl says as she also doesn't pull her hand away. She seems to be enjoying the fact that this man is taken by her. "Oh doubt it really..." Ntokozo says with a blush as he finaly lets go of the woman's hand.
"Hahaha...you are so kind. Nothing a bath can't fix hahaha..." Pearl jokes.
For a second there they just stare at each as though they are in the world of their own. They seem to have forgotten that there are other people passing by them. "Uhmm...so you dissapeared from the area...are you now back?" Pearl asks as he fixes her eyes on him. Ntokozo thinks for a second before saying, "Uhmm...yeah i believe I am...for now, that is" Ntokozo says with a smile as he snaps out of that little heaven he had created.
They then begin to slowly move towards Ntokozo's home. Both of them have their hearts pounding at this moment as it is clear that there's chemistry building. "So...a lot has changed in this place huh? Some faces I don't recognize hey..." Ntokozo says as he looks at people in their yards and those who are moving pass them. "Oh yeah some people you grew up with moved out of this place. You know what they...'if you live in the same place for too long you won't be able to see your growth', so people move for a better life" Pearl says with a smile as he takes a look at Ntokozo who nods and says, "But you didn't move out and judging by how you look life turned out just fine for you hey...."

"Well, they also say 'if you are going to stay in the same place, you better grow yourself'...so that's exactly what my family did I guess" Pearl says as she looks pleased with herself. "Well that's true..." Ntokozo says as he nods. "So miss Pearl Ngubeni, after many years later what are you known for in this area besides the obvious fact that you are the most beautiful woman here?"
"Uhmm...well, uhmm...I'm involved in the family business. And you? What are you known for after so many years, besides being a charmer? Hahaha..." Pearl says jokingly which makes Ntokozo blush for a second as he looks at the passing people. "Well, uhmm...I'm a curious traveller...I think that what best describes me hahaha..." he says as he jokes back. "A curious traveller? Wow I don't think I have ever heard that before...what does a curious traveller do?" a visibly charmed Pearl asks. Ntokozo thinks for a second before saying, "Uhmm...I guess, I'm just a person who doesn't like to stay in the same job for too long, or the same place for too long, so I travel a lot all around the world...to experience different cultures."
Pearl seems to love this as she think about it with a smile. "That sounds really interesting..." she says, "Ive always wanted to travel as well, but time just never allows. But I hope that one day you will allow me to tag along...so that I enjoy the beauty of the wolrd like you"
They then stop and look at each other in eyes when they reach Ntokozo's home gate. It seems as though they have a lot they are saying to each without uttering a wowrd and understand each other as well. They are these close to risking it all and just kiss each other right there on the street. Ntokozo never felt this about any other he has met before and Pearl feels like this man is the person she has been waitng for all her life. They stand so close to each other that a slight move forward from either of them will bump their chests...and their eyes are fixed on each that they don't wanna look anywhere else.

But that instense moment is interrupted by Lungile's car which slowly passes past them. When Ntokozo realises that his sister has her car window down and looking at them in a way that suggests she doesn't like what she sees, he snaps out of it and says, "Uhmm...well I guess I will see you around Pearl Ngubeni" with a smile.
"Yeah uhmm...I guess I will see you around Ntokozo Gumede..." Pearl says as she smiles back at Ntokozo who stands there and watch this lady walk away. After a few metres out Pearl turns around and notices that Ntokozo is still looking at her. She smiles and waves at him and he waves back. She then turns and walks away and Ntokozo opens the gate and gets inside.

***

Later on during supper the family is all together on the table but Ntokozo mind is still on Pearl, the lady she met earlier on his way home from the shop. He himself can't discribe how and what he is feeling inside but all that keeps playing in his mind this beautiful woman's smile and her beautiful eyes. He can still feel the warmth of her palm when he held her hand and couldn't let go. While he can't be certain about it, he can assume that Pearl felt something too but now one thing he regret is not not getting her number. But since she doesn't live far from his home they are bound to see meet again. *'We shall surely meet again'* he thinks to himself.

His thoughts are interrupted by his sister who calls out, "So uhmm...do you know the girl you were talking to at the gate earlier?" she asks with a straight face as she takes a sip of her dry red wine. Ntokozo thinks for a second before saying, "Uhmm...you mean Pearl? Uhmm...not really, but she said she knew me from back then. I don't remember her though..." as he takes a sip of his juice.

"Well, I suggest that you paly far away from her big brother..." Lungile says as she looks a little annoyed but Ntokozo quickly cuts in, "Uhmm...why?" he asks curiously as he raises an eyebrow. "Well, where do I start? How about the fact that her family is dangerous?" Lungile says as she raises her voice a little bit but Ntokozo's eyes pop out as he is a littpe shocked by that. When Lungile sees that she continues, "Yeah they are drug dealers..." she says as she looks at her mother who looks down as though she doesn;t want to be part of this conversation. It's a good thing that Lungile's daughter Mbali is sitting in the lounge watching TV because this conversation is going to be tense.

"Oh well uhmm...that's not the sense I got when I spoke to her...she was very nice" Ntokozo says with a low voice but his sister quickly interjects, "Oh...is it becaue you are such a good judge of character? You don't know her Ntokozo...you just met her." she says as she throws her hands in the air. Lungile is always irritable.

"Oh well, why don't you tell me?" Ntokozo says as he puts his glass down, clearly he is also becoming irritated by her sister who is always triggered. "Well, your new friend's father is a drug dealer..." Lungile says as she looks at her brother in the eyes trying to read his reaction. "His drugs has hooked so many youths here in the area and many people have died at his hand around here. His people sell drugs to young school kids and we have seen many of them turning into pharas as a result. So there you have it, is that good enough for you? That girl that you were with works for her father so I don't want her near my child because of you."

"So if Pearl's father has killed many people or hooked the youth into drugs, why isn't he behind bars?" Ntokozo asks curiously as there seems to be a little shock in his eyes but his mother interjects, "Your sister is right mfana wami(my son)..." she says politely. "Jabulani Ngubeni is a very dangerous man and, making friends with his daughter is not a good idea"

"Yeah and why he isn't behind bars? Who will make him when he has police in his pockets?" Lungile adds. "Who can snitch on him when he kills everyone who talks? Do you remember Qaqamba

Magubane? You used to play soccer with here on the streets...he was your childhood friend. Well, he tried to report bra J to the police and he got a bullet in the head. There are many others like Qaqamba who have been killed for talking. So who will have that man arrested then? Geez that man kills even the police who investigate him...Everyone is scared of him, so I say to you befriending his daughter is dangerous...not only to you but to this family"

Ntokozo is in disbelief of what he is hearing here in this table because the picture of the woman he met erlier is still in his mind and she looked like a very kind and warm lady. But he also knows that he's been away for too long to dispute what his sister and mother are saying. He is a little dissapointed because he was looking forward to seeing Pearl again.

"Excuse me guys, I need to make a call..." he says as he leaves the table goimng upstairs to his room, much to the shock of his mother and sister.

Chapter 4

Dark

The follwoing day on a Saturday night Ntokozo is in this seemingly abandoned warehouse in the middle of nowhere and he looks to be in a different mode as he is dressed in a black shirt, black pants and a black leather jacket. The place could have been an old steel manufacturing warehouse some decades ago as it's almost falling apart and Ntokozo has a man tied up in chair in the middle of the hall. He looks terrified as he tries to free himself but it's no use as his hands are tightened into the armchair. He can't scream either because his mouth is taped. Clearly he has been getting a beating for a little while since he has blood on the side of his left eye. Ntokozo pulls down the tape from his mouth and says, "Okay are you ready to talk now or you still want to play tough, huh?" as he punches him hard on that left side again that the man falls down to the floor with the chair, but Ntokozo helps him up. Judging by the blood on the floor, this has been happening atleast for a few times now.

"Please sir I don't know what you are talking about okay? You got the wrong person, please...please let me go..." the man shouts as he looks to be in agony. His teeth are red with blood from Ntokozo's fury punches. His left eye is beginning to swell a little bit and a few more punches, it will close. Ntokozo on the other hand looks a little scary as his eyes are red with rage. He is nothing like the Ntokozo whose heart was soften by a beautiful lady yesterday. Tonight he looks like a deadly mecenary that is on a mission.

"Oh so you think I'm stupid huh? You see, I know all about you surgent Sbongiseni Nxumalo..." Ntokozo says as he looks at his target in the eyes. "I am asking you to tell me what happened to docket opened for a rape case against Philani Masondo two years

ago? I swear to you, if you don't give me the information I'm asking for I will do things to you that you have never imagined."
"But sir we have many rape cases everyday and I don't know who Philani Masondo is..." the police officer screams as he begins to cry in fear but Ntokozo cuts in, "Oh but you will know who Philani Masondo is..." he says softly as he goes to the wheel table that is next to the chair that Sbongiseni is tied in. On the table are are different kinds of instruments that if you didn't know you'd think someone is in surgery and being operated upon. Ntokozo picks up what looks like a little sharp knife, he looks at it and then puts it down. He then picks up what looks like a pair of ceasers...he looks at the Sbongiseni and then looks at the instrument before putting it down. Lastly he picks up a plier and comes back to his target.
"Now listen to me carefully police officer, if you do not give me the information I need things will get really bad for you, you hear me?" he says as he looks at the mini plier. "Now, what happened to the docket opened against Philani Masondo who was charged for rape in 2021 September 11? Are you going to tell me that or we should begin?" He shouts at his target with rage.
"But I told you sir, we deal with many rape cases every single day I wouldn't know which case was that..." the terrified and crying police officer says but Ntokoz once again cuts in, "Oh so you mean to tell me making dockets dissappear is your thing huh? You do this all the time that's why you don't even remember which docket I'm talking about, huh? You corrupt bastard..." he shouts as he presses Sbongiseni's hand down on the armchair and use the plier to pull a finger nail from his thumb, leading to the police officer to scream on top his lungs in agony. "Oh no please no...please no...I don't know no what you are talking about..."
"Don't worry Sbongiseni, your memory will come back soon..." Ntokozo says with a calm voice. "You see...you have 10 fingers so we will play your game and you will tell me when you are tired of

playing it, okay? I have all day for this and you can scream all you want...no one will hear you from this place."
Drops of blood from Sbongiseni's thumb start driping to the floor as he looks to be in excruciating pain but Ntokozo has no sympathy for him as his eyes are filled with rage. He is beginning to run out of patience as he holds the officer's hand down again and says, "Should we continue?" as he fiercely pulls another nail from the index finger leading to a loud scream from the police officer, "Aaah...Please stop, I will talk okay? I will talk...I'm begging you, please stop..." he shouts as tears fall down his face. Blood is all over the floor as it drips from his tied hand.
"Alright then, you will talk? Okay good...talk" Ntokozo says with a calm voice as he wipes sweat from his forehead but suddenly Sbongiseni looks hesitant as he shakes his head in fear. "Look here...I don't have all day okay? You said you will talk right? Now talk damnit..." Ntokozo shouts in frsutration as he goes over to the table to see what other effective instruments he can use.
"Alright sir look...I'm just a low level police okay? I do what I'm told...I don't ask questions" Sbongiseni says as he cries in pain but Ntokozo says "Oh you do what you are told while you take bribes to make dockets dissapear, right?" as he comes back to him. Sbongiseni nods to the question as he looks sto be running out of breathe.
"Alright then who gave you money to make the docket disappear?" Ntokozo asks with an angry face, "Look, I don't care about all the sh*t you do with whoever...but I'm asking you about this particular case okay? I know that you have been doing this for a very long time because you are a useless pice of sh*t, but I don't care about all that. I wanna know who paid you to disappear the docket of Phlani Masondo..."
The bloody-faced Sbongiseni thinks for a second as panic sets in his eyes. "Okay look, I will tell you..." he says with a trembling voice. "Uhmm...it was a gentleman by the name of Luke Collins a white

guy. I think he was Philani's lawyer or something like that. He gave me R10,000 to make the docket disappear...I was desperate for cash, so I took the money okay?"

"You useless piece of sh*t, did you even think about the victim, huh?" Ntokozo shouts as he punches the police hard across the face again. "How many people do you think this guy has raped and got away with it huh? He does this to women all the time because he knows he has rubbish police officers like you, right? Where is this Collins guy now? And where is Philani Masondo? I want their address and particulars, right now..."

"Look, I don't know where Collins is but Philani Masondo is a known businessman I'm sure you can easily get his particulars..." the panicking police officers says with a trembling voice. "All I did was taking the money and got rid of the docket...sir I am not part of any criminal syndicate with these people, please believe me." he says but Ntokozo cuts in, "No, you didn't just take the money...you denied justied by getting rid of the docket..." he says as he pulls a gun from his back and points it at Sbongiseni's face. Suddenly his face changes to being a face of a killer.

"Please sir, I have a family...I have already told everything I know..." Sbongiseni begs with a trembling voice as he looks at the burrel of the gun pointed at him. "You should have thought about that before you denied my sister justice, you pice of sh*t..." Ntokozo says as he squizes the trigger to put two bullets in the officer's forehead.

***

Later on that night at the Gumede mansion Ntokozo arrives home just in time for supper. He has changed from what he was wearing earlier on at the warehouse and now in his smart casual outfit of a white shirt, blue jeans, brown shoes and crem blazer. He walks into the dinning room where his mom, his sister and an unknown man are sitting. '*This must be an occassion of some kind...*' he thinks to himself as he lets out a half smile. "Good evening everyone..." he says as he pulls a chair and sits down opposite the stranger who is sitting next to Lungile. This man smiles at him so he smiles back just to be polite.

"Well, right on time...we almost started without you..." Lungile says with a smile, which Ntokozo find a little strange because she is usually cold towards him. *'Maybe we should have a stranger in this house every now and then...'* he thinks to himself as he smiles back at his sister.

"Uhmm...so I would like to introduce you to Thulani Zulu, my boyfriend..." Lungile says with a nervous voice as she avoids eye contact. She looks a little embarrassed or worried about her brother's reaction to this and certainly Ntokozo looks a little caught off guard by this. After what he had to do a little earlier to find people responsible for his sister's pain, his trust levels are on an all-time low it comes any element near his family. On the other hand Dora and Lungile are a little anxious about his reaction as they wait breathlessly to hear what he is going to say.

"Oh uhmm...it's nice to meet you Thulani Zulu, I'm Ntokozo..." Ntokozo says as he extend a hand to shake, which Thulani accepts nervously as he looks like a guilty person. Immediately, the moment becomes a little awkward in the room as it seems everyone has run out of something to say.

"Uhmm...sweetheart can you come help me in the kitchen please?" Lungile says as she looks at her daughter Mbali who was sitting next to Ntokozo. Mbali duly oblidges as she quickly stands up and follows her mom to the kitchen, leaving Ntokozo, Thulani and Dora on the dinning room. "Uhmm...so Thulani, where are you from man?" Ntokozo asks as he pours himself a glass of orange juice. "Oh uhmm...ngokokuzalwa(by birth) I'm from Ndwedwe but now I live in Umhlanga..." a nervous looking Thulani says as he takes a sip of his dry red wine, probably to calm his nerves.

"Oh uhmm...I see. How old are you?" Ntokozo probes as he wears a straight face. "35..." responds Thulani. "Only child?" Ntokozo throws another one. "No, I have a younger sister who is 28..." Thulani says as he seems a little uncomfortable with the questions a little bit. "I see...What do you do again?" Ntokozo probes some more but before Thulani could respond, a voice coming the kitchen calls out "If you must know, he is a medical doctor..." Lungile says with a smile as she and daughter come in with platters of food to the dinning room. "Oh really? That's really nice..." Ntokozo says as he forces a smile.

This seems to be a little relief for Dora who didn't want things to turn awkward in the table but as Lungile and Mbali sit down a call comes through for Ntokozo. "Oh uhm...excuse me guys, I have to take this." he says as he looks at his phone. He gets up and goes through the glass sliding door off to the veranda.

Ntokozo: "Hey man..."

Man: "Hey bro...I thought I should check in..."

Ntokozo: "Okay but before we even go there, I need you to check somebody out for me alright?"

Man: "Oohkay...who?"

Ntokozo: "Uhmm...his name is Thulani Zulu. I will give you his full details in a moment..."

Man: "Uhmm...I don't see any problem in that man..."

Ntokozo: "Okay good...So what were you saying?"

***

A day later, on a Sunday afternoon, Ntokozo and Dora are sitting in the lounge watching the news on TV, while Lungile and Mbali are in their respective rooms. It seems dinner with Lungile's boyfriend Thulani went well without any akward moments, even though Ntokozo had asked his contact to do a background check on the man who is dating his sister. Now he is hoping that nothing sinister

comes up because by the looks of things Lungile really likes this guy. But he feels obligated to do this after he failed to protect his sister on three occassions and now he feels prssed to make up for it.
"Son, can you please up the volume on that..." Dora says as her eyes pops from what is being said on the news.
'48 year-old Surgent Sbongiseni Nxumalo who was found dead with bullet wounds in his head and his body burned inside his car that was also torched was a husband and a father of two teenage girls. The police spokesperson in KZN that we spoke to earlier on says the motive for this gruesome murder has not yet been established as the forensic team is still swifting through things to try and establish what exactly may have happend to the police officer who was tortured by having his finger nails removed...' the news anchor says,
"Lungile...Lungile....Please come quick..." Dora shouts for her daughter as she is shocked at what she is hearing on the news. Lungile comes down as fast as she can, "Mama what's wrong? What's happening?" she says as wonders about what could be important that her mother had to shout that like.
"Look who it is...the police officer that was investigating your case two years ago..." Dora says as she points to the TV. Lungile comes and sits down on the couch to listen what is being said on the news.
'KZN Police Commissioner Mthokozisi Ncube has vowed to find the perpetrator and bring him or her or them to justice because the department has lost a great servant of the people...' the news anchor continues but this seems to upset Lungile a little bit as she says, "Great servant my ass. I say good riddence...That man got what he deserved, corrupt bastard..." she says as she looks away from her mother. "Oh baby, come on now..." Dora says with a low voice but Lungile cuts in sharply, "No mama, it's true alright? That man deserves this..." she shouts as she looks upset. "I say welldone to whoever did this to him. Do you forget that he lost the docket that

would have taken Philani behind bars? He probably was killed for one of his corrupt activities..."
"I know sweetheart what that man did but I was just saying that..." Dora says but doesn't finish as Lungile interrupts her again, "No mama...the world is a better place without that man nxa..." she says as she stands up and goes back to her room, leaving Dora a little shock. But perhaps though not as shocking as seeing how calm her son is about all this.
"Are you okay my boy?" she asks with a raised eyebrow. Ntokozo looks at her and says, "Yeah mama...why you ask?" while fixing his eyes on the TV. He is clearly avoiding eye contact. "Oh no...nothing son...I was just thinking that, why would anyone kill a police officer like that..." Dora says as she looks at her son who is still looking at the TV. "Just like Lungile said mama...if he was a corrupt person, maybe the world is a better place without him...excuse me" Ntokozo says as he stands and goes upstairs to his room, leaving his mother confused by that reaction.

Chapter 5

Meeting new people

Six days after the breaking news on murder of a police officer nothing has been laid at Ntokozo's feet and the police investigations are still on going. While Dora has a gut feeling that her son may know something about this, considering that she had given him the contact details of the police officer, she can't really link him to any of this. But it has however ressurected the desire to want to know about Ntokozo's life in the past 12 years he was away, but part of her is scared to find out...and the death of the police officer doesn't make this any easier for her.

But today is a joyous day as it is Mbali's birthday and her mother Lungile has invited her friends and their kids over to celebrate this day. In fact there's quiet a lot of Mbali's friends and kids from the area in the yard today because the Gumede's are known to throw a very good party. Since it's a sunny Saterday the tables and a tent are set up in the yard by the pool area where kids can swim or play in the jumping castle that is also erected next to the tent.

"You Gumedes really know how to throw a party don't you? If I didn't know better I'd think it's your party hey..." Lindiwe says as she looks at the lot of kids in the yard playing. "Oh wait until my birthday comes in a couple of weeks time my friend, you ain't seen nothing yet, hahaha..." Lungile says as she jokes at her friend. The three friends are sitting inside the tent next to gifts section, with a cooler box full of refreshments. This party became a perfect excuse for the girls to have their own little party in the tent since it is empty-kids are outside having fun.

"So, where's the good doctor today? What...he doesn't like children parties?" Nompumelelo asks as she takes a sip of her sparkling white wine. "Oh no...he is working today and he feels bad about it but, he actually left a gift for Mbali." Lungile says, "Speaking of which let me quickly go and fetch it, I almost forgot" She quickly leaves the tent and goes inside the house.

***

At the gate, Ntokozo who is coming back from a gift shop at the mall wants to get inside and give his niece the present, but as he opens the gate someone calls out, "Hey stranger..." It's Pearl with the brightest of smiles. These two haven't actually seen each other since the day they met a while ago and Ntokozo's eyes immediately brighten as he sees who is calling out. This is the woman he couldn't stop thinking about when he met her bu then suddenly his face changes when he thinks about what his sister had to say about her. He is now conflicted and not knowing what he should follow-his heart or his mind.

He gets out of the car and goes on to hug the beautiful Pearl who, as usually dressed beautifully in a lime short summer dress and sun glasses. "Hey to you too stranger...how are you?" he says with a bright smile. Pearl takes off her glasses and looks at Ntokozo, and it is clear that they both want to kiss but perhaps it's to soon for that. Their hearts beating fast with the excitement of seeing each after a little while. By the look of things, Pearl has been thinking about Ntokozo too.

"So how have you been? It's been a minute..." Pearl says with a smile as they both come to lean against Ntokozo car which has it's nose inside the gate on the driveway. "Yeah it's been a minute hey...I've been okay, how about you?" Ntokozo asks as he bumps his new friend with a shoulder before smiling at her. "I've been good hey...but honestly, I didn't think it was going to take us this long to see each again..." Pearl says as she blushes away. "Oh yeah? Well, you actually didn't leave me your number hey..." Ntokozo says as he

shrugs his shoulders but Pearl quickly interjects, "Well you didn't ask for it, did you? Hahaha..." she jokes back.
"Yeah I didn't wanna get all weird about it you know? I didn't want you thinking I'm some kind of psycho hahaha..." Ntokozo says as he laughs loud. "Hahaha...You are so silly..." Pearl says as she laughs back. "So I see that your home is in full party mode huh? But then again, the Gumedes are known to throw a good party...so what's the occasion?"
"Oh uhmm...it's my niece's birthday and I'm actually coming from buying her a gift...let's hope she's gonna love it." Ntokozo says with a little of a blush. "Ncooh uncle Ntokozo...so sweet of you" Pearl says as she bumps Ntokozo's shoulder. "So where's yours?" she asks. "Where is what?" Ntokozo asks as he raises an eyebrow. "Child...do you have a child?" Pearl asks as she blushes as the question which makes Nokozo thinks for a second before saying, "Oh no I don't have a child...not that I know anyways...hahaha..." as he laughs loud. "What? Are you kidding me? A catch like you? Gosh...what have you been doing all this time?" a pleasantly surpised Pearl asks. Ntokozo once again thinks for a second... "Arg, you know...I just never found the person I can settle and have a child with I guess. Before I knew it, I'm 37..." he says as he seems a little embarrassed by that. "You? Do you have a child? A man?" he probes as he clearly wants to change the subject.
"Uhmm...no child, no man..." Pearl says as she looks down as though she is embarrassed but Ntokozo quickly interjects, "What? No ways...you? No man? The most beautiful woman in this community has no man? I can't believe that for one second" he says as he smiles as though this is pleasing. "Hahaha...I'm serious hey" Pearl says as she bursts out laughing. "But seriously though...I think that people are just scared of my dad. He can be really intimidating for guys to even think about approaching me hahaha...so yeah, I struggle to find anything that is serious. I guess it comes with being a Ngubeni."

"Is your dad dangerous?" Ntokozo asks as he raises his eyebrow, which makes Pearl to think for a second before saying, "Uhmm...he is very protective of his kids and he'd do anything to protect them" as she shrugs her shoulders. "Well, that sounds dangerous...perhaps I should just stay away from you then hey..." Ntokozo says with a raised eyebrow.
"No man, don't be silly okay? Hahaha..." Pearl says with a laughter as she tries to brush that off but it leads a little awkward silence as both of them seem to have run out of things to say to each other.
Ntokozo really wants to invite Pearl inside but he knows that won't go well with his sister, who had warned him about this woman.
"Well, I better go in and give this gift to my niece..." he says with a blush. "Oh yeah, for sure..." Pearl says as she looks a little dissapointed that she has no been invited inside. "Oh uhmm...here's my number, you know...incase you wanna take me out for lunch some time..." she says with a blush. "Oh yeah for sure...I will surely do that" Ntokozo says with a smile as he takes a piece of paper from Pearl and looks at it. "Alright then, we will talk..." he says as he gets in his car and off to to the party in the yard, while Pearl walks back home down the road.

***

Ntokozo gets out of the ca with a wrapped box and goes straight to the birthday girl, his niece who is turning 12 today. "Where is birthday girl? There she is...there she is..." he says with much excitement as Mbali comes running to her uncle. "Happy birthday my girl..." Ntokozo says as he gives a beautifully wrapped box to his excited neice.
"Oh wow...ngiyabonga malume(Thank you uncle)..." Mbali says as her eyes brighten before giving her uncle a warm hug. "You are welcome sweetheart..." Ntokozo says as he squeezes a light tight on that tiny body but suddenly his face changes to being a little serious

as he breaks the hug and looks into his niece's eyes. "Okay now I want you to listen to me sweetheart" I know that I wasn't throughout your childhood and your life...and I want to say I'm really sorry about that, but I'm hear now and I will be present in your life until I die, I promise. I also want to know that if ever you need anything...anything at all, I'm here okay? Lastly, if anyone intends to harm you in any way never ever hesitate to come to me okay?"
"Okay malume(uncle)..." Mbali says with a smile. "Okay then...go on and have fun with your friends, alright?" the visibly emotional Ntokozo says with a smile as he watches his niece excitedly showing her friends the wrapped gift box. He then looks around and realises that he is the only man in this party and thinks he will just go inside the house and watch some football, but he then realises that his sister and her friends are in the tent. '*There we go...*' he thinks to himself as he goes in.
"Hey everyone..." he says nervously as he approaches the ladies who are in front of the tent having ciders. "Well, well, well...finally, I get to meet Ntokozo Gumede..." Nompumelelo says with a naughter smile that makes Lungile roll her eyes in disbelief of her friend. "Uhmm...this is my friend Nompumelelo and ofcourse you know Lindiwe..." she says as she looks a little embarrassed. "Oh hey...how are you guys?" Ntokozo says with a nervous smile. "We are good thanks...please grab a chair" a vissbly smitten Nompulelo says, again making Lungile to role her eyes. "Drink?" Nompumelelo asks as she doesn;t even wait for Ntokozo to respond but pulls a cider from the cooler box and gives it to him.
Ntokozo takes it as he sits down. "So uhmm...welcome back Ntokozo...long time hey" Lindiwe says with a smile. "Thank you...yeah, it is a very long time. How have you been wena(you)?" Ntokozo responds. "Arg, I've been okay thanks..." Lindiwe responds but Nompumelelo interjects, "Nice ride you have there...I take it

you are doing well...?" she asks as she takes a sip of her cider. Clearly she has had one too many.

But just before Ntokozo could respond, Lungile cuts in, "Uhmm...excuse us guys..." she says as she takes Ntokozo by the hand so that they go outside the tent. Ntokozo knows this can't be good as her sister doesn't look happy at all.

"Uhmm...thank you for the present...you know, for Mbali." Lungile says with a little of a blush but Ntokozo cuts in, "Ofcourse, she's my niece...I missed out a lot on her over the years I'm just trying to make amends sis..." he says with a low voice as he looks down. This seems to soften his sister a little bit as she smiles without responding to it. "So...I saw you at the gate with your friend Peral?" she says as she suddenly looks annoyed. "But I thought we spoke about this Ntokozo..." she looks around to see anyone is listening to their conversation. She looks unhappy.

"What? Come on sis...we were just talking okay?" Ntokozo says as he throws his hands in the air. "Look if you need to talk to a woman just come to the tent...there's Lindi and Ntombi there, not that girl" Lungile says as she looks away as though she can't she just said that. Ntokozoko is a little taken aback by this statement. For a second there he actually thought they'll have a descent conversation. "Sisi...I really think you are overreacting okay? There's nothing going on between me and Pearl..." he says with a little smile because part of him is happy that his sister is protective of him. "Yes there's nothing happening right now but how about later?" Lungile asks as she throws her hands in the air as well. "I mean, don't you see that girl wants you? Ntokozo, her family is dangerous...her father is dangerous. I don't want her near my child or mom...or even you for that matter. You guys are the only family I got so when a daughter of a dangerous drug dealer starts playing around my brother, how long before her father starts sniffing around this family?"

This makes Ntokozo to think for a seond as he looks at his sister. "I hear you sis okay?" he says as he takes a deep sigh. "Okay tell me this, how well do you know Pearl?" he asks as he also looks around the yard but his irriatble sister quickly interjects, "But that's just the thing alright? The point is to not know her because knowing her is dangerous for this family"

"Look sisi...I promise you, I will not allow anything to happen to you, my niece or mom okay?" Ntokozo says with a smile as he takes his sister's hand. This makes Lungile think for a second as she looks at his brother before saying, "Do you have a girlfriend?" which shocks Ntokozo who says, "Nope..." as he raises an eyebrow. "Do you need one?" Lungile probes. "Uhmm...everyone needs love at some point okay? But why? Why are you asking?" Ntokozo asks curiously. "Well, there's nothing wrong with finding love bhuti(brother) but please I beg of you okay? Can it please not be Pearl? I don't trust her..."

Ntokozo thinks for a second and smiles before saying, "Okay look, let me watch some game, you guys enjoy the party..." as he kisses his sister in the forehead and walks into the house. This was a pleasant surpise for both siblings as they haven't had a talk like this before. Ntokozo is happy that finally he and his sister are talking at all while Lungile is beginning to think maybe she has overreatcted to this whole thing of her brother coming back home.

***

Later on at night Ntokozo is parked somewhere on a street that is a 30 minutes walk from his home under a tree. This road is dark because street lights are not working and it is very quiet at night because its a dead end road. Where Ntokozo is parked is a ring where where cars make a u-tur and go back to th direction from where they came. Beyond the ring is a huge dark bush field where people can't walk through to get to the other side of the twonship.

DARK VENGEANCE

Ntokozo looks a little anxious as he keeps taping his thumb on the steering wheel while also checking his watch. The time is around 20h: 45 and he doesn't want to worry his family about his whereabout because he left home around 18h:00 saying he is going to see his friend Sthembiso who doesn't live far from his home. He sits up straight when he sees a coming to park next to his car. A guy who looks to be in his early 40s gets out of the car and approaches Ntokozo who takes a deep breath and lowers the window. "Eyi mjita(dude), ngiyiphethe impahla yakho(I have your stuff) as agreed on the phone." this tall and dingly man says as he keeps looking to see if anyone is seeing him out here. Ntokozo thinks for a second before pulling out his wallet and takes out a few notes. He gives them to the man who gives him what looks like a plasting bag that has something on it. He looks at the contents in the platic and nods.

But as the man turns around to walk back to his car Ntokozo quickly bends and pulls a 9mm gun with a silencer from under his seat and shoots him in the back of the head. The man falls down without moving at all. Ntokozo waits for about 5 seconds before coming out of his car...he probably wanted to make sure there was no one else emerging from that other car. He stands over the body lying down and puts another on the side of his head.

He then goes to the other car and opens it...when he sees that there's no passenger he pops the trunk and goes to see what he could find. He opens the trunk and see a big black bag...he opens it and his eyes pop when he see what's inside. He decides to take the bag to his car and drives off, leaving the dead body laying in the pool of blood.

Chapter 6

Up a notch

Few days after he took out a drug dealer on a Saturday after his niece's birthday party, Ntokozo is once again in his killer mode and this time, it's the man who raped his sister two years ago-Philani Masondo. Thanks to the information he got from surgent Sbongiseni Nxumalo Ntokozo was able to track down Masango...he grabed him from his apartment in Amanzimtoti and took him to this abandoned two-story building further down South Coast in the middle of nowhere. This building could have been a factory of some kind that hasn't been used for years. Luckily for Ntokozo there are no houses or business establishments around it, so there are no people to witness anything hapenning inside.

As usual, Ntokozo is wearing black clothes from head to toe...it makes him look very scary, but that's just the way he likes it.
"So, Philani Masondo...you thought no one will ever find you huh?" Ntokozo says to a Philani who is tied to a chair very tight, just like officer Nxumalo was. It looks like he has also been beaten up pretty bad and it could have been going on for hours. Ntokozo's infamous table of dangerous instruments is also next to Philani's chair, and this time it has scary looking objects including an ex and a pounder.
"Sir, sir, sir...I really don't know who you are or what you want okay? Please let me go..." The crying Philani begas as he bleeds from the mouth and forehead. His white shirt is almost completely red with blood that is coming from every part of his body. "Oh you don't know what I'm talking about huh? Aren't you the piece of sh*t that rapes women and get away with it because you have money? Huh? Aren't you that piece of sh*t?" Ntokozo shouts in anger as his eyes turn red with rage and he is thristy for revenge. Once he gets in this mode, he can't be talked down untill his thrist is quenched.

"Sir...I don't know what you are..." Philani shouts in agony but doesn't finish as Ntokozo plunges a bug knife through his thigh and judging from his scream, it must have reached the bone.

"Aaaah...please no sir...you got the wrong man, I swear you got wrong man..." he cries uncontrollably in a scream but that doesn't seem to move Ntokozo whose eyes are red with rage.

"Philani...you think I'm here to play, huh? You think I'm playing with you?" he shouts as he spits on the man who has a knife plunged deep into his thigh. He goes over to the table and looks at the instruments again. He thinks for a second before picking a small axe and a huge hammer which terrifies the crying Philani as he looks on.

"Now, let me jog your memory a little bit Masondo..." Ntokozo says as he puts the hammer down and stands in front of his victim. "You scambag raped my sister Lungile Gumede back in September 11, 2021 and then paid the officer in charge Sbongiseni Nxumalo to make the dockect disappear...isn't that what you rich people do, huh?"

Philani who is in pain looks like he is trying to recall the event that his accuser is talking about as he looks up in panic but without a moment's notice, Ntokozo had swung his axe hard on Philani's hand, cutting three of his fingers in an instant. The rapist screams so loud that he could have been heard across 10 blocks down the road if there any houses around.

"Aaah...my fingers...aaah please no sir...aaah...I'm so sorry, I'm so sorry...please forgive me...Aah..." he screams in agony. "Oh...forgive you? So what am I forgiving you for Masondo? That you raped my sister? My sister? You piece of sh*t?" Ntokozo shouts as as he spits on the man's face.

"Please sir forgive okay? I will never do it again...please sir, please..." the sobing Philani begs in excruciating pain. At this point the whole floor is covered in blood as it gushes off from Philani's hand, thigh and just about every other part of his body. His once white shirt is

now soaked in red. Ntokozo looks at him and thinks for a second, "What gives you rich people the rights to abuse women and get away with it huh?" he shouts as he swings his axe on Philani's hand again cutting off the remaining thumb and index finger, much to Philani's scream, "Aah...aah...aah...please sir stop...please I'm begging you please...aah..." he screams.
Ntokozo looks tired from swinging the axe as he breathes heavily while wiping a sweat from his his face. He throws the axe down and goes over to the table to look at what he has there while Philani looks on in agony. "You know what, I don't want you to go into shock before we are done here...so I will give you a little something to keep you awake okay?" he says as he picks from the table what looks like a syringe.
He comes over to Philani and plunges the syringe on the side of his forearm, making his eyes pop as though he's just waken up from deep sleep. "There you go...that will help stay awake a little longer Masondo..." Ntokozo says with a smile as he looks into Philani's eyes and sees that he is now wide awake. It doesn't look like the injection has taken any away though as the man looks to be awake to every bit of pain in his body, but that's exactly the kind of reaction Ntokozo was looking for.
"Sir, please...if I had done something wrong to you...please I apologies...I'm begging you, please..." in-pain Philani begs as he breathes heavily. Tears are falling down his face and he can't even wipe them because he is tied tight to a chair and missing five fingers from one hand. "it is not me you should be apologising to Masondo...it's my sister" Ntokozo says as as he picks up the hummer from the floor which terrifies Philani as he begins to sob all over again, "Sir please...no, I beg you okay? Please...uhmm...please tell me what you want me to do okay? I will do it. Uhmm...I have money and my family has money. How much do you want sir?"

DARK VENGEANCE 51

Well, that seems to set Ntokozo off as he smashes Philani so hard with a hammer on his right knee, leading to deafening scream, "Aaah...aah...my knee...aah...please sir aah, no, God no...aah..." Well, that knee is definately broken now...there is absolutely no way it can ever work again as Philani screams in agony. At this point he is probably feeling that death is the only thing that will relieve from the pain.
"So you rich people think everything is about money huh?" Ntokozo shouts as he spits on the man. "Did you think you can buy your way out of this? Huh? Do you think your money is any good to me or my sister? Huh?" he smashes his hammer so hard on Philani's knee again...the left one this time, leading to another uncontrollable scream from him,
"Aah...aah...aah...aah...aah...aah...please stop...I'm sorry...please stop...aah..."
From how those knees look, that man will never ever walk again as Ntokozo throws away the hammer in a rage. He takes a breathe as he wipes his sweat. "Now I want you to say her name..." he says with a low and seemingly tired voice. "But sir I don't know what..." the in-oain and panicking Philani says but he doesn't finish as Ntokozo cuts in, "You say her name right now or else I will cut off your balls and feed them to you, you understand?" he says as he points a finger at him. Well, no man wants to hear those kind of words, as Philani's eyes pop in panic. After what this man has done to him already? He knows he is not bluffing.
Now he is trying to recall all of his victims' names as he looks up while tears fall from his face. Ntokozo pulls a gun from bis bag and points it at Philani, "I said...say her name goddamnit..." he shouts as his eyes also become teary. "Alright, okay..." Philani says with a trembling voice as he closes his eyes in terror. "Her name is Lungile Gumede..." he says as tears gush from his eyes. Ntokozo thinks for a second as he takes deep sigh. "Yes, her name is Lungile Gumede..."

he says before squeezing the trigger, putting two bullets in Philani's forehead and watch his body falls lifeless to the pool of blood.

***

Somewhere else, Jabulani Ngubeni is furious over what happened to one of his drug dealers a few days ago and what frustrates him even more is not knowing who could have done this to him. Drug business is a very shaky one and it's hard for one to not have enemies and rivals, Jabulani knows that very well, but what puzzles him is why now? He has been king of this area for a very long time...he has always been the one terrifying the comminity and everyone is scared of him. He has never had anyone in their right senses try to challenge him in any way and this is not something he will allow now.

"Are you saying up untill now you haven't found anything? Anything at all?" Ngubane shouts at his people as they hold a meeting in the garage of his double story mansion. In this meeting there's about 8 people including the boss himself. Everyone looks a little anxious because they all know that Ngubeni can be a little trigger happy when he is angry.

"No Bra J...no one saw anything or, atleast no one is talking..." one of his man leaning against the boot of one of the cars in this huge garage says with an anxious voice, leading to an outburst from the boss, "Are you trying to tell me that all seven of you don't know what the hell is going on?" he shouts as he looks at all the man in the room who all look down like school kids in front of the head master. "What about Majola? Does he have people assigned to the case already? And what are they saying? Someone has got to know something about this whole thing alright? Because I am not going to be taken for a fool, you hear me?"

"Yes, Majola said he is handling this one himself and will let me know once something comes up..." another man says but Ngubeni cuts in, "Oh he will...damnit...when will that be?" he shouts. "What's the point of having the police on the payroll if they can't give you the information you need when you need it, huh?"

The garage goes quiet as the men look at each other, not knowi ng how to respond to the question but Ngubeni continues, "Do you know how much cocaine was with Ntuthane? Huh?" he asks as he opens his eyes wide. "5Kg of cocain, okay? Bloody 5Kg...That's worth a lot of money and it's all gone...the worst part being the fact that we don't know who's got my f*cking cocain, alright?" Out of nowhere, he smashes the glass of whiskey that he had in his hand against the garage door, which makes everyone take cover from the debris that fly all over the garage.

That leads to a dead silence in the room as men once again look at each other. Ngubeni takes a deep sigh before asking, "Okay where is Pearl? Why isn't she in this meeting?" as he looks around the room. There's a little silence in the wroom before one of the men says, "Oh, she should have been part of this meeting, Bra J? I didn't know that she is..." but doesn't finish as Ngubeni cuts in, "No she is not in this side of the business okay? But I wanted her here because one day she will be running things here" he says with a controlled temper. "But sir are you sure that's a good idea? I mean, if this is not her idea then maybe its..." another man stabding in the corner says but Ngubeni loses his patience and says, "Hey, hey, hey...don't you dare tell me how to deal with my own daughter alright?"

That certainly leaves the room dead quiet, I mean who can dare challenge this authoritative man? His people know better than to prolong the argument with him. "Dismissed guys...let's get back to work and find my drugs okay?" Ngubeni says with a firm voice, to which everyone quickly leaves the garage.

***

At the Gumede mansion everyone is still shocked about the news of the death of Jabulani's man and while it comes as a relief there's fear of a drug war that might erupted from this. While Ntokozo is away Lungile and Dora are on the couch watching the news, while Mbali is in her room upstairs.

"Hey mom...you know, I was gonna ask you if you saw on the news that Ntuthane who works for Bra J is dead...yeah they shot him over the weekend" Lungile says as she turs down the volume on the TV.

"Oh yeah I saw that mntanami(my child)...infact I was going to ask you about it" Dora says as she shakes her head in disbelief. "But ofcourse it's not like it's a bad thing that they killed him...those people have been terrorising this community for a long time now. They have hooked so many kids into drugs, it's about time that they got what was coming to them"

"yeah that's very true but I just wished that you know...it would have been better had he been killed by the police, because then the war would have been between the police and the drug lords." Lungile says as she shrugs her shoulders, "But if he was killed by other drug lords then soon we may find ourselves in the middle of a drug war and you know, these streets won't be safe for our kids here in this area. And you know how drug wars can turn like hey" She suddenly looks worried as she lifts up her head to see if her daughter can hear her from upstairs.

"I know sweetheart but whether it was the police or other gansters it makes no difference because the very police work for these criminals, so I say let them eat each other up..." Dora says as she shrugs her shoulders, to which Lungile seems to be in agreement with the statement.

"Hey uhmm...any news about the police officer that was killed?" Dora asks curiously but a vissibly annoyed Lungile quickly cuts in, "Why? Who cares? The corrupt bastard is dead mom..." she says as she throws her hands in the air but her mother raises in eyebrow

and looks at her. "What?" Lungile asks as she shrugs her shoulders, "I'm serious...who cares about what happened to that police officer? He probably was killed during his many corrupt activities and I can tell you now, he won't be missed by anyone. The world is a better place without him...I'm not bothered and neither should you" Dora raises an eyebrow again as she is in disbelief of what her daughter is saying. While she understands why she this may be trigering for her Dora is just not used to seeing her daughter this cold about someone's death. "No honey I was just thinking that, it was strange how he was killed...I mean, tortured first? It's as though it was a revenge killing, don't you think?" she persists as she tries to read her daughter's eyes.
"Well...lucky bastard to whoever killed him for whatever reason..." Lungile says with an annoyed face, "But why are you so interested in this guy mama, hey? I mean, we were just talking about corrupt police now and Nxumalo was most definately one of them, so why should we care if one criminal dies, huh? Look, I know that you are probably thinking about what happened two years ago and yes, Nxumalo's death doesn't give me closure but it still does feel good that he is dead because he probably had been denying many other women justice by making dockets disappear...so yes I'm happy that he is dead. You know what? In fact I need a bottle of wine to toast to it"
Dora thinks for a second as she looks at her daughter because the last thing she wants to escalate this talk to another level. "You know, speaking of which...has your brother spoken to you about the uhmm...you know, cases lately?" she asks with a calm voice which makes her daughter raises an eyebrow in wonder. "No, why?" Lungile asks curiously. "Oh uhmm...I thought he had spoken to you..." Dora says as she looks down as though she is embarrassed. "The thing is that uhmm...he thought it might be a good idea that you re-open the cases."

"Oh geez not this again mama...what now?" an annoyed-looking Lungile says as she throws her hands in the air. "Why would Ntokozo suggest something like that now, huh? I mean, what will that solve? He just came back home now and he is already wanting me to re-open these cases? I spoke to him and told him what this trauma did to me, wasn't she listening? And now I must re-open cases, what...so that he may feel good about himself after leaving us? No, no, no...I obviously need to set him straight with that. Besides, the office in of the case just got killed, so that case won't go anywhere now except opening up old wounds"

"Look sweetheart, I'm with you okay? I also told him the same, alright?" Dora says as she takes a daughter's hand as Lungile begins to be a little teary. "I told hi to speak to you first and hear what you have to say about this alright?"

"Yeah I will also tell him the same...how dare he suggests something like this after he had been gone for so long..." an upset Lungile says as she wipes one tear. "Shhh...It's okay baby, I'm with you okay?" Dora says as she brushes her daughter's hand. "Uhmm...you know what, I think I really do need that wine..." Lungile says as she quickly stands up and goe goes to the kitchen.

***

Well, speaking of the devil...after meeting with Philani Masondo Ntokozo is on a dinner date with Pearl at the Pavillion Mall and by the look of things, it's all going well betwen the two. Ntokozo couldn't tell his family where he was going because he knows how they feel about Pearl and he figured that if he had to stop seeing her he'd have to find out the truth for himself. One thing is certain, these two can't hide how they feel about each other.

They are in this beautiful cosy little restaurent that doesn't have a lot of people but has a very good menu for people going out on dates. This isn't something Ntokozo does a lot so he really didn't know how to dress up, so he figured smart casual of Jeans and a white shirt will do just fine. Pearl on the other hand, perhaps maybe out of excitement she came a little over-dressed with a beautiful red boobtube dress, red lipstick and red hills or maybe she just wanted to make a first impression.

"Uhmm...so you actually called huh?" a vissibly smitten Pearl says as she sips her dry red wine. "Yeah ofcourse I called, told you would hahaha..." Ntokozo says with a laughter. "Well I actually thought you know...you'd be like every other guy and chicken out, hahaha..." Pearl says jokingly as she takes another sip. "Oh no mam, I never chicken out hahaha..." Ntokozo says as he laughs back at tyhe joke.

"Okay so what dd your family say when you told them that you went out on a date?" Pearl asks curiously as she raises an eyebrow with a smile, which catches Ntokozo offguard as he almost chokes on his drink. "Uhmm...actually, they don't know that I'm here with you" he says as he looks a little embarrassed by even saying that but that seems to make Pearl a little dissapointed as she says, "You didn't tell them? What, you are embarrassed about me?" she asks with a low and dissapointed voice. This also makes Ntokozo feel bad as he looks down for a second.

"Oh come on don't be silly alright?" he says as he makes eye contact and sees that this may cause awkwardness in the table but Pearl raises an eyeborw as if to say *'really?'* He thinks for a second and says, "Okay look...honestly? You know that I just got back, right? And uhmm...I have heard from a few people about your family, your father inparticular..." He looks down as though he is embarrassed. "Oh you mean your sister?" Pearl says as she raises an eyebrow again. "Amongst them, yes..." Ntokozo says as he shrugs his shoulders. "I thought you said you worked for your family business...you din't tell me what kind business it is Pearl..." He takes a sip of his wine as he looks at his date in the eyes but Pearl quickly interjects, "Hey look, I got nothing to do with whatever my father is accused of okay?" she says as she throws her hands in the air. "Yes I said I work for the family business which includes establishments like the Butchery, Hardware store, Car Wash etc....Anything else has got nothing to do with me"

This conversation threatens to make things a little akward and both of them would really love to avoid that because they were really looking forward to this date.

"Okay look, uhmm...I would really love it if you saw me as an individual, Ntokozo...not jut as my father's daughter" Pearl says with a calm voice. "We don't choose the families we are born to but I am capable of making my own choices and one of them being to not be part of whatever my father is doing. I run other businesses at my discretion and my father doesn't interfere with that."

"But Pearl, I hear he and his people have been terrifying the community here and that young kids are hooked from drugs and some have died...Have you ever tried to talk to him?" Ntokozo asks curiously but this seems to irritate Pearl a little bit as she takes a deep sigh before saying, "You know...I really thought this dinner was about us Ntokozo but clearly I was wrong..." with a sad face, which makes Ntokozo feel bad. "You are right, I'm sorry..." he says as he looks at her with begging eyes which seems to do the trick as Pearl lets out a little smile before taking a sip of her dry red wine.

That is follwowed by a little silence as the two seem to be thinking about what to say next.

"You know Ntokozo..." Pearl says with a calm voice, "In life you meet people who suddenly change your perspective on life, people who make you want to become a better person and make better decisions..." Pearl says with a low voice as she smiles. "Such person is you Ntokozo...from the first day we met I knew there and then that there could be something here that will change my life forever. Since then, I had never stopped thinking about you and all I have wanted

is to get to know you a little better and, maybe if you felt the same, we could even start a relationship"
Ntokozo's heart is suddenly warmed by these words as he smiles while taking a sip of his wine. Deep down he knows this is what he wanted to hear all along but he is trying to control his emotions. "Wow uhmm...that's, that's uhmm...that is the most beautiful words I have ever heard..." he says with a blush as he stutters out of nerves.
"So? What do you say?" Pearl asks with a nervous smile. She is seems worried about being rejected after pouring out her heart like that but Ntokozo thinks for a second before saying, "Uhmm...Pearl, your father will never approve of us you know that and my family will certainly never approve." with what sounds like a sad voice but Pearl quickly interjects, "But we are not kids anymore Ntokozo, can't we make our own decisions?" she says as she looks a little dissapointed. She was expecting Ntokozo to jump into this without any hesitation but maybe that was too much to hope for.
"Look Pearl, this isn't just about us okay? How we feel about each doesn't matter. It is not the question here..." Ntokozo says with a low voice. "The problem here is with our families...I mean, I will never approve of what your father does and at some point he will see me as a threat. On the other hand, my family worries that if I get involved with you I also involve them in it because if me and your father dissagree on something it may put their lives in danger. You see how that complicates everything for us Pearl?"
Pearl can;t honestly say there's no truth in what Ntokozo is saying because she know how and what her father can become but this is a tough pill to swallow.
"So what now?" sh asks with a sad voice. "Ngyakuthanda(I love you) Ntokozo and I know you feel the same about me...this is so unfair"
Now she her eyes are beginning to be a little teary as she looks at Ntokozo in the eyes. "Look Ntokozo, if I have to disown my father I will okay? I have never approved of anything that he does so, if it

means that I move out of his house then I will...because all I want is to be with you and you alone"

"Whoa, whoa, whoa...if you do that then he will really come after my family, don't you think?" Ntokozo says with a low voice as he looks around to see if anyone is watching their intense moment.

Pearl knows once again that Ntokozo is right about this so she thinks for a second before saying, "So what? We just give up on us, just like that Ntokozo?" as she looks really sad. "We must just pretend that we don't exist or that we don't love each other? I'm sorry but I can't do that Ntokozo...I just can't. I love you and I am willing to fight for you and I am willing to fight my father fo you" Ntokozo can't help but smile at those words as he finds them cute. "You are crazy, you know that?" he says with a smile as he shakes his head. "Yeah, I'm crazy about you Mr Gumede..." Pearl says as she smiles back at him before taking his hands across the table. "I really am crazy about you and it feels so good..."

Ntokozo thinks for a second before saying "Alright then Miss Ngubeni, what's the plan here?" with a smile as he looks at this brave woman sitting acroos him. Pearl dosn't respond to that but leans forward 90% across the table to invite Ntokozo for a kiss. He can't resist this moment even though there are people on the other tables. He accepts the invitation as they kiss slowly and intimately.

Chapter 7

Suspicion

"We apologies for showing up like this unnounced...we understand that it's a Friday evening and everyone just wants to chill and relax after a very long week..." a gentle who is walking in to the Gumede lounge with a woman says as they sit down on the couch opposit Dora and her daughter Lungile. "Uhmm, I'm detective David Skhosana and this is my partner detective Lindiwe Zulu..." he says with a low voice, much to the Gumede's confusion. They are wo dering what could this be all about because the last time they have interacted with the police was when investigations were on-going on the cases that Lungile opened.

"Yes, uhmm...you are welcome officers, can we get you something? Tea? Cold drink? Water?" Dora asks as she looks at her daughter. "Oh uhmm no thank you..." David says with a smile as he looks at his partner who nods in agreement. "Oh okay. Uhmm...sweetheart do you mind going upstairs? Momy and granny want to talk to the officers here, really quick okay?" Dora says to Mbali who was sitting in the lone couch focusing on the TV. She obliges as she quickly goes upstairs to her room.

This is a few days after Ntokozo had put two bullets in Philani Masondo's forehead before he went on a date with Pearl a few hours later. Between that time and now nothing out of the ordinary had happened in the Gumede household. Things between Lungile and Ntokozo had been a little better because they are atleast now talking to each other. Pearl never told his father where she went on Tuesday because she had to think long and hard about what Ntokozo said. The last thing she wants is to put him and his family family in danger because she knows how her father can be sometimes. The

two have however been calling and texting each other since date night.
"Uhmm...so how can we help you officers?" Dora asks anxiously as she looks at her daughter. David looks at his partner before clearing his throat. "Uhmm...oh yes...I'm sure you may have been follwing the story about the death of a police officer Surgent Sbongiseni Nxumalo, yes?" he says with a low voice. "Yes ofcourse, what about it?" Lungile asks curiously as she raises an eyebrow.
"Uhmm, you may also want to know that that Philani Masondo was found brutally murdered on Tuesday night somewhere in South Coast..." David says, much to Lungile and Dora's shock but as they attempt to respond, David's partner Lindiwe interjects, "Uhmm...we understand that there's a connection between you and Philani Masondo, no?" she asks looking at Lungile as she pulls out a small note book and a pen from her shirt pocket. "Excuse me?" Lungile says as she raises an eyebrow but David qickly cuts in, "Oh uhmm...what she means is that uhmm...we understand that you opened a case of rape against Philani Masondo back in 2021..."
"Yes? So what?" the irritable Lungile says as she shrugs her shoulders. "So uhmm...we thought that maybe you could answer a few questions for us seeing that officer Sbongiseni Nxumalo was linked to you as well..." David says but quickly corrects himself before Lungile could respond, "Oh, I mean that uhmm...when you opened the case against Masondo, officer Nxumalo was the one investigating the case, am I right?"
"Yes ofcourse and as I recall, that case never went on because the docket mysteriously went missing..." Lungile says as she shrugs her shoulders. This leads to a moment of silence as the two officers look at each other. "And that didn't sit well with you did it?" officer Lindiwe asks but Lungile jumps to it, "Excuse me?" she says as she looks at her mother who is just as puzzled by the line of questioning. "I mean, you were angry that the docket went

mysteriously missing...right?" Lindiwe asks as she writes something down but Dora quickly jumps in, "I'm sorry, are you implying that my daughter had something to do with the death of that police offcer?" she asks as she raises her voice a little bit.

"Oh no uhmm...ofcourse not...but we'd just like to ask her a few questions regarding these two murders seeing that she has a history with those two men. Anything she can tell us may help in piecing together what may have happened to them..." David says with a nervous smile but his partner who, quiet frankly seems to have an attitude towards the Gumedes interjects, "But perhaps we should start by asking where were you on Tuesday, say between 15:00-22:00 in the evening?" she asks witha straight face.

Lungile thinks for a second beofore saying, "Uhmm...In the morning I visited some of the family businesses spread across the city...you are free to check logs for that. I then came back home afterwards, and for that you are free to check our CCTV footage." as she looks at her mother who nods in agreement. "Uhmm...and you Mrs Gumede, do you remember where you were?" David asks as he looks a little nervous. "Oh yeah...I work from home everyday. We have an office down in the basement and my daughter goes to sites when there's a need to do so but she is largely here at home as well. If I need anything from the Mall I send my son and if I need anything from the tuckshop I send my granddaughter " Dora says with a certain level of calmness that makes David and his partner look each other.

"Uhmm...you said your son, Mrs Gumede?" officer Lindiwe asks curiously as she looks at her partner. Dora looks at Lungile as she wonders wherether she should have mentioned that. "Oh yeah, uhmm...yeah my son Ntokozo, he just got back home from overseas a couple of weeks ago." she says with a rather nervous voice.

"Oh, is he here? Can we talk to him as well?" David asks curiously as he looks upstairs. "Oh no, he isn't here right now...I think he is out"

Dora says with a nervous smile. "Oh that's a shame because we'd loved to hear from him as well..." Lindiwe says as she shrugs but Lungile quickly interjects, "I'm sorry officers...are we suspects or, am I suspect in this?" she asks curiously as she looks at her mother but David quickly cuts in, "No uhmm...the thing is that, it's the nature of these murders that we find perculiar" he says as he looks at Lindiwe but Dora probes, "Perculiar how?"

"Well uhmm...we are not saying that they are actually linked to one another but, both victims were serverly tortured before being killed." David says. "I mean, it's still early to tell but it suggests to us that these could have been revenge killings. Whether they were completely separate incidents, the perpetrator or perpetrators had a score to settle"

"Oh, that perpetrator being me huh?" Lungile cuts in. "Or it have been just two criminals killed by other criminals...isn't that possible?" She seems a little irritated by the two officers who seem to be suggesting something to her. "Well, you did open a case of rape aginst Mr Masondo and surgent Nxumalo was the officer in charge where the docket was lost..." Lindiwe says as she shrugs her shoulders but Lungile gives her a sharp eye without saying nothing. "Alright look officers, we have answered your questions the best way we can, so if there's nothing else, we'd like to go on with what we were doing as family" Dora says with a straight face as she stands up, to which the two officers stand up as well. "Uhmm...thank you for your time Miss and Mrs Gumede" David says with a smile as they walk towards the door.

***

The following day Lungile and Dora work up to the news of another drug dealer in the area having been killed and this is beginning to spok them a little bit. They actually thought today since it's a Saturday, they'd just relax and maybe have a braai as a

family but waking up to these news after they had a visit from the police last night is making them wonder about a few things.
"Mama I'm telling you, something ain't right with these murders it's beginning to make me a little edgy" Lungile says as she turns the volume down. "Yeah I know okay? Something is going on..." Dora says with a worried face as she sips on her cocktail. She has had an early start since it't around 10:00 in the morning and they are busy making salads that will go nicely with the meat.
"Yeah I mean, are we having a drug war right now? How ;long before this escalates to gun battle on these streets where our kids are playing?" Lungile asks in a panic as she continues to look at what is playing in in TV. "What are the chances that Bra J is involved in all this? Everybody knows who is the drug dealer in these streets and everything that is illegal happening in this area involves him"
"Yeah, no doubt Ngubeni is involved in all this my child...but it's his drug dealers that were killed, right?" Dora asks as she looks a little curious. "I mean, we all know Sticks worked for him and also Ntuthane worked for him, so this means one of his rivals could have done this. But my worry is that they will turn this are into a drug war zone and we and our children will pay a heavy price for it. On the other hand, it's actually not a bad thing that these drug dealers are off the streets and I wish they all kill each other so that our children can be safe. The community need to stand up against this as well""
"You see why I don't want Ntokozo to get involved with Bra Ja's daughter? He will end up getting hurt. If he wants a girlfriend, I'd rather hook him up with one of my girls instead..." Lungile says with a sigh, much to her mother's surprise. "Oh, you actually do care about your brother huh?" she says with a smle as she points at her daughter.
"Why would you think I don't care about Ntokozo? Ofcourse I do...he is my brother mom..." Lungile says as she rolls her eyes. "Oh

no uhmm...It's just that I never hear you sounding like you care for him, that's all..." Dora says with a smile as she shrugs her shoulders.

"He just got back home mama okay? Plus I was still angry at him...but it doesn't mean I didn't care" Lungile says as she throws her hands in the air. "Anyways, back to him and his...friend Pearl, I just don't think it's a good idea that they make friends, or even talk to each other...and you also should discourage that from happening mama..."

"Okay look, I will talk to him okay? But I don't think there's anything untowards there okay? But you are right..." Dora says as she thinks for a second. "Speaking of which, where is your brother vele(by the way)? I thought he'd have started fire by now..."

"I don't know...probably with Pearl?" Lungile says as she roles her eyes. "Come on mama let's finish up these salads...Ntokozo will start the fire when he gets back, hopefully before we both get drunk from this wine, hahaha..." They burst out laughing as they head into the kitchen.

***

Somewhere else in Umhlanga, Philani Masondo's father Judas is mourning his son and is in a rage when visited by Police Commisioner Mthokozisi Ncube at his home where the mood is sombre. Philani had two sisters who were both younger than him and they also live here in this house with their father and mother. The Masondo family which is in the mining sector has a networth of over R5b and is well connected politically.

As relatives and friends of the family keep coming in and out of the house to pay their respects, Judas and the commisioner are sitting under the tree on this huge green lawn and are having whiskey. "What do you have for me Ncube?" Judas ask with a low voice as he looks far where visitors are mingling. They are in a bit of a distance because they didnt want to get disturbed.

"Uhmm...at the moment, nothing Mr Masondo..." the commisioner says nervously as he takes a sip of his drink. "Nothing? Nothing? Really? What is the job of the police if you can't find the people who killed my boy, huh?" a furious Judas asks as he finishes off whatever was left on his glass. "Someone killed my boy Ncube and I wanna know who and my wife and daughters won't get closure if they don't know why this happened, you hear me?" he says as he raises his voice a little bit.

"Uhmm...do you think perhaps that your son may have had enemies? Or people who may have wanted to harm him for a sepcific reason?" the nervous commissioner asks but that just seems to annoy Judas as he says, "If I knew that those people would have been found already, okay?" before pouring himself another double. "Okay then, I guess my people willl keep looking then sir..." Ncube says but Judas quickly cuts in, "Yeah you do that alright? But when you find those people you bring them to me okay? I will deal with them. They need to feel my own justice since yours takes long" he says as he takes a stiff.

"I'm sorry sir but I can't do that alright? That's not how law works..." Ncube says as he looks down but Judas quickly cuts in, "Don't tell me about law okay? My son is dead and you have not found the killer yet, five days on" he raises his voice. "All you people do is making statements and promises while families mourn their loved ones"

"I understand your frustrations Mr Masondo, but you got to allow us to do our jobs okay?" Ncube says with a calm voice. "Interference in this case will only make things delay further and ultimately delay the closure you and your family so need. Now trust me when I say that I have very capable people on this case to help find the people who did this to your son...now, are you sure that your son didn't have enemies that would want to harm him? Please try and think if

there's anything, no matter how small it is. It may just lead to something that we need to make a break through"
"What with you and that nonse? My son didn't have enemies okay? He was a business man just like me and the rest of his family" the annoyed Judas says as he finishes off his drink. Ncube thinks for a second before saying, "Well, it's just that your son was uhmm...he was tortured first before he was short. This suggests that this was not random but was a targeted killing...revenge killing to be exact." Judas thinks for a second before saying, "Well...my son didn't have any enemies I knew of okay?" as he looks away. "Alright then if you say so..." Ncube says as he pours himself another double, much to Judas' annoyance as he looks at him. But this moment is interrupted when they see Judas' wife coming from the house and approaching them. Now the two must be on their best behavior because Mrs Masondo can be a very strict woman and since she is mourning the loss of her son she won't accept any shinanigans from anyone, especially guest who are here to pay their respects.
"Sweetheart, there is a gentlement in the house who is here to see you..." Mrs Masondo says calmly. "Oh honey please tell him I will be there in a minute, I just want to..." Judas says but doesn't finish as his wifes cuts, "No baby, you will do this now okay?" she says as she makes her voice a little firm, to which Judas quickly gets off the chair and heads to the house, leaving his wife with the nervous commisioner.
"Uhmm...Mrs Masondo please let just say how sorry I am..." Ncube says with a low voice but he doesn't finish as Mrs Masondo cuts in, "Oh, please just call me Jessica okay?" she says with a humble smile which seems to put Ncube at ease as he lets out a nervous smile. "Uhmm...Jessica, let me say condolances for the loss of your son..." he says as he bows his head. "Uhmm...yeah it's really been tough commisioner Ncube, but thank you for your heart-felt condolences. Anything on the people who committed this crime on my boy?"

DARK VENGEANCE 69

Jessica asks with a low voice as she watches her husband gets inside the house with a guest.

Ncube thinks for a second before saying, "Oh uhmm...as I have already explained to your husband, my officers are still looking into the matter and they haven't linked anyone to the crime as yet" with a low voice as he looks a little embarrassed, which seems to disappoint Jessica a little bit as she nods.

"But uhmm...like I asked your husband earlier, do you think your son had any enemies or any person that would wanted to harm him?" Ncube asks with a nervous voice. He doesn't want the same response he got from Judas but Jessica thinks for a second as she raises an eyebrow. "Uhmm...not that I know of, no..." she says calmly as she looks at the commisioner's eyes. "You think this was personal? Perhaps someone settling a score with my son?"

"Well, how he murdered suggests that it was personal...revenge killing..." Ncube says as he looks away which makes Jessica to take a deep breath. "Uhmm look Commissioner...my son was not perfect alright? He was sturbon and uncontrollable most of the time so I won't be surprised if he indeed had enemies..." she says as she looks emotional. "But I guess the only way to know for sure what happened to him is finding out who killed him, right? Please Ncube, we as a family need closure over this...we can't move on not k owing who did this or why they did it. Living with anger is not a very healthy way, I'm sure you can understand that Commissioner..." Ncube thinks for a second before saying, "Yeah I get it Jessicca but please, like I said to your husband earlier...please allow us as the police to handle this matter. When the perpetrators are caught they shall be dealt with within the confines of the law, right?" as he looks at the grieving mother. "Oh yeah ofcourse Commissioner, do what you have to do okay? Just do it quickly"

"I got to go Mrs Masondo...please tell your husband that I will be in touch." Ncube says as he bows his head to Jessica before leaving her under the tree.

***

Elsewhere, the Masondos are not the olnly ones feeling agrieved a death of their own but Judas Ngubeni is spitting fire as well, as he meets his men in garage as usual. The last meeting in this place was really tense and anxious but this time it's even worse as Ngubeni is spitting fire from the latest incident. This time around, Pearl has been forced by her father to attend the meeting so she is here physically but her mind is somewhere else-the man she loves. "Now I need someone to explain this to me okay? What the f*ck is going on here? Who is taking out my people and why haven't they been found yet, huh? Someone better answer me very fast..." the furious Ngubeni shouts that his terrifying voice resounds across the walls of the garage, but no man wants to dare say anything as they all look at the daughter-Pearl. They are perhaps hoping that her presence will buy them another day with the dragon boss since he hasn't drawn his weapon just yet, but Pearl herself knows that there's no controlling her father when he is angry about something. "Okay since none of you want to talk, I want all of you to go out there and find out who is killing my people and then find my goddamn drugs okay. This including you Pearl alright?" Ngubeni says as he looks at his daughter who is shocked at hearing that instruction but she thinks it is not best to challenge her father when she is in a foul mood and in front of his men.
"Now get out of here and find those people and bring them right here with my drugs, you here me?" Ngubeni says to the men who quickly leave the garage lest the boss loses his mind and starts shooting around. "Baba(dad), can we talk?" Pearl says politely while watching the men leave the garage. "What is it Pearl?" Ngubeni says

angrily as he pours himself a double of whiskey, not even looking at his daughter. "Uhmm...I had told you before dad that I am not getting involved with your business okay? So please don't involve me in this nonsensem because I don't even know why you called me to attend this this meeting."

"Hey, hey, hey...you are still a Ngubeni right? So you will do what you are told okay? You are part of this business and one day you will run it..." the angry Ngubeni says as he downs his double in one go but the rebelious Pearl interjects, "No, no, no dad...I said I am not getting involved in your dirty bisiness that shed blood okay?" she says as she approaches her father firmly.

"Oh? How do you think the other businesses you are now running were built huh? Where do you think money to start them came from? You think your hands are clean then? Don't be naive little girl..." Ngubeni says as he shakes his head, my to Pearl's irritation as she also shakes her head. "I'm serious dad, I am not getting involved with drugs..." she says as she begins to feel a little emotional. Part of her is feeling guilty about what her father is doing and how he started the businesses that she now runs. After the conversation she had with Ntokozo a few days ago, she is more and more feeling guilty about even living in this house, under the same roof as her father.

"What the hell happened to you Pearl, huh? You used to be so ambitious and wanted to take on the world alongside me, but now I don't understand you anymore..." Ngubeni says as he looks into his daughter's eyes to try and read her. "What? You found a man? You fell in love or something? Someone who is influencing you against me?"

When Pearl sees how her father's face changes when asking the question it terrifies her because she knows what she is capable of. The conversation she had with Ntokozo about how unsafe their relationship is, is now playing on her mind as she begins to look a little terrified. Jabulani can see that his daughter is hiding something from him as he raises an eyebrow. "Oh so there is a man in your life now huh? Ofcourse there is..." he says as he shakes his head in disbelief. "Now I want you to listen to me very carefully Pearl, okay? You have to put whatevr childishness you are going through now and focus on the task at hand okay?" he says with a firm voice. "Dad I said I am not going to be part of your criminal activities okay?" Pearl says as she raises her voice a little bit but her father quickly cuts in, "Alright then, you will have to relinquish your position as head of the family businesses and move out of the house to find your own place to stay, right? I will find one of my man to run things from now on, okay?" he says as he raises hos voice even higher, much to his daughter's shock. He knows her father is a diffcult man but she also knows that he loves her very much. She thinks for a second as she looks at her Ngubeni in the eyes to try and read if he is bluffing or not...nope he is not bluffing. "Alright then, I'm resigning as head of family and I will move out in the next few hours to go find my own place to stay..." she says with a firm voice as she tries hard to not show emotions on this. Her heart is pounding so fast because she never thought she and her father would ever be in this kind of position. Ngubeni himself didn't expect to hear his daughter talking like this but will his pride allow allow him to admit that he perhaps was too harsh on his little princess?

There's now a little uncomfortable silence in the garage as the two look at eah other like they are strangers but when Pearl turns around to walk out of the garage her father calls out, "Sweetheart wait..." he says with a rather subdued voice. "Uhmm...ofcourse I didn't mean that. I don't want you to move out of the house okay? And you don't have to resign as head of family businesses, you are doing a fantastic job. You know how much I love you, right? After losing your mother, I don;t wanna lose you too...you are the only

DARK VENGEANCE

family I got now and if anything was to happen to you i'd never be able to live with myself..."
Pearl listens to her father and thinks for a second as though she wants to say something but she turns around and walks out of the garage, leaving her fagther scratching his head.

***

Elsewhere, Ntokozo who is already late for a family braai day is on his killing mode as he has found yet another one of those 3 people who raped his sister without facing any concequences. This is the guy who raped Lungile in University but got away with it because his family was rich. It's unclear how Ntokozo found him but like the other two targets, he has him tied up in a chair in some dirty apartment in the middle of noewhere. It looks like he has been beating this guy up for a little while now as his face and clothes are soaking in blood. He is also missing an eye that is now placed on Ntokozo's favourite table of deadly instruments.
"Now look here Akhona Velenkosini Lukhele, I don't have a lot of time okay? I'm already late for a family braai day, my mother is depending on me to prepare the coals..." Ntokozo says to the man who is in pain as blood flows from every part of his body. "Here's what I need you to do okay? You will tell me about the incident that happened 6 years ago while you were still at the University of KwaZulu-Natal. You scambag raped a girl named Lungile Gumede but you never paid for it because your family is rich, right? Well boy, alukho usuku olungafiki (No day doesn't arrive) you hear me? Yours is today...to pay for your sins and your family money won't save you this time"
"But angazi ukhuluma ngani(I don't know what you are talking about), you got the wrong man..." Akhona cries loud in agony but that irritates Ntokozo as he plunges his favourite 8-inch knife deep into the rapist's right thigh and Akhona screams on top of his lungs

in pain, "Aaah...please sir, no...I don't know what you are talking about, aaah..."

But Ntokozo quickly goes to the table and comes back with a little bottle, "Are you ready?" he says as he looks at his target in the eye. He pours what looks like liquid into Akhona's knife wound, leading to another scream that is so loud could have been heard miles out. "Aaah...aaah...aaah...please stop I'm begging you, I don't know what you want from me...aaah...aaah...aaah, please, please please...I'm begging you..." he screams as he continues to bleed all over the place from every part of his body. The screams don't seem to move Ntokozo one bit as he looks at him with eyes of hate and digust. "Akhona, do you think I'm stupid, huh? You think I'm stupid? Well guess what...we can play this game all day long until there's nothing left of you to identify you as human. You see...I will take you piece by piece, you hear me?" he screams at the suffering rapist. "Now let's see what else is on that table of pain..." he says as he goes over to the wheel table to take a look.

He picks up what looks like a very sharp cutting knife. "Well, this loooks like a very good instrument that I can use to cut your balls..." he says as with a low voice as he looks at the knife, which terries the one-eyed Akhona as ge begins to beg for his life, "Please, please, please sir I'm begging you okay? I'm really sorry..." he cries hopelessly as he feels the pain from the bone-deep knife wound. "I will stop if you answer this one question for me and it better be the truth Akhona, you hear me? It's better be the truth..." Ntokozo shouts at him before taking a deep breathe.

"Now tell me...how many women have you raped in your life?" he asks as he looks at Akhona in the eyes. "Uhmm...uhmm...sir please I don't know what you are..." Akhona cires out but without a moment's notice Ntokozo cuts his left thigh so deep that it tears open which leads to another loud scream. He is almost running out of voice since this has been going on for a little while now. Ntokozo once again pours the liquid to the wound, which makes the pain worse for Akhona as he almost chokes from screaming.

"Are you going to tell me what I need to know or we should cut your ears?" Ntokozo screams at the man's face. "But I already told that I don't know anything..." Akhona shouts in agony as his thighs bleed from the cuts. Ntokozo looks up and takes a deep breathe before saying, "You know what...f*ck this. You think I'm joking with you, don't you?" He then holds Akhona's head up and turns it on the side before cutting his left ear off, leading to the loudeest scream he has made so far. At this point the blood is just gushing out from cut that it has sprayed on Ntokozo's hands as well, which doesn't seem to bother him at all.

"Alright...are you ready to talk now or we are going for your balls?" he says with an angry face which terrifies Akhona because he now realises that this man has no limits at all. "Oh no sir please don't...okay? Alright, I will talk...I will talk..." he says in agony as he breathes heavily. He can't take anymore of this pain and he knows he can't hold out any longer.

"So, how many women have you raped Lukhele?" Ntokozo asks as his voices becomes deeper. "Water...water...can I please have some water." Akhona begs as he breathes heavily but Ntokozo cuts in, "Did you offer my sister water after you violated her?" he shouts at the man. "There will be no water for you untill you answer my question. I asked, how many women have you raped?" He looks at his blood-stained knife before bringing his face closer to that of Akhona's. "How many? How many goddamnit?" he shouts at Akhona with rage. His eyes are thirsty for more blood.

"Uhmm...6, 7, or 8...I don't know....please, I'm sorry..." Akhona begs for mercy as he cries uncontrollably. "So you don't even remember how many women you have violated you sick bastard?" Ntokozo shouts at him. You do this because you always get away with it, right? You think you are above the law, that's it? Talk you piece of sh*t..."

"No, no, no sir...It wasn't like that sir...uhmm...it...uhmm...please sir, it wasn't..." the stuttering and terrified Akhona begs for his life. "It wasn't like that? How was it like, huh?" Ntokozo shouts. "So you rape and throw money...after that you ove to another prey, right? Is that how it is, Lukhele...huh? You think your money will always protect you from being held accountable for your sins? Well, SA justice is too slow...people like you will face my justice now. Yes, that's right...I wasn't there when you traumatised my sister and then threw money at the police so that you will get away with it. I wasn't there for her and I regret that very much...but guess what...I'm here now."

"Please, please, please...I beg you you sir...I will never do it again. Please forgive me..." Akhona begs for his life when he sees Ntokozo pulling a gun from his back. "People like you never change Lukhele, you think you can arrogantly buy your way through everything..." Ntokozo says as he points the gun at the man's face. "This not only for my sister but for every woman you have abused and those you would have abused in the future" he says as she squeezes the trigger and puts two bullets in his forehead.

Chapter 8

Answers

"Well, it looks like we have come back again huh? It's a good thing that we actually found you too Miss Gumede..." detective David Skhosana says nervously as he and his partner sit down on the couch at the Gumede mansion. It's a Monday morning, a couple of days after Ntokozo had killed Akhona Lukhele, the man who raped his sister. And today, both Dora and Lungile are working from home as there are no pressing matters at the sites that need their attention. They actually figured they'll just take it easy today since they had a hectic weekend of fun as a family but as it turns out, it won't happen.

"What are you accusing us of today officers?" the viisibly annoyed Lungile asks as she looks at her mother who sits next to her. "Yeah, we thought we answered all your questions on Friday detectives, what's going now?" Dora probes with a face of worry. This time they didn't offer the detectives anything, perhaps out ofanxiousness.

"Uhmm...actually we are today on another matter, sort of..." detective Lindiwe Zulu says but Lungile quickly cuts in, "Sort of?" she asks curiously as she looks at her mother again. "Oh yeah, uhmm...today we have come to ask you questions about another murder..." David says with a low voice as he looks at his partner but again Dora cuts in, "You got to be kidding me officers. When did we suddenly become suspected serial killers in a space of three days, huh? Who are you suspecting us of killing now?" she says as she throws her hands in the air in disbelief. Lungile is just as shocked at what the police have to say.

"Uhmm...we are not accusing you of anything Mrs Gumede but it appears that the latest victim is also linked to your daughter here..." David says calmly, which seems to puzzle the Gumedes but Lindiwe adds, "Uhmm...do you remember a person by the name of Akhona Velenkosini Lukhele?" she asks Lungile who immediately takes a deep breathe as though she is frightened about something, which makes David and Lindiwe to look at each in wonder.

At that very moment Lungile is transported down memory lane to the day the man mentioned has his way with her at the University resident. She remembers how he hit her on the face several times before forcing himself on her and how made light of it afterward as though it wasn't something serious. She remembers the trauma of wanting to kill herself as result of the humiliation she had had to endure at Akhona Lukhele's friends. As all of those emotions come flooding her memory, tears begin to fall down as her hands begin to shake.

When her mother notices this she quickly embraces her daughter and says, "Oh sweetheart, are you okay? Shhh...let me quickly go get you some water okay?" as she quickly goes to the kitchen to fetch some water. At that point officers David and Lindiwe don't know what to say as they look at each other but they can see how this has triggered Lungile.

"You see now what you two have done to my daughter? Are you happy now?" Dora shouts at the officers as she comes back to sit down next to her daughter with a glass of water. "Here sweetheart, drink..." she says as she gives water to Lungile who drinks up quickly to a point of almost choking on it. "Alright baby, easy okay?" the worried Dora says as she brushes Lungile's back. "I think you two should leave okay? Beacuse you two have really uoset my daughter. Are you enjoying this? Huh? Are you enjoying this right now?" the upset Dora shouyts at the police who look at eah other not knowing how to respond.

"Uhmm...we are sorry Mrs Gumede, it was really not our intention for this to happen..." David says with a low voice as he looks at his partner. "Perhaps it's best if we left...we can come back some other time when Miss Gumede has calmed down." he says as he stands up but Lungile calls out, "No it's okay...I'm okay" she says as she wipes her tears.

"Sweetheart, are you sure about that?" a surprised Dora asks as she brushes her daughter's back. "Yeah mama, I'm sure..." Lungile says as she nods. "It's not like we have anything to hide, right? So let the officers do their jobs and get this over and done with. So what are you here to say officers? You asked if I knew who Akhona Lukhele is? Yes I know who that scambag is...what about it?"

"Uhmm...so yeah. His body was found dumped in some field somehwere in Verelum. He looked to have been tortured badly before he was killed and he was missing some parts of his body" David says with a nervous voice as he looks at his partner who nods in agreement to the statement, but Lungile interjects, "And so you suspect that I am the one who killed him?" she asks as she shakes her head in disbelief. "Well, I didn't but I certainly would have to be the one who killed him but I guess some lucky bastard got to him first before I did. I suppose life is unfair like that"

The officer are shocked at the statement Lungile is making as they look at each other. Even Dora's eyes pop as she fears that rhe statement may be misinterpreted by the police.

"Well uhmm...considering that all three victims were linked to you somehow and the MO was the same it does race suspicion...and it does make you a person of interest in this matter..." Lindiwe says as she shrugs her shoulders. "Oh well, I will let you know that I had nothing to do with the murder of these people officer okay? Yes they were scumbags who deserved to die, all of them...but I didn't kill them. You are free to do your investigations officers and when you are done come back and tell me who did it so that I can thank them for doing the job you police can't seem to get right."

"Okay can you atleast tell us where were you on Saturday afternoon?" David asks as he pulls a little notebook from his jacket pockets. "I was here with my family having a family braai..." Lungile says as she looks at her mother who nods in agreement. "All of you? What about your brother? Was he here too?" Lindiwe probes as she looks at David but Dora cuts in, "Yes he was here with us. He went to buy meat in the morning and prepared the coals for us, and we had a fun day as a family." she says with a straight face. "Is he around, so that we can ask him a couple of questions as well?" David probes. "Oh no, he went out but you can always come back later when he is back if you want to ask him some questions." Lungile says as she shrugs her shoulders, LIndiwe and David look at each other not know how to respond to that. This leads to a moment of silence as David writes some notes down while Lungile and her mother look at each other.

"So you said when was the last time you saw Akhona Lukhele?" Lindiwe asks with some level of curiosity. "The last time I saw the scambag was the day he forced himself on me some 6 or 7 years ago..." Lungile says with a straight face as she looks at Lindiwe in the eyes while David writes something down. "Uhmm...and between then and now you have never had any form of contact with him?" David probes. "None whatsover..." the vissibly annoyed Lungile says. "I didn't even know where he was or what he was doing, with who...I just couldn't couldn;t careless..."

"But you remembered his name, no?" the seemingly cheeky Lindiwe asks as she raises an eyebrow. "Would you forget the name of a person who violated you or your daughter, or your family member? Woild you?" Lungile asks as she raises her voice a little bit, clearly irritated by the question she deems condescending.

"Alright, alright...please, let's all just calm down okay?" David please as he sees that this could soon get out of hand. "Uhmm...I think we have all that we need so far and if there's anything more we need clarity on, we know which door to knock on..." he says with a smile. "Well, you are free to come by anytime officer. Oh uhmm...and you

are also free to ask neighbours who saw us on Saturday. I think we are all interested in the same thing right? To have criminals and scambag off the street, ör off the earth...no?" Dora says sarcastically as she also forces a smile back.
The detectives don't respond to that but stand up and walk out the door...

***

Somewhere else, things haven't been great between Pearl and her father since that day at the garage where Ngubeni threatened to disown his daughter. Even though Ngubeni made an about turn, Pearl has been doing everything to avoid her father. Jabulani on the other hand wishes he hadn't done something like that but his sturbon heart will never allow him to try and make peace with his daughter.
"Pearl mntanami(my child), can please I have a moment with you?" he says with a calm and voice and a smile to his daughter who has come down from her room to have some milk from the kitchen. He is hoping that she is agree so that they will have a mature conversation. "Dad, I'm a little busy with something upstairs and I have to go check things at the hardware..." the visibly irritated Pearl says as she takes a deep sigh, knowing how this may just turn out.
"Oh sweetheart I understand that but please...I will not take too much of your of your time okay? I promise..." Ngubeni says with a begging voice, to which Pearl gives in and comes to sit down on a couch opposite her father.
At that very moment an awkward and tesne atmosphere seems to settle in as the two look at each other. Ngubeni clears his throat before saying, "Uhmm...so speaking of business, how are things going that side?" with a nervous voice as he fixes his eyes on his daughter. "Uhmm...everything is okay dad, especially with the

Butchery, Car wash and the bricks site...but I have to go check things out at the Hardware"Pearl says as sh shrugs her shoulders. "Oh, that's very good my baby. You know...you are doing areally great job there hey..." Ngubeni says with a smile which makes Pearl raise an eyebrow as if to say, *'oh really?'* but her father quickly interjects, "Uhmn...look, I know that the other day I didn't speak well to you and I'm sorry about that okay?" he says with a low voice as he looks down, which surprises his daughter as she raises an eyebrow in disbelief. "Yes I know that you don't believe me swetheart but I mean it..." Ngubeni continues. "You are doing great with running the family businesses, I shouldn't have threatened to take that away from you..."
This is not what Pearl expected from his father because he usually never folds on anything, so she lets out a little smile but Ngubeni continues, "You know, you are the only family I've got now sweetheart and I hate it when we fight sometimes." he says calmly. "Yes there are other people in this house but you are the only child I have and I don't wanna lose you..."
"I hear you dad..." Pearl says with a calm voice and a half smile no knowing if her father is just saying this for the sake of peace or what? "Alright so uhmm...let me go to the hardware, I will be back later..." she says as she stands up but her father calls out, "Oh uhmm...sweetheart, I need you to stop seeing that boy you are seeing okay? Gumede, is it?" he says with a straight face which catches her daughter off guard as she sits down again. She raises an eyebrow at her father as she didn't expect this. "Dad...?" she calls out as though she has no idea what her father is talking about.
"I'm asking you to stop seeing that Gumede boy okay?" Ngubeni says, with a firmer voice this time and a straight face. "How do you..." a shocked Pearl says but her father quickly cuts in, "Oh come Pearl, I'm in this kind of business so I have enemies...you think I wouldn't ensure that you are protected, or check elements hanging

around you?" he says as picks up a glass of whiskey from the table and start drinking.
"No,you have me followed dad...you can't do that okay?" the visibly upset Pearl says as she raises her voice a little bit but her father cuts in, "Hey, hey, hey...I'm a father and a father does everything to protect his family..." he says as he finishes off what was left from his glass but Pearl jumps in, "Protect from what baba(father), huh? Protect me from what? Ntontozo? What has he done? He is not one of your drug enemies dad..." she says as she raises her voice a liitle bit but Ngubeni once again cuts in, "Hey don't you dare talk to me like that okay? I'm still your father damnit. Now I am telling you to stop seeing that Gumede boy, that's it..."
"But why dad, huh? Why? Ntokozo is no threat to you...his family is actually a very good family" Pearl says as she stands up but her shouts, "Sit the f*ck down..." as his eyes turn red with rage, which seems to scare Pearl a little as she quickly sits down. Now this moment is threatening to get out of hand as the two look at each other in the eyes.
"Listen here...I know the Gumede family well okay? And I'm not saying they are a bad family but look, what happens when boyfriend starts to starts to interfere with my business? You think I'm going to spare him just because he's with you?" Ngubeni asks as he tries to calm himself down before things get out of hand. "What do you mean about that, dad?" a terrified-looking Pearl as as she raises an eyebrow. "Well, you better use your imagination okay?" Ngubeni says as he looks away from his daughter, which makes Pearl feel a little uncomfortable with her father's statement not wanting to even imagine what it could mean.
"Look dad, I love Ntokozo okay? And I am going to be with him..." she says as she looks at her father in the eyes but Ngubeni fires back, "Well child you gonna have to learn to unlove him okay? Because the two of you won't happen..." he says with a firm voice. "I'm telling

you, okay? I know danger when I see one...and this...that boy is danger Pearl..."
"But you don't even know him dad, okay? He is actually a very good person okay? Must I now reamin single forever because you think every man I date is a danger to me or this fmily?" a puzzled Pearl asks as she throws her hands in the air. "Oh yes, I don't date...since your mother passed on, so what's wrong with you also not dating?" Ngubeni responds as he shrugs his shoulders. "Look, we are building an empire here Pearl, okay? We can't have people coming and distracting us from achieving that. I thought you and I agreed that we are a team...we should stick together with that okay? There will be plenty of time for you to date okay?"
"When, dad? When I'm 50 years old? No...I love Ntokozo and I'm going to be with him, otherwise I'm going leave you here alone..." Pearl says as her face turns really serious to show her father that she means business. "No, you will do no such thing okay?" Ngubeni says as she raises his voice a little. If you insists on continuing to see this boy, don't blame me for anything that happens to him okay? Are you sure you wanna be responsible for anything that happens to himor his family? Because if he indeed interferes in my business I will kill him and his entire family...I don't care if he's your boyfriend"
"Dad, I'm warning your okay? Don't you dare touch Ntokozo okay? Or his family...or I swear...I swear you and I are done and you will never see me again..." a furious Pearl shouts as her eyes turn red with rage at her father. "Don't be silly...you and I are family okay? We shall always be a family and this Ntokozo boy is not. Now stop being childish and focus on things that really matter okay?"
Pearl knows better than taking these threats from her father lightely as she looks at him in the eyes. She is beginning to wonder if it's a good indea to get involved with the man she loves hence risking his life or to test the saying that says love conquers all. She also knows that escalating this any further with her ruthless father may not end

well. At this point in time she really hates everything about her father as she gives him a look of disgust towards him. Ngubeni on the other is not willing to fold from this as he pours himself another double of whiskey. "You want one?" he asks his daughter who looks at him in disbelief.
At that moment Pearl stands up and rushes to her room upstairs, leaving her hardened father enjoying hos drink as though he is feeling nothing towards the conversation he just had woth his daughter.

***

Back at the Gumede mansion, Lungile and Dora are still shocked and worried about the visit from the police a little earlier they haven't even be able to focus on the work they had planned to do. While they haven't discussed this since the police left they both know something isn't right about this whole thing.
"Mama, I know that we have not talked about this but I know that you can see something ain't right about this murders..." Lungile says to her mother as she brings her a glass of cold drink in the lounge.
"Yes I know mntanami(my child) something just ain't right about this whole thing..." a worried-looking Dora says with a sigh as she receives the glass of a cold one from her daughter who sits opposite her. "And the elephant in the room mama..." Lungile adds to which Dora raises an eyebrow as though she has no idea what her daughter is talking about. "I mean...uhmm the very fact that these murders all seem to be linked to me and happen after Ntozoko came back hom?" Lungile says as she shrugs her shoulders.
"What are you trying to say Lungile?" a puzzled Dora asks curiously.
"Oh come on mama, don't pretend that you haven't been wondering about thisn too okay?" Lungile says as she raises an eyebrow. "The very fact that we have no idea where Ntokozo has been the past 12 years and doing what and now he comes back people linked to my

cases start dying? You told me the other day that he asked that we re-opened the cases right? But he never asked me about it...but suddenly everyone is dying one by one? Come on, something is going on mama..."

"I thought you believed that these deserved what happened to them, so what has change now?" A worried-looking Dora asks as she takes a sip of her drink but her daughter quickly interjets, "No, that hasn't changed, alright? I stand by my word on that but what worries me is that we could be living with a stranger in this house okay?" Lungile says as she shrugs her shoulders. "What if Ntokozo is the one who killed these people because he is trying to make up for the time he wasn't here to protect me? Yes I know mama what you are thinking alright? The Ntokozo we know wouldn't have done something that" This makes Dora think for a second as she looks at her daughter. "Okay, okay, look...yes this has been bothering me for a little while too okay?" she says as she tries to keep her voice down. "I started paying attention the day news broke about the police that was murdered. I was watching the news with him and his reaction to it was very strange...like, very cold towards the whole thing..."

"Oh God mama, are we living with psycho?" a panicking Lungile says as her eyes pop but her quickly cuts in, "wait, wait, wait...you don't know that yet, alright? It could just be a co-incidence, right? Come on, you know Ntokozo...he is not that kind of a person Lungile...he isn't capable of doing something like that. And when would he have done these things because he was practically here all this time in my sight?"

"You are talking about the Ntokozo of 12 years ago mama, okay?" Lungile says as she throws her hands in the air. "Seondly, he wasn't here all the time...I mean, he isn't here even now" She looks really worried in her face. Her mother thinks for a second before saying, "But why do I get the feeling that you desperately want it to be Ntokozo, huh?" as she raises an eyebrow. "How can you say something like that mama?" Lungile protests in disbelief. "I'm just uneasy about my brother turning out to be cold-blooded killer. I mean, where did he learn to torture people like that? He was never a troubled child, so don't you think we should be asking him about where he was the last 12 years and doing what?"

This leads to a little silence as Dora takes a sip while thinking about what her daughter is saying. "Look my child I hear what you are saying okay? The thought of it terrifies me too..." she says with a worried face. "But there has to be an explanation into all this Lungile...I mean, it's hard to believe that Ntokozo can become a killer in just 12 years. Something must have happened to him where ever he was..."

"Or maybe it's just one person that can change your life within a day..." Lungile says as she rolls her eyes as though she is annoyed by something but that seems to confuse her mother. "I'm talking about that girl Pearl, mama..." Lungile says as she throws her hands in the air. "I mean, don't you think Ntokozo is always with this girl when he is not here in the house? Her father is a drug dealer and a murderer...for all we know she could be having bodies of her own. I think she is a bad influence on Ntokozo that girl and we need to find a way of getting rid of her in my brother's life for good. If Ntokozo is indeed involved in these deaths, what are the chances that she is also?"

Dora thinks for a second before saying, "Arg, I don't know Lungile...maybe that girl isn't like her father, you know..." much to her daughter's surprise as she raises an eyebrow. "Oh really now mama? So you now see a daughter-in law in her now? That's not gonna happen okay?" Lungile says as she is clearly annoyed by this. "Don't be dramatic okay? I'm not saying I trust that girl but I'm saying she may just not have anything to do with what's been happening." Dora says as she shrugs but Lungile cuts in, "I will hook Ntokozo up with one of my girls..." she says as she looks up as

though she's thinking about something. "What? Tell me you are joking..." a shocked Dora says as she can't believe what her daughter just said. "What? My friends are very good people okay? And I think they can ground Ntokozo and make him become a better person" Lungile says as she shrugs her shoulders. "Mpume really likes him but I have been blocking that, and Lindi and Ntokozo know each other since childhood..."
Dora is just in disbelief over what her daughter is saying. "So you wanna pimp your brother now?" You are so unbelievable my child, wow..." as she claps hands once but Lungile doesn't look bothered by this as she quips at that statement fro her mother.
"Alright look...so are we going to ask your brother about all this?" Dora asks as she finishes off her drink. Lungile thinks for a second before saying, "Uhmm...look i think we should first ask him about the past 12 years years, right? And then perhaps from there we can learn something that may suggest whether he is involved in these killings or not..." as she shrugs her shoulders. "Alright then, that's sounds like a good idea...where is he anyways? I wanted to send him to the mall..." Dora says with a sigh but Lungile quickly cuts in, "Where else can be besides that girl Pearl? I'm telling you mama, that girl is trouble..." she says visibly annoyed.
"Stop it okay? You don't know that..." Dora says with a smile as she shakes her head in disbelief. "Look, I'm going down to the study okay? I will see you later. Please inform me when Ntokozo is back okay?" she says as she stands up from the couch but Lungile interjects, "No it's fine mama I will go to the malls okay, because I have to go fetch Mbali from school..." she says as she also stands up and grabbing her keys.

***

Speaking of the devil, Ntokozo is in the car of some mysterious guy parked in the some field in the middle of somewhere and things look a little serious. He is sitting in the passenger seat next alongsie this guy who just has this mystery about him. He is in his usual smart casual self with a black shirt and blue jeans and grey jacket and his car is parked behind this mysterious man's car.

"So you have it?" Ntokozo asks as he keeps his head forward where the car is facing. The man pulls out a brown A4 envelop from the side of his door and hands it over to Ntokozo before saying, "You have been very busy, I see..." with a deep voice as he also looks forward. Ntokozo takes the envelope and opens it, "Yeah well you know me, I don't like to sit idle..." he says as he pulls out what looks like a file from this brown envelop.

"Any trouble from the police yet?" the mystery man asks with a low voice. "I thought I was the one who should be asking that..." Ntokozo says as he turns around and grabs a bag from the back seat, "This is for you my friend..." he says as he gives this man the black bag. He takes it and opens it to see the contents. "6Kg huh? You did great..." he says with a smile of satisfaction. "Don't you worry about the police okay? They will do what they are trained to do, which is to ask question but it really won't go anywhere beyond that I promise. But you better wrap this up very quickly man okay? Eventually people will start asking serious questions?"

"Understood..." Ntokozo says as he looks forward. "Have you explained anything to your family yet?" the man asks as he turns to look at Ntokozo who takes a deep sigh before saying, "Uhmm...not yet hey...I actually thought I'd just deal with the matter at hand first before I sit down with them. I know they are asking themselves questions by now..." a worried-looking Ntokozo says as he looks on his side of the window.

"Yeah it's good that you stay focused on this first and then we will see how best we tackle anything else alright?" the man says as he taps on Ntokozo's shoulder. "So are you now happy about your sister's boyfriend after the info I gave you? Was it of any help?"

"Yeah man, uhmm...I think I have nothing to worry about, as far as this guy is concerned. I guess it was just paranoia that's all..." Ntokozo says as he shrugs his shoulders. "Alright good...so now stay focused please okay? We can't have your head all over the place now..." the man says with a rather firm voice this time. "Oh and please get as much information about this Jabulani Ngubeni guy as possible. We have actually been looking for him for a little while but no one has ever been able to get close to him untill now. Are you sure that his daughter won't be a distraction for you? Because that can present a challenge..."

"Don't worry about that man...I know what I'm doing okay?" Ntokozo says as though he is annoyed by that last question. "Aright then...gotta go...I will keep in touch..." the man says with another tap on the on Ntoko's shouler before they part ways.

Chapter 9

Something doesn't add up

"So who the hell is this?" a grumpy looking Jabulani Ngubeni asks one of his men, pointing at a kid as they stand in their usual place of meeting-the garage. "Uhmm...that's that Makhathini kid down the road by Vusi's corner..." one of his man responds. This meeting happens a few days after the police had visited the Gumedes regarding the latest murder case and not much has actually happened since as Ntokozo continued to act as though everything is normal. Pearl who is actually on this meeting today has had a cold relationship with his father over the argument they had a few a days ago. Since then she hasn't spoken to Ntokozo, perhaps out of fear of what her father might do to him...he is not a man that makes idle threats.

Ngubeni himself seems to have his heart hardened by that argument he had with his daughter that he is less and less bothered by the fact that they are giving each other a cold shoulder in the house. He has some of his men watching his daughter's moves to see if she's still seeimng Ntokozo or hid his order to never see him again.

On the other hand Dora and Lungile haven't had time to sit down with Ntokozo and get answers from him as they committed to do a few days ago. It could be that they don't know how to begin the conversation or they are just scared to find out anything scary about him. They still sit in the dinner table together as a family and they are always puzzled at how warm he can be and perhaps that throws them off a little bit.

"So what's your name kid?" an irritable Ngubeni asks the boy who looks nervous and scared. "Uhmm...I'm a Qaphela Makhathini..." the boy responds with a trembling voice as he looks around the room full of Ngbeni's men. "How old are you?" Ngubeni probes with an intimidating voice, but before the boy could answer Pearl, "Dad, umfana wakwaMakhathini ufunani lana?(what is Makhathini boy doing here)?" she asks with eyes of panic as she looks at the boy is scared out of his mind. She knows this can't be a good thing when she saw one of her father's men bringing the boy through the gate so she followed them to the garage.

"The question is, what are you doing here Pearl? Didn't you say you don't want to be part of this business?" Ngubeni asks as he fixes his eyes on the young boy. "Yes , I'm not part of your business but you have this terriied boy in here dad...what did he do? What do you want with him, huh? Please leave him alone...his parents must be terrified not knowing where he is." a terrified Pearl tries to pleade the boy's case.

"Stay out of this okay? If you don't wanna be here just close the door on your way out okay?" Ngubeni says as he raise his voice a little bit.

"Not without that boy baba(dad), okay?" a defiant Pearl says an angry face but her father ignores her as he looks at the by, "I asked how older are you kid..." he says with a straight face.

"Uhmm...I'm...Uhmm...I'm 17...uhmm...16..." the scared boy says with a trembling voice as he looks at Pearl as if to pleade with her to intervene. The other men also look a little uncomfortable with how their boss is doing things but non of them dare challenge him once he sets his mind of doing something.

"So Qaphela, I hear you refuse to work for me boy...do you wanna tell me why?" Ngubeni asks teh boy wo is still in his school uniform but Pearl once again quickly interjects, "Dad, are you insane? He is a kid, a school kid..." she shouts. Please don't do this okay? Just let the boy go...I'm sure you can find people who are grown that can do this dirty work for you, alright?"

"Pearl, I said stay out of this, alright? Stay out of it..." an angry Ngubeni shouts at his daughter as he gives her a sharp eye. "So boy I asked you, why are you refusing to work for me? Do you know how many kids will jump at this opportunity to make some money and become kings at their school?" he probes the terrified boy who looks at Pearl one more before saying, "Uhmm...my parents will never allow me to do this sir and I also don't want to deal drugs. Please sir I beg you...please let me go and I will not even tell my parents abot this. Please I beg you...please let me go home to my parents..."

In a move that seems to shock everyone in the garage including his men, Ngubeni pulls a gun and points it at the young man but his daughter quickly gets in front of him, "Dad...what the hell are you doing?" she shouts in disbelief of what her father is doing. "I am not going to let you kill this kid dad...no. If you want to do that, you better start with me then" she says with a trmbling voice as she looks at the barrel of the gun.

Even Ngubeni's men don't seem to know what to do at this moment, whether to call out on their boss or grab his daughter aside. "Get out of my way Pearl..." Ngubeni says with a low voice as his eyes turn red with rage. "Get her out of here..." he shouts, and when one of the men approaches, Pearl shouts, "Don't you dare touch me wena(you)" and the man steps back. He knows better than laying a finger on the boss's daughter, especially when he is trigger happy.

"Dad, you are not going to kill this boy in front of me...you hear me?" Pearl says with a firm voice as she continues to look through the barrel, with the terrified boy behind her for cover. "You are losing your mind dad...are you going to go around killing every teenager that doesn't want to do your dirty work? No, this has got to stop dad and it has to stop now. No more bullying of kids..." She quickly grabs the kid by the hand as they head towards the exit door but without a moment's notice, Ngubeni shoots the kid at the back of the head and he falls down dead in an instant. At that moment everyone had taken cover not knowing where the bullet has flown to but when Pearl realises that Qaphela had been shot by her father, it's as though her whole world has come crushing down. "Dad, what the hell did you just do huh? Are you crazy or something?" she shouts on top of her voice as she kneels in front of Qaphela's dead body laying on a pool of blood. When she lifts her head to look at her father, she sees a man she can't recognise.

At this point she is starting to cry as her mind can't process what just happened. She is suddenly feeling dizzy and neausious as she stands up to look at all the men standing in the room. The fact that none of them are doing anything about this shocks her. One of the things that is crossing her mind is that she is now a witness to a murder and that alone is enough to make her more dizzy as she looks at her monster father.

She quickly goes out the garage without turning back but she doesn't seem to know where she is going as she walks out the gate. Ngubeni wants to stop his daughter from leaving this house but he realises that at this point the priority is the this body that is laying on the pool of blood. "Clean this up..." he commands his men as he leaves the garage to go inside the house.

About 2 or 3 hours later when the Gumedes are having an early supper, there's a knock on the door. They all look at each other wondering who could that be at this time. Lungile and Dora are probably thinking that it is the police that came in the morning since they had promised to come back. "Ndodana(son) please go check who that might be..." Dora says to Ntokozo who quickly heads to the door. His eyes can't believe who is standing on the other side of the burgler gate.

"Pearl...? Uhmm...what are you doing here? Uhmm..I mean, are you okay? What happened?"

He seems shocked and caught off guard by this but he also notices that Pearl has been crying and by the looks of it, for a little while. She has a back pack with her which looks to have clothes inside. "Uhmm...Ntokozo I'm sorry for showing up just like this. Your small

gate wasn;t locked so I used it. I really didn;t know where else to go..." the crying Pearl says with a trembling voice as she looks like a person who has been through a very traumatic experience.
"Oh uhmm...sorry please come in..." the worried-lookibg Ntokozo says as he opens the door for Pearl to come in, but now he is suddenly anxious knowing how shocked his family will be when they see this. He leads leads her to the dinning room where everyone else is, "Uhmm....everyone...this is Pearl..." he says with a trembling as he clears his throat, much to to everyone's shock in the room.

***

The following day day on the afternoon is Lungile's birthday and she has invited her friends to celebrate with her. Everyone at the Gumede's is still shocked by the guest that showed up at at night unnounced and they still not quiet sure how to react to it or handle it considering that she is not just any guest in the house but it's Pearl, the daughter of a dangerous drug dealer. But when Dora and Lungile saw how traumatized Pearl looked when she knowcked on the door, they just couldn't chase her out the door even though they certainly feel some kind of way about her. They are just hoping Ntokozo will sort this out quickly.
So this afternoon as Lungile is celebrating her birthday with her friends outside on the beautiful green lawn, Pearl has been locking herself up in the guest bedroom upstairs all day, probably out of shame...and Ntokozo has invited his friend Sthembiso to hang out with him for a little while. It's really not a party of any sort with tents and loud music, even though that's what Lungile promised but she seems to have changed her mind. They are just having camp chairs and a cooler box full of ciders and champagnes while Ntokozo and Sthembiso are sittinng by the gate with a cooler box full of beers and playong music from Ntokozo's car.

"So friend, what's been going on with you? We haven't seen you in a while, even though you said something about dealing with a family crisis on WhatsApp...is everything okay?" Nompumelelo asks curiously as she looks at Lindiwe who nods in agreement with the question. They look really worried about their friend.

"Eish guys, you really wouldn't believe what has been happening hey..." Lungile says as she shakes her head in disbelief. "But before we even go there, Mpumi...do you still want my brother? Because he is available and he would really love to go out with you..." She takes a huge sip of her cider, which seems to confuse her friends as they look at each other. Nompumelelo is probably feeling that her friend has had way too many ciders now as she looks at Lindiwe who jumps in, "My friend, what's going on? Why are you pimping your brother to Mpumi? What happened?" she asks curiously but Nompumelelo quickly interjects, "What? You also wanted him?" she asks with a naughty smile.

"Don't be silly wena(you), ofcourse not...but I'm worried about this one here. Sweetie, what's going on with you? Talk to us..." Lindiwe pleads with a worried face, which makes Lungile to think for a second before saying, "Eish guys you won't believe who showed up at our doorstep last night...Pearl" with a huge sigh, much to her friends' shock.

"What? Pearl?" a stunned Nompumelelo asks but Lindiwe quickly interjects, "I didn't know bayathandana(they are dating)..." she says as she raises an eyebrow. Lungile takes a deep sigh before saying, "Look, I don't know if they are dating or not but...uhmm...yeah they are friends, sort of. I actually don't know what's going there between the two but Pearl showed looking in bad shape last night and she was crying...I'm assuming it got something to do woth back home. She said she had nowhere else to go so we couldn't let her sleep on the street, so we took her in...she's actually upstairs right now in the guest bedroom..."

"What? She slept here? In your home? Doesn't she have relatives or something? Why here?" a puzzled Nompumelelo asks as she looks at Lindiwe who is just as confused. "I really don't know much of anything right now guys honestly..."Lungile says as she yawns as though she is sleepy. "But we will obviously find out more from Ntokozo who might know just a little more than us"
"But do you guys trust her? I mean she is a drug dealer's daughter...if she'd run away from home, don't you think her father will come here guns blazing and knock down your door looking for her?" a worried Lindiwe asks as she takes a sip of her cider and Nompumelelo nods in agreemet to the point. "Ofourse we don't trust her Lindi...I mean, as you say, she is a drug dealer's daughter." Lindiwe says as she shrugs her shoulders. " Mom and I will speak to Ntokozo about this later tonight...he will have to get rid of her as soon as possible. I can't have an element like that around my daughter. If she can't find other relatives she will have to book herself a hotel."
This makes the shocked Lindiwe and Nompumelelo to look at each other in disbelief.
"Anyways, that's not even in the middle of the family crisis I was talking about guys..." Lungile says as she shakes her head, much to her friends' shock. They must be thinking, *'What could be more than this?'* as they look at each other again. But they think it's best to wait for their friend to tell them what else is going on in the Gumede family.
"Well, guess who is the number one suspect on multiple murders..." Lugile says as she throws her hands in the air bjt her friends are very confused. "What the hell are you talking about?" Lindiwe asks curiously as she looks at Nompumelelo who adds, "Yeah friend, what are you talking about?" she asks. Lungile takes a deep breathe before saying, "Well, you guys know about my story right? And all that I had to go through, and the the cases I opened with the police...I have told you this many, many times." Her friends don't

respond to the question but wait for their friend tp continue with the story.
"Anyway uhmm...I think you have already seen on the news about the death of police a few weeks ago? Well, the police cam, to question me a couple of weeks ago..." Lungile says as he shrugs her shoulders, much to her friends'shock, "What? What on earth for?" Lindiwe asks in disbelief as she looks at Nompumelelo who quickly adds, "Yeah I mean...friend, why didn't you tell me about this mos? You know I would have been there for you..."
"They haven't charged me yet guys okay? So relax..." Lungile says as she takes a sip of her cider. "The police says they were questioning me because the police officer that died was in charge of the case I opened against one guy and the docket dissappeared. But when the guy I opened the case against also died few days after...brutally so, it seems, the police came knocking on my door"
"What? Lungile are you serious? This is not good...and you are certain you are far from this, right?" Nompumelelo asks as her eyes pop in disbelief. "Ofcourse I had nothing to do with this Mpume, what do you take me for?" Lungile says as she throws her hands in the air as she looks a little irritated. "But that's not all guys..." she continues, "Also...do you remember the other guy I also opened a case against...Akhona Lukhele? Uhmm...yeah he was also found dead and he was also tortured badly before being shot dead in the head. The police are now questioning me because all three are connected to me and they think these are revenge killings..."
Her friends are so shocked by these revelations as they look at each other. "My friend, this doesn't look good..." Lindiwe says with a worried face. "I know Lindi but this has got nothing to do with me...I didn't kill those people. As much as I really wishe I could have been the one who killed them, some bastard beat me to it..." Lungile says as she looks a little annoyed.

"But who would have killed these people though? I mean, unless they have done this to a number of other people before..." Lindiwe says as she tries to makes sense out of this but Lungile cuts in, "That's exactly what I said...these people must have raped other people before, people who revenged against them" she says as she takes a sigh. "And that police officer must have taken may bribes before, which means he is a dirty cops and dirty cops always have enemies. For the record, I'm happy that the three of them are dead."
"Okay look, if they charge you at any stage please call me okay?" a worried looking Nompumelelo says as she takes a strong sip. "I will do that my friend..." Lungile says with a smile. "So you see why that girl upstairs is the least of my worries right now? Ntokozo will have to deal with her cause I just can't." Lungile says as she rolls her eyes. "But enough about that guys...this is my birthday, can we please enjoy it?"

***

Right by the gate, Ntokozo is chilling with his highschool friend Sthembiso whom he hasn't seen in a little while since he's been on a revenge spree lately. Ntokozo and Sthembiso have known each other since high school and were very close, untill a couple of years before left home. They didn't have a way of keeping in touch afterwards so when they saw each other for the first time in 14 or 15 years they knew they had a lot to catch up on.
Sthembiso is now a 36 year-old engineer who makes a very descent leaving but decided against leaving home...instead he rebuilt his parents' home and made big. He has a 28 year-old sister who moved out when she got married 3 years ago. His parents are both still alive and he lives with them in the house.
"So my man, how much were you making overseas that you could afford a beautiful car like this? I mean, how are you mentaining it now that you are back? Did you join the family business or working

somewhere?" a pleased Sthembiso asks as he brushes the bonett of Ntokozo's new metalic black BMW. "Arg man...it was actually a very descent earning my friend hahaha..." Ntokozo says with a laughter and a little blush. "Well I made good savings while I was travelling the world but I'm working on opening my own Data Solutions company and the plan is coming along very well..." He takes a sip of his beer as though he is downing those news.

"Wow, that's really great man...you certainly will get contracts with both private and government. Data analysis is really big deal these days." Sthembiso says with a smile as he lifts his beer up. "And over there? Are you lucky with any of those ladies over there?" he asks as he looks ovwr where Lungile and her friends are seated having drinks.

"Oh come on man...those ones?" a blushing Ntokozo says as he shakes his head. "First of all, I've known Lindiwe from when we were kids it would be weird...and the other one, Nompumelelo seems okay but I don't know man, I don't think she's my type" He shrugs his shoulders which makes his friend to raise an eyebwrow, "Not your type huh? And your type would be...?" Sthembiso asks with some curiousity, which looks to make Ntokozo as little uncomfortable as he looks down blushing. "Uhmm...actually, it is Pearl Ngubeni..." he says with a low voice which almost sends his friend tumbling to the floor in shock.

"What? Are you insane man?" a disbelieving Sthembiso says as his eyes pop. "I know that you have been away for a little while man but you actually know who that girl is? Do you know who her father is? As your good friend man, I'm asking you to stay far, far away from that girl...you hear me? Stay far away from that girl bro..."

"Don't worry man, I know all about her okay?" Ntokozo says calmly with a smile but Sthembiso quickly interjects, "Alright then, so if you know all about her then you already know that it's bad news to get involved with her...for your sake and that of your family, okay?"

he says with a face of worry. Ntokozo doesn't want to entertain this topic very much because he has already much of it at home with his sister and mother, but whoelse can he talk to if it's not his friend? He probably is the only person that can understand or atleast see where he is coming from with this.

"Uhmm...look man, Pearl is upstairs right now...in the guest bedroom" he says with a low voice as he avoids eye contact. "What?" a shocked Sthembiso shouts as he looks at the upper room window of the house. "What on earth is she doing there? Man, what the hell are you doing? Do you really wanna die? Talk to me man, what are you thinking?"

Ntokozo thinks for a second before saying, "Look man, she showed up at my door last night unexpectedly and she was in bad state. She said she just had to get away from home but hd nowhere to go, so we had no choice but to take her in..." as he shrugs his shoulders but Sthembiso cuts in, "What are you talking about you had no choice? Ofcourse you had a choice man..." he says as he tries to whisper. "Why didn't she go to her relatives or at the hotel even? What is it that she had to run away from that she thought you were her refuge? You need to get rid of her man...I mean as soon as possible"

"Look man, I don't have much details on everything just yet..." Ntokozo says with a deep sigh. "She has locked herself in that room since yesterday when she set foot in the house. She looks terrified over something man and I thought that maybe I should allow her to calm down first before asking her about what's really going on at her home..."

Sthembiso thinks for a second as he shakes his head, "Look man, I really hope that you know what you are doing okay?" he says with a low voice. "Do you realise that when her father finds out that she is here he will come guns blazing to knock your front door down? You will become his enemy number one and trust me dude, you don't want that. That man is ruthless and can get away with everything because he has police and politicians in his pockets. Even parents who have tried to snitch on him for using their kids as drug mulles have either died or dissappeared somehow. I don't want you to get mixed up in something like that man"

What Sthembiso says seems to really upset Ntokozo as his face changes. "Hey man, I was meaning to ask you...who are his political friends?" he asks curiously as he takes a sip of his beer which makes Sthembiso to think for a second before saying, "Uhmm...you know Sbusiso Vilakazi, the MEC for Economic Developement right? Uhmm...Nonceba Nkosi the MEC for Higher Education, and a few other guys like those...why do you ask?"

"Arg man...I just wanted to know who esle I'm f*cking up with that is linked to this guy..." Ntokozo says as he shrugs his shoulders. "And the police commissioner? Is he also one of Ngubeni's friends?" This question seems to catch Sthembiso off guard as he wonders why his friend asks but he ignores that by saying, "I don't know man, but with this guy? You may never know hey. But I'm just asking you to stay away from him...starting with that girl upstairs, before you get her pregnant...hahaha" as he bursts out laughing, but Ntokoz wants to quickly dismiss this topic so he says, "Wanna say hi to the ladies over there? Let's go..."

Sthembiso is a little relunctant but he agrees as they go over to Lungile and her friends to have a great time.

***

Later on in the evening after Lungile's friends and Ntokozo's friend Sthembiso have left, the family is having supper, while Pearl is still locking herself in her room. At this point she seems even ashamed to come out and eat with her hosts in the same table, but Dora didn't want her to be pressured. At this point Dora and Lungile still don't even know why she Pearl is here and they are hoping that Ntokozo will give clarity to since he has been in her room a few times to check on her. One thing is for certain though is that there is a level of discomfort in the house which needs to be urgently addressed.

"Sweetheart did you send food to aunt Pearl's room?" Dora asks Mbali who is sittong with them in the table. "Yes gogo(grandma) I did..." Lungile's daughter answers. "Alright then my baby...can you please take your food to the lounge and eat there sweetheart? Grandma wants to have a word with your mom and uncle...please" Dora says with a smile and a begging voice, to which Mbali nods as she takes her plate to the lounge.

"Auntie Pearl? Really mama?" a vissibly annoyed Lungile says as she rolls her eyes but her mother interjects, "Oh come on stop it...you want me to teach your daughter to disrespect elders?" she says as she throws her hands in the air, to which Lungile rolls her eyes again as though she is saying, *'Oh whatever'* but Dora ignores that as she turns her attention to Ntokozo. "So son, what's the story with your friend? She's been in that room since yesterday but I didn't wanna force her to come down and eat with us without knowing her story. So why did she come knocking on this door? Who is she running away from? Do we need to be worried about our saftey?" This question makes Ntokozo to think for a seconmd as he looks at his sister who is also interested to hear what he has to say. "Uhmm mama, I don't have all the details at the moment but in a nutshell, she is running away from home. She says she can't be there at the moment but she didn't have anywhere else to go..." he says with a low voice as he looks down as though he is embarrassed by this. "Running from home? Does that mean she is bringing trouble to our doorstep? How long will she stay? Because you know, I have a chid here...I don't want any troble landing itself to our doorstep. What did she do?" Lungile throw all these questions to her brother, to which her mother nods in agreement. She also is wondering about the same things. The fact that they know who that is upstairs makes them very nervous and want to have all the answers before they decide what to do with the situation. This is what Ntokozo was worried about when Pearl stood in front of him at the adosor last night.

"Uhmm...guys, I say that let's give her atleast a day okay? At the moment she looks terrified about something and I don't wanna push her too far." he says with a nervous voice as he avoice eye contact with his family. "I swear I won't do anything to risk your saftey guys okay? I promise. So I will speak to Pearl tomorrow and try to understand what's really going on with her."

Lungile and Dora look at each as they try to digest what Ntokozo is saying. They may noyt like what he is saying but it's not like they have much of a choice on this.

"Alright look, let's just...we will talk about this matter later ndodana(son) but uhmm...there's another matter me and your sister want to discuss with you okay?" Dora says with a rather nervous voice as she looks at her daughter who nods, which makes Ntonkozo wonder a little bit as he raises an eyebrow. He knows that his family has questions about a lot of things and at some point they'd have to sit down and talk about stuff. Judging form the look in ther faces, this might just be the day for such sit down but whether he is ready to do this or not is another topic all together as nerves suddenly set in.

"Look son...few weeks ago you showed up at my door after 12 years you had dissappeared..." Dora says with a low and shaky voice. "While I'm really happy that you have come back home, we still don't know what happened to you Ntokozo...or where you were, doing what. A lot of things happened durimg the time you were away. Your sister went through the worst traumatic experience ever and it really was hard for her and we feel that if you were here to protect her she wouldn't have gone through all that. So yeah she needs needs closure on that, and I need closure on that. We need to know why abandoned us Ntokozo..."

These words stab Ntokozo's heart as the feelings of guilt come flooding his heart as he looks down in shame. He surely must have expected to face this at some point but now that his family is telling all this in his face he is feeling ashamed and embarrassed for having abandoned them...for having let his sister go through all the trauma alone.

At this point Lungile has come to full tears as she gently lays on her mother shoulder for comfort. All the memories of what she has had to deal with for the past 12 years have come to flood her mind as she cries uncontrollably. "Shhh sweeteart, I'm here okay? No one will hurt you anymore I promise, shhh..." Dora says as she gently brushes her daughter's shoulder which makes Ntokozo so guilty as he watches on. This is the first time he witnesses effect of his leaving and the pain he is seeing in her terrified sister is too much to bare as his now also begin to be teary. If he could turn back the clock, he would in a second.

"You see what your leaving has done to this family mfanawami(my son)?" Dora asks with a sad voice as she looks into her son's eyes. "This is the pain and hurt we have had to live with all the years you were not here wondering if any of it would have happened had you been home with us. This is it Ntokozo...what we are asking for now is for you to atleast explain to us why you did what you did. Perhaps then we shall have closure."

Ntokozo takes a second to think as he breathes a deep sigh. At this point he knows that there's no running away from this, he will have to deal with this matter one way or another. The problem now is that he doesn't even seem to know where to begin or what to leave out, if any but one thing he knows for sure is that he can't take the pain his family is feeling right now.

"Uhmm...mama, you guys are right...you deserve to know the truth..." he says with a low voice as he looks down in shame. "But uhmm...firstly I would love to apologies to you my sister for not being there when you went through all of that, I really failed you as a big brother. I know that I don't deserve your forgiveness and I can understand that. I wish there was a way of fixing all this and make things right...I will do anything to make it up to you sisi. To you mama as well, I'm really sorry...I know that's not how you raised me to be a man. I failed you and I failed this family. I shouldn't have done things the way I did."

Lungile doesn't say anything but continues to lay at her mother's shoulder as tears continue to fall down. "Then why did you do it son? Please make us understand okay? I think you know that we deserve to know that part..." a sad Dora says with a low voice as she continues to brush her daughter's shoulder.

Ntokozo looks up to the cieling and takes a deep breathe before saying, "Okay uhmm...12 years ago dad suggested that I join the army..." much to his family's shock as Lungile sits up straight and wipes her tears before looking at her equally shocked mother. "What?" Dora exclaims. "Why did your father suggests something like that?" she and Lungile are a little puzzled by these revelations and it's not something they expected when they said they wanted to know the truth about what happened. Now they are both curious to know about everything that Ntokozo will tell them.

"Uhmm...actually it's something he and I discussed a lot of times, I had always wanted to join the military." Ntokozo says as he takes a deep sigh. "But dad didn't know how you'd take this so once he had arranged everything for me to enlist he felt that it's best that we don't inform you about it cause you may try to persuade me..."

This is suddenly making Dora upset about this and begins to wonder if this is the kind of truth she really wanted to hear. To learn that her husband knew all along where her son was but never cared to mention it infuriates her. Perhaps what's more infuriating is that he is no longer here to speak for himself so that she can punch him in the face.

"Anyways uhmm...I was in the army for about 6 years during which I was in special taskforce missions across Africa and Europe and South America..." Ntokozo says as he scratches his head but his sister interjects, "I'm sorry...Are you saying to us that you were in the military travelling across the globe all the time you were away?" she asks in shock as she looks at her mother in disbelief. "And the missions you were in were dangerous? As in like, how we always see in the movies? That kind of danger?" This is not what she expected to hear from her brother and it's so hard to believe.

"Yes sis...something like that..." Ntokozo says with a low voice as he looks down but his mother interjects, "So your father sent you to risk your life all across the globe and for what? Huh? For what? Was he insane or what? Who sends his son to endanger themselves out there and not even have guts to inform the mother?" she asks as she raises her voice a little bit. She is just in disbelief over this.

Ntokozo wants to ignore his mother's questions as he continues, "Uhmm...anyways, after those 6 years I joined a government special program where I worked with other law enforcement agencies across the globe..." he says but his sister interrupts, "what kind of special programs? Doing what exactly?" she asks as she raises an eyebrow. This makes Ntokozo think for a second as he wonders if he should tell or not. "Uhmm...we prevented bad things from happening..." he says as he looks away but his mother quickly cuts in, "Things like what?" she asks curiously as she looks at Lungile who also wants to know.

"Bad things mama...things like, uhmm...terrorism, insurrection, coups etc., but uhmm...we did it covertly..." Ntokozo says as he takes a huge sigh but things suddenly dawn on Lungile as her eyes pop, "Oh my God...so you are a spy?" she asks in disbelief as she looks at

her mother who looks lost in all this, but Ntokozo continues, "I was not allowed to make contact with any member of my family or friends...except my handler."
"Your handler?" Lungile asks as she raises an eyebrow. "My dad..." Ntokozo says, much to his sister and mother's shock. "What's a handler?"a confused or, rather numb Dora asks. Ntokozo thinks for a second before saying "Uhmm...mama, a handler is a go to person...someone who is like a broker, the in-between guy that will represent the company that needs a job done and then represents you to the company after the job is done." as he looks down, knowing how this will make him mother feel as she is in shock and in disbelief.
"No, I don't believe you Ntokozo...your father was never like that okay?" Dora says as her voice begins to shake. She is almost in tears as though she is feeling the betreyal of the worst kind. "I guess we never know a person, do we?" Ntokozo says as he shrugs his shoulers but Lungile cuts in, "So dad knew all along where you were when we were worried sick about you? Damnit that bastard..." she shouts out of frustration but Ntokozo interjects, "Sisi he was just trying to protect you okay?" he says but Lungile doesn't wanna have it as she cuts in again, "If it was that dangerous why did he allow you to go there in the first place and let us believe that you had deserted us? He was a bloody liar, that's all he was..."
"Now the mood is really sense in this room as a shocked Lungile can't believe what her father did. Dora on the hand is struggling to even imagine any of this being true as her eyes begin to turn red and teary. If she had known the truth was going to be painful she wouldn't have aksed for it, but now she can't unhear what she's just heard.
"Guys, please believe me when I say that I wanted to come back home and see you but I couldn't..." Ntokozo says as he looks at both his sister and mother who are in shock. "But you know, dad kept me

informed about your lives and what you were up to...I suppose he didn't tell me about what you went through sis because he didn't want me to lose focus and end up quitting and coming back home." he says as he looks at his sister with begging eyes but suddenly his mother stands up says, " I need a minute okay? I can't take this anymore, I just can't..." with tears coming down as she goes upstairs to her room, leaving Ntokozo and Lungile glued on their chairs.

Chapter 10

Unhinged

A day after Ntokozo droped a bombshell on his mother and sister, things are a little tense at the Gumede home. After Ntokozo detailed his time away from home Dora went straight to bed where she cried herself to sleep. Apart from shockingly learning about Ntokozo's past which almost gave her hard attack, it is really hard to accept that her husband; the man she had been married for years could lie to her the way she did. Her husband was always a very open person to her and there was never any sense that he was hiding something from her, so to learn that he knew all along about her son's whereabouts is hard to accept.

At this point she is questioning everything about her marriage to Bongani and she is struggling to find a way to best deal with this. The conversation she had with her son last night kept playing in her mind throughout the night and she is strugglinf to deal with the pain she is feeling. For the longest of time she had longed for the truth on why her son Ntokozo left home, but now that she knows, she is kind of regretting seeking for it. Finding out that her son is a government spy is so unsettling for her but a little comfort is in the fact she had actually thought of the worst regarding Ntokozo's disappearance.

Lungile on the other hand, while she is just as shocked as her mother over Ntokozo's revelations, she is a little relieved that her brother didn't just abandoned them but was serving a course. She is however, like her mother, angry at her father for having kept all of this from them which led to her hating her brother for years. Ntokozo feels a huge burden has been has been lifted from his shoulders after the conversation he had with his family but he worries how this will affect relationships in the house. He hasn't seen his mother since last night and he knows how heart broken she is over the revelations regarding him and his father but, he wants to give her space to digest all of this before engaging her. The timing of all this couldn't have been the worst for the family since there is still a matter of Pearl Ngubeni, the daughter of a ruthless and feared drug dealer. It does complicated things in the house a little bit because they wouldn't want a guest to witness tensions in the house. Pearl has been locking herself in the room since arriving at the Gumede home, the only time she seems to get fresh air is when she goes through the sliding door to the balcony. She is carefull though that no one on the streets sees her here, that's why she doesn't want to leave the room, but luckily for her the guest room has the bathroom and the toilet. She eats breakfast, lunch and supper right here from this room, it's as though she is a prisoner of choice in this house. It could also be though that she is ashamed to face Ntokozo's family, knowing how they feel about her and about her father. This morning Ntokozo is sitting on the cement bench under one of the huge trees on the lawn and is thinking about all that has happened since he came back home when a voice calls out from behind him, "Hey Jason Bourne..." his sister Lungile says jokingly as she taps him on the shoulder, This is not what Ntokozo was expecting especially after last night family talk.

"Hey sis, how are you doing this morning, considering?" he says with a nervous smile as he looks at his sister's to try and read her. "Arg, you know...after last night? You can imagine how everyone is feeling...especially umama(mother). I'm sure this wan't easy for you as well hey..." Lungile says with a low voice as she comes to sit down on the opposite bench across the table. "I think to be fair on anyone, it will take a little bit of time for everyone to have this sink in properly...especially the thing about dad. I still can't believe dad actually kept your whereabouts from us when we at some point were ready to concede that you were dead"

"Yeah, don't be hard on him sis he was just trying..." Ntokozo says with a low voice but his sister cuts in, "Yes...to protect us, you mentioned that last night..." she says as she rolls her eyes in irritation. "He had no right to do that to us Ntokozo, okay? He had no right. Do you have any idea how much I hated you for leaving us? For leaving me? Dad heard me crying everyday and venting to mom and him about it but he chose to keep quiet and let me believe that you abandoned us. How can that ever be right, Ntokozo? He could have explained things to us and we would have understood. Serving your country can never be wrong...it's a heroic thing to do." Lungile is now becoming very emotional as she looks away from his brother who is feeling ashamed of this whole thing and this leads to an awkward silence. They are both trying to not escalate this to something more, just incase their mother or Pearl are watching up there.

"Uhmm...sis, I just want to say I'm sorry for everything you have been through and Im really sorry that I was never here to protect you..." Ntokozo says with a nervous voice as he clears his throat, but Lungile cuts in, "No, no, no brother...now I know better. It's not you I should have been angry with all these years..." she says with a low voice as she lifts her head to look at her brother. "Dad did not even tell you about what I was going through...such a father he was. But I am actually shocked that you didn't even come to his funeral. Did you even know he had passed on, or your people never told you?" Ntokozo thinks for a second before saying, "Uhmm...actually I was at the funeral..." with a low voice as he looks embarrassed. "What? You were at the funeral? But Ntokozo why would you..." a shocked Lungile shouts but Ntokozo quickly interjects, "Uhmm...I know sisi but I couldn't..." he says but he also doesn't finish as Lungile cuts in,

"Yes I know...you couldn't show yourself." she says with a dissapointed voice. "Yeah sis, i couldn't be seen here...It wasn't safe. It

really broke my heart to not be able to reach out to you guys but your saftey was more important to me..."
This leads to another silence as Lungile thinks for a second. "Okay now, why did you come back? Are you done working for these people?" she asks with a curious face as she raises an eyebrow. Ntokozo thinks for a second and says, "Uhmm...well, nobody ever officially retire with these people sis..." as he shrugs his shoulders, making his sister even more curious, "What do you mean?" she asks as she raises an eyebrow again.
"Look you don't have to worry about that right now okay? What's important is that I'm here now sis and I will never leave you and mom ever again..." Ntokozo says as he intends to completely ignore his sister's question which she can see but elects to not pay attention to it. "So a spy huh? How is it like? Running around the world like James Bond and killing people? You like it? I mean who would have thought I'd have my brother as a government agent, not in a million years..." she says with an excited face but Ntokozo just smiles and shakes his head without saying a wowrd. Clearly that's not a topic he is willing to get into and Lungile can see that as she throws his hands in the air as if to say *'Okay fine, I'll drop it'*
Ntokozo takes a deep breathe before saying, "Look, it's not something you can say you love to do or you don't. It's about serving your country but even in that, sometimes you feel that you have seen enough and maybe it's time to move on. Sometimes you make enemies and or you just become an enemy to some because you know just a little too much" as his face becomes a little serious. "Anyways, I'm happy to have you back brother..." Lungile says with a smile which Ntokozo returns as he smiles back but she continues as she becomes a little serious, "So tell me something...you know that I have to ask right?" she says with a rather nervous voice. "Uhmm...so these bodies that have been dropping like flies since you came

back...did you do it? And please brother tell me the truth, I really need to know..."

Ntokozo knew at some point this question was going to come but he was hoping that it wouldn't because it would be so difficult to lie to her.

"Come on sis...why does it matter huh? Those scambags are dead and they deserved it, whether I did it or some other lucky guy did..." he says as he looks away from his sister who raises an eyebrow as if she is confused by that response. To Lungile, this is a confrimation of sort even though the response from her brother was very vague, true to the spy that he is...but she knows better than pushing this issue. Perhaps it's better for her if she doesn't know anything about it. Part of her really wishes that her brother did it because revenge feels better than karma, according to her. But she also worries that her brother could have turned into a monster just to revenge for her.

"Uhmm...so Mr super spy, what is your plan about that other problem upstairs?" she asks with a smile as she looks up to Pearl's guest room. "What are you going to do with because you know, we need to know what's going on with your friend. If her father finds out that she is here, he will send his kill squad that will come guns blazzing"

Ntokozo thinks for a second before saying, "Look, I will speak to her emini(during the day) to get all the necesary facts about her situation" as he shrugs his shoulders. "But sisi, as you can imagine now, I won't let anyone hurt you or mom okay? I have actually added few cameras as well to ensure that every area of this house is covered. I will handle Pearl sis, don't worry..."

This comes as a relief to Lungile as she lets out a little smile before standing up, but Ntokozo calls out, "Hey uhmm...Can I ask that you and mom please go easy on her?" he says with a begging voice.

"Look I know your concerns about her and they are valid but...Uhmm...I'm just asking that you cut her some slack a little bit

DARK VENGEANCE

so that she doesn't feel like...uhmm...you know what I mean" He looks down as though he is embarrassed but her sister just smiles as she shakes her head and says, "Oh Lord...soft spy, hahaha..." as she walks back tok the house.

***

At the police stations detectives David Skhosana and Lindiwe Zulu have been given the task of investigating the myserious killings in the last few weeks and it has proven to be such a tough assignment. While Lungile has so far been thier primary person of interest, they have nothing to concrete to prove she is involved...maybe except a possible motive. Also her alabies have checked out, making this a very tough case to deal with. It is hard to tell whether these officers are also on the payroll of criminals and politicians like sone of their colleagues or they are amongst the few good ones, but they seem to have a passion for their job.

48 year-old David is married with two teenage daughters, while Lindiwe is a 35 year-old single parent of a 10 year-old son. The two have been partners for about 5 years now and there seems to be a great level of trist between them. Their captain gave them this case because they have proven to be good investigators who follow evidence wherever it leads them.

"So my friend, what do you think about this case? What is your gut telling you?" David asks his partner who sits opposite him at the station office. Lindiwe thinks for a second as she chew on the tip of the pen. "Well, so far we have got nothing but, my gut? My gut tells me that Lungile Gumede is our man...well, women in this case..." she says as she shrugs hee shoulders but David interjects, "Oh come on...we have nothing on her yet, okay? So we are not sure about that..." he says as he raises an eyebrow but Lindiwe cuts in, "Hey, you asked about my gut feeling okay?" she says as she also raises an eyebrow. "I'm telling you D...Miss Gumede is our person for sure..."

"Look, we are not sure hey, it's just an untetsed theory that's it..." David say as he throws his hands in the air but Lindiwe quickly interjects, "Well, Lungile Gumede has a motive against these three men okay?" she says as she rolls her eyes. "Who wouldn't want revenge for what they did to her? Remember that these three men were brutally tortured first before being shot in the head." David thinks for a second as he takes a deep sigh, "Well, we do need the murder weapon, don't we?" Without it, it will be hard to prove any theory that we might have." he says with a face of worry but Lindiwe interjects, "There is one thing that bothers me with all this though..." she says as she looks to the ceiling to think. "What is it?" David asks curiously. "Look, I think we have established the killer's MO, right?" Lindiwe says as she takes a sight. "But what bothers me is that the killings of torture like this are always linked to people with military training, so this couldn't have been an ameture. What we need to establish is a link between these victims, their businesses, associates and stuff like that..."

"So you agree now that Lungile Gumede is not the killer?" David asks as he shrugs his shoulders. "Not in the least. Look, she is so far the only person with a motive alright?" Lindiwe says as she also shrugs. "So until we find something else, she should remain out primary person of interest. We just need to thoroughly verify her alibi and check out her bank statements to see if we can find any abnormal transactions..."

"Alright then..." David says with a sigh. "Anything about her brother?" he asks curiously as he gently chews a pencil. "Oh sh*t I almost forgot about that..." Lindiwe says as she bumps her head aginst the desk. "Uhmm...yeah I actually did check him out but guess what...nothing shows up on the data base, nothing..." She looks worried as she looks into the ceiling but David cuts in, "What the hell do you mean 'nothing'?" he asks curiously as he sits up staright and then leaning forward. "I mean there's info about his life

ofcourse but nothing for the past 12 years...it's strange man, very strange..." Lindiwe says with a concerned face.
"Well, clearly we have go there and question him..." David says with his eyes pop out. "Yeah definatley we have to. Buy I'm also curious about another thing here..." Lindiwe says as she looks to the ceiling again. "What is it now?" David says as he throws his hands in the air which makes Lindiwe to think as though she is hesitating about this one.
"Uhmm...I'm sure you have heard rumours about surgent Sbongiseni Nxumalo, right?" she says with a low voice as she looks around to see if anyone is listening. "Well...what if his murder had more to do with his shaddy dealings than anything else?" She knows that this may not go down well with her partner but this was something she needed to get out of her chest.
"Look, how is speculation going to help us here Lindiwe? It's all hearsay and we can't do anything with that. Besides, Nxumalo is dead now so he can't defend himself, can he?" David says with a low voice as he looks a little uncomfortable having this discussion here at the office. "Oh come D, I know you know that this isn't just hearsay okay? You have heard many accusations against Nxumalo and you have also heard other colleages talk about him." Lindiwe says in a whisper but again David interjects, "yeah sure I have heard talks and assumptions but where is evidence of all that, huh?" he whispers back. "We need to focus only on what we can prove, okay?"
"Alright fine..." Lindiwe says as she rolls her eyes. She can be a little defiant sometimes and goon to do things her way. David knows what his partner is saying is true but as a family man he fears for the saftey of his loved ones, so he doesn't want to rock the boat and end up irritating the wrong people about this.

***

Somewhere else, Ntokozo is face to face with the man he has been warned many times to stay away from-Jabulani Ngubeni. Ngubeni's men picked Ntokozo up from the Mall when they saw him while he was buying a few things for the family. It is possible that they have been following him for a little while now at the instruction of Ngubeni. Clearly a very capable Ntokozo could have handled these men but he chose to go with them instead so that he can meet the drug dealer face to face. Obviously this was a risk for him since he didn't know whether Ngubeni will just kill him on the spot or not but he banked on the hope that he will just want to talk only, more than likey about Pearl.

Unlike like how he usually does things, Ngubeni had Ntokozo brought inside his living room instead of the garage and with only two of his body guard in the house. The house has cameras installed in every corner and by the looks of things, there is a CCTV monitoring room somewhere. That can only mean that there are people watching the room Ntokozo and Ngubeni are in right now, so there's no way of trying to do something funny here.

"Uhmm...drink?" Ngubeni says as he pours a double of whiskey for himself. "Oh no thanks...Ntokozo says with a calm voice as he keeps looking around the walls where he notices some pictures on the wall. He doesn't seem anxious or nervous about being here, even though against his own will but rather he seems to sizeing up the situation for whatever eventuality. He has seen worse in his life as soldier, this doesn't come close to any.

"Oh yeah, that's my late wife...Pearl's mother, she passed on a few years ago. Now it's just me and my little girl in this house..." Ngubeni says as he comes back to sit down opposite the calm Ntokozo. He then takes a huge sip of his drink before putting the glass down but Ntokozo just looks at him without saying a word.

"Alright, so I guess you are wondering why my men picked you up and brought you here..." Ngubeni says as he raises an eyebrow. "Well

you should add that it was actually against my will. I Could have them arrested, you know that?" Ntokozo asks with a straight face so that his host will know he is not intimidated.
"Oh come on Gumede, I'm sure you know who I am so it leads me to believe that you also know that calling police on me wouldn;t have worked out very well, especially for you..." Ngubeni says with a smirk on his face as he picks yup his glass to take a sip. "But look, all I wanted was for us to talk okay? So why don't we just do that, like...man to man?"
Ntokozo takes a deep sigh before saying, "Alright then...why am I here Mr Ngubeni?" as she sits up straight so that he can look at Pearl's father in the eyes. Ngubeni finishes off what was left on the glass before putting it down. "Alright straight to it huh? I like that..." he says with a half smile. "First of all I wanted to say that I actually knew your father. He was one of the most respected people in this communities...all of us looked up to him as he led the way in changing people's lives in this area. He truly was an astute businessman...I'm really sorry for his passing, I hope the familly has managed to steer the ship"
At first Ntokozo doesn't really know how to respond to this as he looks at this man in the eyes, so he takes a sigh before saying, "Uhmm...thank you very much" to which Ngubeni smiles with a nod. "So, what is it that you wanted us to talk about? Cause you know...your men pulled me from important chores that I was busy with..." Ntokozo says calmly.
"Well uhmm...it's actually quiet simple Gumede..." Ngubeni says as he leans back on his couch. "I am aware that you and my daughter Pearl are friends and I know that sincxe she left home a few days ago she's been staying with you..." He stands and goes to the side table to pour himself another double. "Uhmm...is that a question or a statement?" Ntokozo asks with a calm voice but Ngubeni quickly interjects, "I'm actually telling you Gumede...that my daughter left

home and I know that she's been staying with you. I want her back in this house, tonight..." he says as his voice becomes a little firmer as though he is ordering one of his men.

Ntokozo knows that he needs to be smart about this whole thing by thinking carefully before responding to what Ngubeni is saying. He is outnumbered here by his men in and outside the house. He didn't have his gun with him when Ngibeni's men picked him up from the mall. Perhaps that actually worked in his favour because it would have raised alarms about who he really is if they'd recovered it.

"What happened between the two of you?" Ntokozo asks with a calm voice which makes Ngubeni to think for a second before saying, "Uhmm...you know fathers and their daughter? Sometimes they disagree on things but it doesn't mean they stop loving each other." as he lets out a little smile. "So Pearl and I disagreed on something and out of emotions she left the house and came over to you. What did she actually tell you?"

"Well, she actually didn't say anything to me or atleast she hasn't said anything..." Ntokozo says as he shrugs his shoulders. "What I noticed though is that she looked very terrified when she came knocking on my door and I can't imagine that being something good. So what happened between the two of you?" Now he is also becoming firm in his voice as he looks at Pearl's father in the eyes.

"Look Gumede...this has got mnothing to do with you, alright? Now I want my daughter back here tonight. Otherwise I might have no other choice but to come over to your house and get her by force..." Ngubeni says with a rather intimidating tone.

This is one thing Lungile has been warning Ntokozo against, that Ngubeni may just want to do things this way. Ntokozo himself doesn't like this Ngubeni's tone and it sounds more like a threat to his family. Suddenly he remembers that his family has been sternly warning him about this and should anything happen to them he won't be abe to forgive himself.

"I don't think that would be a good idea Mr Ngubeni..." he says calmly. "Why not?" Ngubeni probes. "Well, because you and your men would be tresspassing and I'm allowed by law to do what I can to protect my family..." Ntokozo says as his face changes to being serious. He wants Ngubeni to know that he is not going to be pushed over. "Well, you can try Gumede...you can try." Ngubeni says as he shakes his head. "Look, no one wants to see blood being shed okay? So all you have to do is bring my daughter back here and you and I can forget this conversation ever happened...alright" "Did you just threatened me Mr Ngubeni?" Ntokozo asks calmly as he raises an eyebrow. "Oh no...ofcourse not Gumede..." Ngubeni says with a smile. "All I'm saying is that there's no ned for tensions between me and you or your family as it were. I just want my daughter to come back home so that she and I can try to work things out..."
"And what if Pearl doesn't want to come back here to live with you?" Ntokozo asks as he looks at the drug dealer in the eyes. "Well, you gonna have to convince her, for all of our sakes okay? You make her see reason..." Ngubeni says with a straight face. "Look, I don't want to fight with you Gumede okay? Because, like I said earlier, I respected your father very much. He and I had never bee on the cross roads before and I don't want that to begin now with his son. It just won't be right. The past few weeks there has been a lots of deaths in this area and it's our responsibily for families such as mine and yours to ensure no more blood is shed..."
This makes Ntokozo to think for a second as he looks at this man in the eyes knowing that this is a veiled threat. This is bigger than him or his ego now but it involves his mother, sister and niece. Even if he wanted to kill Ngubeni rigght here and now it may put his family in danger so he has to think carefully about his next move.
"Uhmm...I will surely speak to her and hear what she says..." he says with a low voice as his heart is filled with rage that he could reach

out across the table and snap the man's neck in an instant. "Okay you do that Gumede and make it very convincing please..." Ngubeni says with a smile as he takes a sip of his drink without standing up. Ntokozo looks at him one more time before turning around but Ngubeni calls out, "Oh my men will drive you back to where you left your car okay? We don't want anything happening to it..." he says as he stands up to walk Ntokozo out of the house.

***

Back at the Gumede house, it is the first time that Pearl is leaving her guestroom to go to the kitchen for some water because Ntokozo or Mbali who usually are there to help her are not in the house. She had assumed that no one else was in the house because Lungile and Dora might be at work, so this will allow her to stretch her feet a little bit since she's been locked up in that room for a couple of days now.

So as she closes the fridge door she almost drops the glass of water in her hand when she realises that Lungile is right there in the lounge room sitting in the couch. Suddenly her heart races faster as she doesn;t know what to do, you'd swear she just stole something.

"Uhmm...I'm really sorry I didn't see you. Uhmm...uhmm...I was...Uhmm...I was just getting myself some water...Uhmm...sorry..." she stutters with a seeming terrified voice as she looks so embarrassed at being in someone else' kitchen.

She quickly moves out, but as she approaches the stairs Lungile calls out, "Uhmm...no, you don't have to run out okay?" she says with a calm voice but with a straight face that is hard to read. "In fact, I actually wanted to talk to you about something...so why don't you join me? Have you had breakfast yet?"

This is coming as a surprise for Pearl who didn't expect that from Ntokozo's sister who she knows doesn't like her very much. She is even struggling to read her since she is not showing any emotion.

'This feels like an ambush...' she thinks to herself as she nervously approaches the lounge. She comes in and sit on the edge of the couch opposite Lungile's. She looks down as she tries ti avoid eye contact because she is embarrassed, leading to a very awkward silence. Lungile herself is trying to read this woman sitting opposite her but if she were honest, she'd see that she's terrified or atleast anxious a little bit.

"Uhmm...so, are you comfortable here at the Gumede home?" she asks with a low voice as fixes her eyes on Pearl who eventually lefts her head and says, "Uhmm...it's been the most peaceful few days I have had in a very long time..." with a nervous smile as she looks at her host back. "Uhmm...I'm sorry for invading your space, I actually thought there was no one in the house because Ntokozo had mentioned that he'd go to the mall in the morning. I thought you and your mom were actually at work so I needed water from your kitchen. You almost gave me a heart attack..."

"Oh uhmm...I'm sorry about that..." Lungile says as she lets out a nervous smile. "Oh yeah uhmm...mom usually works from home, her office is down in the basement. I do oversight visits to our businesses for most part of the week but I also do work from home in some days because we have managers to handle the day to day running of the establishments..."

"Oh wow...Uhmm, that's kinda like how I do it with my family businesses as well..." Pearl says with a blush but Lungile raises an eyebrow as if to say, *'Oh really now?'* but when Pearl sees that she interjects, "Look, I know that you may believe this but, I'm not involved with my dad's shaddy business...I've got nothing to do with that." she says with a low voice. "I, just like you run family businesses like the Hardware store, Car Wash and the butchery but, I suppose I am invloved with my father's shaddy business if you consider that the money to start these businesses came from whatever shaddy business he does" She suddenly looks sad embarrassed by this as she

looks down and lungile herself looks down as she is feeling sorry for her.
"But you know that you always have a choice Pearl, right?" Lungile says with a calm voice as she looks at her guest in the eyes. "Just because someone is father it doesn't mean that you have to do anything they want okay? I mean, everyone in this neighbourhood knows about your father and what he does. What do you think people say about you when they see you drive down the street?" Pearl thinks about this for a second as she looks at the Lungile sitting oppsotie her. She knows what she is saying can't be dismissed easily. "Uhmm...look, I might not even be working there anymore anyays since I'm here and not there..." she says with a sad face as she shrugs her shoulders. "Did you and your father had a fight? When you knocked on our door a few days ago you didn't look okay?" Lungile probes with keen interest as she looks at a sad Pearl who is looking down. This leads to a little silence as Pearl takes a second to think of a response. She is wondering whether telling the Gumedes what actually happened at home the day she ran away is a good idea or not.
"Uhmm...yeah, something like that..." she says as she shrugs her shoulders but Lungile quickly interjects, "Does your father know that you are here?" she asks curiously with a somewhat worried face. "Uhmm...I think it's safe to say he probably know...that one always has people all over the place. That's why I haven't set foot outside since I came here..." Pearl says as she takes a deep sigh.
"But do you realise how this puts my family in a very difficult position, Pearl?" Lungile asks with a worried face. "If your father knows that you are here then it's just a matter of time before he and his men knocked down this down guns blazing. I have a little girl here Pearl...I don't want her caught in a crossfire. You know how dangerous your father is...what if he thinks we have kidnapped you?"

When Pearl sees how worried Lungile is she starts to feel bad just as she is embarrassed. "Uhmm...I'm really sorry for putting you guys in this difficult position. It really was never my intention to do so..." she says as she looks down in shame. "I just...uhmm...I just didn't know where to go...I had left home in a hurry and my mind wasn't in the right frame. I did n't stop to think how this would affect you guys, I'm really sorry. I will go and get my stuff and leave immediately..." She stands up quickly but as she approaches the stairs, Lungile calls out. "Please wait...Please let's talk a little..." she says with a somewhat begging voice.

Pearl comes back to sit on the edge of the couch and looks down in shame. "Look...where will you go? I didn't mean that you should leave okay?" Lungile says with a sad voice as though she is feeling sorry for the embarrassed Pearl who lifts her head and says, "But you were right Lungi...me being here does put your family in danger. I don't want you guys to go to war with him over me..." with a sad voice.

Lungile thinks for a second before saying, "Okay look, let's wait for Ntokozo to come back so that we decide together as family okay?" with a little smile which comes as a surprise to Pearl who is now beginning to feel a little emotional. She didn't see this one coming and Lungile herself is beginning to feel that maybe she had judged Pearl a little harsh over the sins of her father. When she tries to read her she can see that she is genuienly scared of going back home, but she is no really convinced that it's because of a mere fight. *'There must be something more than that...'* she thinks to herself as she looks at Pearl who is looking down.

"Uhmm...and my brother? What's the story there?" Lungile asks with a low voice as she clears her throat. Pearl thinks for a second before nervously saying, "Uhmm...believe it or notg Lungile, I love your brother...As it turns out, quiet a lot actually. That is why I'm willing to stay away from him if it means that will keep him and you guys safe from my dad..."

That catches Lungile offguard as she raises an eyebrow before asking, "And...how does he feel about you?" curiosuly. Pearl thinks for a second..."Uhmm...well, I think he loves you guys more..." she says as she lets out a little nervous smile. "You know, he really worries about you guys...a lot. I have never asked him about his past or his relatinship with you but everytime he talks about you his tone changes or his facial expressions. You know, growing up I knew him from a distance, but when we met for the first time a few weeks ago it really changed my life. From that day on, my heart decided he was the person I wanted to spend my life with...but also a person I will make sacrifices for to keep him safe..."

Lungile may not bring herself down to admit it but she is a little warmed by these words as she lets out a little smile and Pearl herself is feeling emotional but a like shy realising that she has poured out her heart to Ntokozo's sister. But this moment is interrupted when someone walks through the door-It's Ntokozo carrying a few groccery plastic bags.

***

Later on during supper, Ntokozo is a little pleased that Pearl is this time sitting with them in the table, *'Clearly something must have happened Pearl and my sister a little earlier...'* he thinks to himself as she looks at her across the table next to Lungile. He is sitting next to his niece while his mother is at then head of the table like the queen she is. By the look of things supper went well because there doesn't seem to be any akwardness in the table. Even Dora seems to be a little uneasy she is trying hard to not make things awkward by keep talking about stories of Ntokozo and Lungile growing up.

"Do you mind helping me with this?" Lungile says to a pleasantly surprised Pearl as they both stand up and take dishes to the kitchen.

Ntokozo himself is a little surpised because a few days Lungile couldn't stand Pearl, so to see them going to the kitchen to wash dishes together is very unexpected.
"Uhmm...son, can I talk to you for a minute in the veranda?" Dora says as she interrupts Ntokozo from looking at the ladies in the kitchen. "Sweetheart, why don't you go assist mommy and aunt Pearl in the kitchen okay?" she says to Mbali who quickly gets up and head to the kitchen where Lungile and Pearl are washing dishes and tidying up. She and Ntokozo go outside to the veranda where there's a table and chairs. It is actually not a cold evening, with a full moon to light up the dark. Dora had brought with her a bottle of wine and two glasses, which makes Ntokozo feel a little curious about the nature of conversation they will have out here.
"It's nothing son, I just wanted to ask you about this girl, Pearl...what's really going on there Ntokozo?" Dora asks with a curious face as she pours wine in two glasses. "Look, it's been a little while since she's been here but we still don't know why she is here or if we are in any danger. Geez we don;t even know what's going between the two of you baby..." She gives her relunctant son a glass and then takes a sip of hers.
Ntokozo figures that if he will have this conversation with his mom he might as well have some of this wine. Nobody wants to have a relationship conversation with their parents, especially the mother and son kinda talk.
"Uhmm...mama, it's my fault...I should have handled this better." Ntokozo says with a low as he takes a sip. "I just wanted to give Pearl some time to settle a bit you know. I don't want to push her too hard, but I can assure you mama, we are in no kind of danger okay? And I will never net let anything happen to you, Mbali or Lungi, I promise."
"You know, a couple of weeks ago I wouldn't have believed that but after you told us about your past I can actually believe it. I know

that you won't let anything happen to us ndodana(son)..." Dora says with a low voice as she looks a little worried. "But the thing is that I don't want to start any war or tension between us and that Ngubeni guy. He is dangerous and you will not always be here with us to ensure he and his men don't knock this door down looking for his daughter. I don't think that you being friends with Pearl can actually save us from that, no?"

Now this makes Ntokozo think for a second because he's just came back from Ngubeni's house a few hours ago and he is not sure whether to tell his family about it or not. He does however remember the threats that man made...that if Pearl doesn't return home by tonight he and his men will come here guns blazing to retrieve her.

"I will handle this mama, okay? You have nothing to worry about." he says as he takes another sip but his mother raise an eyebrow before saying, "So, you like her? I mean, it seems your sister is suddenly warming up to her..." as she also takes a sip. Ntokozo thinks for a second, "Uhmm...actually mama yes, I lke her..." he says with a little blush. "I know what you are thinking mama, but she is not involved with her father's business. As they say, we don't choose our families...so she didn't choose hers. But ofcourse if I were to choose Pearl and you guys, you know I choose you everyday." Dora seems pleased by these words from her son as she lets out a little smile.

"She seems like a nice person...I think it's her father I have a problem with, not her persay. she says as she shrugs her shoulders which seems to please Ntokozo who smiles at his mom. "She is a nice person mama...And I believe that people don't always turn out to be like their parents..." he says as he takes another sip but his mother quickly interjects, "But you know what they say son...blood is thicker than water. Do you think if she was forced to choose between you or us over her father she will choose us? I really don't think so baby..." she says with a raised eyebrow.

Ntokozo doesn't know how to respond to that as he looks down but Dora interjects again, "look, enough about that okay?" she says with a smile. "Now tell me all about your days in the military..."

Chapter 11
Love is blind

"Your family has been really good to me since I have been here...who would have thought?" Pearl says to Ntokozo as they sit under one of the trees at the Gumede home on a Saturday noon, few days after Ntokozo and Dora had a conversation about Pearl. Everyone is home today and the attitude towards Pearl from everyone has shifted a lot since she joined them for supper a few days ago. It is as though they have accepted her as Ntokozo's girlfriend or something. After having a talk with Ntokozo, Dora has decided to give the two some space to work things out on their own. Also, the talk Pearl had with Lungile seems to have eased up tensions bweween them a little bit.

"I had a little chat with your mom earlier this morning and she seems to have warmed up to me hey..what did you say to her?" Pearl asks curiously as she looks a little excited about it. Ntokozo looks up as though he is trying to recall something, "Uhmm...nah, I didn't say anything hey...I just think that she's just warming up to you like my sister is..." he says with a smile that Pearl returns. "There is however something I need to talk to you about Pearl..." Ntokozo says as his tone changes to being a little serious, which makes Pearl raise an eyebrow. "Uhmm...I wanted to tell you the other day but when you joined us for supper and I saw how mom and Lungo started to warm up to you it didn't feel like the right time."

Now this is making Pearl feel a little anxious as she interjects, "What is it?" she asks with a face of worry. "Uhmm...on Monday I was at the Mall and your dad's men grabed and took me to him..." Ntokozo says as he takes a deep sigh but this shocks Pearl and leads her to panic as her eyes pop out, "What? But Ntokozo, why didn't you tell me then? Did they hurt you? What the hell did he want with you?

Oh babe, I'm so sorry..." She panics as her eyes begin to be teary while she covers her mouth in disbelief. This is what she has been fearing all along about her father.

"No, no, no...they didn't hurt me..." Ntokozo says as he takes a panicking Pearl's hand. "He said he wanted to talk to me. He knows that you are here and he had demanded that you come back home or else he is coming here, knocking down my door and take you by force. I could see in his eyes that he wasn't bluffing..."

Pearl can't believe what she's hearing as her head begins to spin. Her heart is now racing faster knowing the kind of man her father is.

"Why the hell didn't you tell me this on Monday Ntokozo, because I'd have packed up and went back home then? I can't have my father harm you or your family on my account..." she shouts in panic but Ntokozo cuts in, "You will please calm down, okay? Nothing happened to my family okay?" he says but Pearl herself interrupts him, "No, no, no...I have to go Ntokozo. I can never forgive myself if my dad would do something stupid to you or your family..."

She stands up in panic as she heads back to the house but Ntokozo follows as he tries to stop her. Everyone else in the house is wondering what's going on when they see Pearl storms in and goes straight up to her room. "What's going on?" Dora, who is seating with Lungile and Mbali in the lounge asks curiously but Ntokozo doesn't know how to answer that as he shrugs her shoulders while looking upstairs.

Lungile quickly goes to Pearl's room and finds her packing up her stuff in haste. "Pearl...? What's going on?" she asks curiously as she watches on in wonder. "I got to go Lungile...I have to go back home before my dad comes her with his men to start trouble..." Pearl says with a trembling voice as her hands are shaking. "What the hell are you talking about? Pearl? Please stop okay?" a confused Lungile pleads as she comes in the room. "Look, Ntokozo didn't tell me this on Monday...but my dad sent his men to grab Ntokozo at the Mall.

He apparently threatened that if I'm not back home that night he and his men will come here to grab me by force..."
"What? But Ntokozo never mentioned anything like that to us..." a shocked Lungile says but Pearl quickly interjects, "Exactly...he didn't mention it to me either...only now when we were sitting outside." she says as she continues to put her clothes and belongings into the backpack that she arrived with.
"Look Lungile, I am really sorry about this okay? Believe me when I say that I would never do anything to put your family's life in danger...me staying here does exactly that, put your lives in danger." Pearl says as her eyes become teary but Lungile interjects, "But maybe your father was just bluffing Pearl okay? I mean, he and his men never came here and today is a Saturday..." Lungile says with a begging voice as though this is making her sad. Who would have thought that she'd actually one day beg Pearl into not leaving her home? Perhaps she was getting used to having another woman in this house.
Pearl takes a deep sigh as she sits down on the bed and wipes her tears. "Look Lungi...the real reason uhmm...I ran away from home, uhmm...is because my father killed a boy in front of my eyes..." she says with a trembling voice which almost sends Lungile tumbling to the floor in shock as she also comes to sit down next to the destraught guest.
"Oh my God Pearl...what are you saying to me...?" she asks with a low voice as she suddenly becomes weak but Pearl doesn't respond to that as she looks down. This leads to a very uncomfortable silence in the room as the two ladies run out of words. Part of Pearl is obviously relived after telling this to someone but she is also worried about how Lungile will handle it. But perhaps her biggest worry is how Ntokozo will react to it once his sister informs him. She had finally found someone who truly makes her happy but all of that could come to an end because of her father and his ruthlessness.

"Uhmm...did you tell the police about this?" Lungile asks with a low voice as she looks down. "Police? What will police do Lungi? They work for my father, that's why he gets away with a lot of things. I don"t want him to come here guns blazing knowing that no one can ever hold him accountable for anything he does..." Pearl says as she stands and slowly picking up her backpack.

Lungile doesn't know what to says as she follows Pearl who out of the room and goes downstairs where Ntokozo and his mom are. "Uhmm...what's going Pearl? Where are you going?" a surprised Dora asks as she looks at her so who is just as shocked at this sudden move by their guest. "Uhmm...Mrs Gumede, thank you very much for the hospitality that you have shown me in your home, I really was comfortable..." Pearl says as her eyes once again become teary with emotions. "But uhmm...I gotta go home now but I hope that I will come visit you guys one of these days soon okay?" she says as she looks down as though she is embarrassed but Dora looks at Lungile who was up there with Pearl and wonders what's going on...Lungile just shrugs her shoulders.

When Dora sees Pearl walks towards the door she looks at Ntokozo as if to say, *'Well, don't just stand there...go after her for Christ's sake...'* to which Ntokozo quickly goes after the woman he loves as she walks out the door, leaving everyone just stunned.

***

At the Masondo home, Judas is visited by Police Commssioner Mthokozisi Ncube to give him an update about the case of his son. Things have been really hard for the rich family even after they had burried their son with a hope that they will get closure. The manner in which their own was killed leaves more questions than answers and Judas Mosondo is becoming impatient with the police commissioner whom he suspect is dragging feet.

"I hope you are here with good news Ncube, not another useless update..." Masondo says as he takes a sip of double whiskey when they sit outside under the tree. "My family can't get closure over this until they find out who killed my boy. My wife and my daughters are inside the house right now waiting for me to come in with some kind of news on this Ncube, so what do you have for me?" He looks very upset. "Uhmm...well, I have an update for you..." Ncube says with a calm voice, which turn Masondo's eyes bright in anticipation.

"We have not made any arrests yet but we do have a person or persons we deem as persons of interests."

"Who the hell are they? Gangsters? Business partners? Or someone who had a vendetta against my son?" the impetient Masondo asks as he takes another sip of his drink. Ncube thinks for a second before saying, "Well actually, the person we are questioning is a woman who by the way, opened a case of rape against your son where the case docket mysteriously disappeared and case closed. Funny thing though is that when I asked you if your son had anyone who woul have wanted to harm him you said no..."

"Hey, hey, hey...I didn't say there wasn't okay? I said I didn't know anyone who would want to harm him..." Masondo says with a firm voice as he is vissibly displeased. "So what are you saying Ncube? This woman is the one who killed my son in cold blood out of revenge for something she couldn't even prove in court?"

"No, no, no...that's not what I'm saying alright?" Ncube says as he motions with hands because he can see how this can easily get out of hand. "She is just a person we are question seeing that she and your son had a history, but her alabi on the night night your son was killed actually checks out...so she may not be involve in any of this..." he says but Masondo quickly interjects, "No, no, no...it has to be her..." he says firmly. "You see...she had the motive. Clearly this woman has been planning this for a very long time Commissioner. Look at the evidence..."

"Oh, so are you then conceding to the fact that she was correct to accuse your son of rape, Mr Masondo? She obviously can't have a motive over something that never happned now, can she?" Ncube asks as he looks away to avoid eye contact but Masonddo doesn't know how to respond to this question as he looks a little annoyed by it.

"Look Commissioner...I have to talk this woman. My family needs answers and closure...so if this woman can provide then she needs..." Masondo says but he doesn't finish his thought as Ncube cuts in, "No Mr Masondo, you are not going to question her, that's police business...I hope we are clear on that..." he says with a firm voice to which Masondo seems very irritated as he finishes off whatever was left on his glass.

"Look, I gotta go...I will keep you posted." Ncube says as he picks up his police hat and wears it. "You do that Commissioner..." the vissibly disappointed Masondo says with a long face as he watches Ncube gets on his car and drives off.

***

Back at the Gumede home Ntokozo is sitting outside having a very sad moment alone after Pearl left earlier in the morning. Dora and Lungile thought it might be best to allow him some time alone as it is clear that he didn't take it very well. Even though he is hurting, Ntokozo knows deep down in his heart that this was probably best for everyone because Pearl's father is a law unto himself...so he can't trust the police to protect hos family, unless ofcourse he will have to do things his way.

So as he keeps going through some of the WhatsApp texts he exchanged that made him laugh a call comes through.

Ntokozo: "Hey my man..."
Man: "Hey bro, how are you doing..."
Ntokozo: "I'm good man, how are you?"

Man: "I'm great...got the file?"

Ntokozo: "Yeah man thanks...this is the last one..."

Man: "Okay good, because people are getting nervous with these unsolved murders. Have the police visited you yet?"

Ntokozo: "No, not me specifically, but they have come twice to question my sister....

Man: "And...? What happened?"

Ntokozo: "Well, ofcourse it kinda raised suspicision when I dropped that Lukhele piece of sh*t. It was too much to be a co-incident so my family started asking questions..."

Man: "What did you tell them?"

little silence

Man: "Are you there?"

Ntokozo: "Yeah manI'm here...Look I had to give them something, so I told them about my military history..."

Man: "Did you tell them about, uhmm...you know...the bodies?"

Ntokozo: "Ofcourse not but, you know...it's safe to say they suspect that it was me..."

another silence

Man: "Okay look, we'll deal with that some other time. So where are you with the Ngubeni operation? That's the guy we really need...him and his associates..."

Little silence

Ntokozo: "Uhmm...bro, there has been a little complication..."

Man: "What do you mean?"

Ntokozo: "Uhmm...Ngubeni's daughter...she and her father had a fight and she ran away from home, and came to live with me..."

Man: "What? Why the hell would you do something like that man? I knew this gir, was going to be a distraction in this operation man."

Ntokozo: "Well, while she was at my home her father's men grabbed me at the mall and took me to him..."

Man: "Wait, what?"

Ntokozo: "Relax man...they didn't harm me...Ngubeni only wanted to talk. In fact he wanted his daughter back with him, so Pearl went back home this morning..."

Little silence

Ntokozo: "Are you there?"

Man: "Yeah man, I'm here...I'm just thinking about how fucked this is now..."

Ntokozo: " Yeah tell me about it..."

Man: "But why didn't you drop that mother f*cker right there in his living room?"

Ntokozo: "Whoa man...first of all I didn't have my gun with me, secondly we said we needed the files, bank accounts, his associates and all his stash...right?"

Man: "Yeah, I know..."

Ntokozo: "Don't worry man, we will get that drug dealer..."

Man: "Not when you are busy going after his daughter...I'm telling man, that girl is distracting you..."

Ntokozo: "Look man, we need her okay? She is a daughter of a drug dealer...she knows a lot. What I need to do is turn her. I need to use the tensions between she and her father. I need her to get me something from her father's office.

silence

Man: "Alright then...but you better start moving fast because I can't hold authorities off for too long. Also we need to move fast before your cover gets blown...if that happens I won;t be able to help you okay?"

Ntokozo: "Relax man, I know how the game works okay? But first things first...I will move with the first phase. I will clean up those accounts so that Ngubeni reacts to it and then it's phase two afterwards.

Man: "Okay good...that's good. Oh uhmm...you may want to know that there's another matter that needs your attention.

Ntokozo: "What is it?"

Man: "You know that we have the police commissioner, Ncube under survaillance right? So guess who he's been visitting this morning-Judas Masondo, Philani Masondo's father.

Ntokozo: "What?"

Man: "Yeah. Judas wants to know who killed his son and he is thirsty for blood. The commissioner has been updating him on the case and your family's name came up.

Silence

Man: "Hey...are you there?"

Ntokozo: "Yeah man I'm here. If Judas comes after my family I will have to tie that sh*t up man...These rich people think they are a law unto themselves and I will show them that it's not gonna be like that for long.

Man: "Is there not any other way you can handle this man?"

silence

Ntokozo: "Well, I'm all ears but I will be damned if I let that scambag Judas Masondo come anywhere near my family, so I'm gonna need your help man.

Man: "Don't even mention it man..."

Ntokozo: "I will be in touch..."

Call dropped

***

Somewhere else Lungile has gone to be with her boyfriend Thulani at the park after this morning's drama with Pearl and Ntokozo. She was getting used to having the drug dealer's daughter in the house, even though she knew the risks...but seeing Ntokozo so sad in the morning when Pearl left makes her sad as well. She and her mother wanted to give Nokozo some space so now she's with her boyfriend to try and unwind. They are at the botanic gardens for a little picnic, which is something they enjoy doing together from time to time when they are both off from work.

"So how was it like staying with that girl there in your home, huh?" Thulani asks as they sit under one of the trees shades on a picnic blunket. They have a cooler box with drinks and a busket of snacks and finger lunch in there...it's a very chilled moment.

"Yeah well...for most days she locked herself up in the guestbedroom, she only came out in the last couple of day..." Lungile says as she taks a deep sigh. "When I finally got to speak to her I find that she was actually an okay person you know. I was getting used to the idea of having her in the house." She suddenly looks sad as she says, which puzzles her boyfriend as he raises an eyebrow, "And now?" he asks..."I thought you didn't like that girl, what changed? I mean, you said it yourself...her family is dangerous and poses a serious threat to your community. Has that changed now? And when?"

This makes Lungile think for a second as she looks at her confused man, "Uhmm look, I'm not saying any of hat has changed at all okay?" she says with a low voice. "But I spent time with her the other day and I saw something..." She shrugs her shoulders but Thulani doesn't say anything but waits on his girlfirend to continue, to which she does, "Look, I saw it in her eyes okay? She doesn't want to be anything like her father and I believe her when she says she loves my brother. Honestly, I hate seeing Ntokozo this way. When Pearl left this morning he was miserable and he wanted to be alone...so we gave him his space."

"Why did Pearl decide to go back home by the way?" Thulani asks curiously as he takes a sip of his orange juice. Lungile thinks for a seconf before saying, "Uhmm...she didn't want her father to come knocking down our door looking for her...I guess she was just trying to protect us from her monster dad..." with a deep sigh as she suddenly look sad.

"Well, that's noble of her..." Thulani says with a raised eyebrow. "Yeah..." Lungile says as she shrugs her shoulders, leading to a bit of silence as both of them take a sip of their drinks. "Anyways speaking of Ntokozo...so now that you know about his past, have you forgiven him?" Thulani asks as he looks a little embarrassed by asking that. "Uhmm, well...first of all, my anger towards him was very much justified, considering what I have been through..." Lungile says with a low voice as she shrugs her shoulders. "I felt that he abandoned us as a family, without even telling us why. My mom cried for weeks and months for him...hell we even accepted the possibility that he was dead."

It looks like this is making her a little angry all over again as she quickly downs her orange juice to calm herself down. "But now that he has explained things to us I guess I'm seeing things a little differently..." she continues. "But the person I'm really angry at is my dad. He watched on as my momwent through depression; we watched on as I cursed my brother everyday for leaving us...for not being there to protect me. All along he knew where he was and what he was doing, what kind of a father does that to his family, huh? I mean, he was highly respected in this community as an honorable man yet he allowed his family to go through all of that? No ways..."

"Yeah but babe don't be hard on him okay? He probably did it for a reason..." Thulani says with a low voice as he tries to calm his girlfriend by gently brushing her shoulder. "You sound like Ntokozo..." a vissibly annoyed Lungile says as she looks away. "I just don't understand why he couldn't just tell us...were we really supposed to accept that Ntokozo had died somewhere? What about getting closure, huh?"

Thulani can see that this may soon turn the mood sombre here at the park so interjects, "okay, okay, okay sweetheart please calm down, okay?" he says as he takes his girfriend's hand. "So uhmm...any updates on the cases the police were questioning you about? What are the chances that Ntokozo knows something abut this? I mean, he comes back home after a decade and suddenly people who abused his sister get dead? Especially now that we know about his military background...really babe, what are the chances he didn't have anything to do with this, huh? Have you asked him about this?"

This is catching Lungile offguard a bit because she has had a conversation with Ntokozo about this and he wan't really fouthcoming. Even though part of her knows for sure that her brother was involved somehow, she doesn't really know if she can tell that to Thulani who seems a little curious about it. Now she has to be careful about her response.

"Look babe, calm down with the questions...one at a time okay?" she says as she shrugs her shoulders. "Firstly, I don't know what's going with the police but they haven't charged me, so I suppose they don't have any case against me. As for my brother....look, Ntokozo is not capable of something like this okay? And yes I asked him about it and he assured me that he is not involved. Remember that those men were scambags, probably other people they did business with got to them first. Personally I wished I could have been the one who killed them for what they put me through, but this will have to do..."

Thulani thinks for a second as he looks at his girlfriend. It's as though he is trying to see of she's telling the truth or not. "Well let's hope you are right babe...let's hope your brother is not involved in all this because you don't wanna lose him for the second time..." he says with a sigh but Lungile doesn't respond to that as she would very much like to avoid this topic altogether.

"Anyways, when am I coming over to your house again?" Thulani asks as he also wants to change the topic, but Lungile thinks for a second before saying, "Uhmm...oh yeah baby, about that...can we wait for the right moment?" with a begging eyes. "At the moment everything is just all over the place between the police making me a person of interest in a multiple murder case to me trying to deal with a few things at work. I hope you don't mind that baby..."

"Yeah, yeah, yeah...sure baby it's okay..." Thulani says with a seemingly dissapointed face but Lungile quickly imterjects, "Oh come on baby okay? You know that you are always welcomed at home and my mom is fond you..." she says but Thulani cuts in quick, "What about your broher?" he asks with a raised eyebrow. "Oh uhmm...you know, he doesn't know well, that's all..." Lungile quickly responds. "Why? You wanna come over to have a man to man conversation with him? Because I can arrange something like that with him if you are up for it , hahahha. You guys would actually have a great time.

" Oh no...I don;t think he and I are there just yet okay? Hahaha..." Thulani says as he laughs back at his girlfriend. "I mean I saw that other day he was looking at me. He had that innate, protective thing about him and now that I know about his military history I don't think it's such a good I dea at the moment for us to sit down and talk..."

"Oh come on...why not?" Lungile asks with a laughter as she shakes her head. "How else will my brother get to know you better? Tell you what...scrap that thimng about not coming over at this particular moment okay? How about I organize a little braai and drinks at home and you can come over? If it makes you feel better, Ntokozo can also invite his friend Sthembiso so that it won't be awkward with just the two of you. I will invite my friends also, to come and hangout with us...so what do you think?"

Thulani thinks for a second as he looks at Lungile with a raised eyebrow as though he is in disbelief. He shakes his head as he smiles at this seemingly insane idea from his girlfriend. Lungile smiles back at him as she lifts a glass to toast.

***

DARK VENGEANCE

Later on, Ntokozo finds himself face to face with the first man who had violated his sister some 12 years ago and got away with it. It was a mission and half to find this guy but through the help of his mysterious handler he finally nailed this rapist down somewhere in Eshowe township. He somehow managed to drung him, put him in the boot of the car and drove for miles to the middle of nowhere. It seems like Ntokozo prefers it when he uses an abandoned factory or a warehouse where there are no people around to interrupt him.

Also he likes places where residential houses are miles away in radious one would have to have a real reason for coming here.

As usual, he has this man tired up tight in the chair and placed in the middle of the room like the previous 3 victims of his. This man's mouth is not tapped because even if he screamed on top of his voice nobody can hear him out here. Again, like the other 3 previously, this one seems to have been beaten up pretty bad for atleast some time now. He is also missing 5 fingernails on his left hand, suggesting that Ntokozo has been at it for a little while now. There's blood all over the floor around the steel chair and the man's swollen face is driping blood like an open tap staining his white shirt red.

"Lungisani Mbhele, so you thought you could actually outrun your sins huh?" Ntokozo asks with a deep voice as he looks at both of his bloody fists. His eyes are like those of a wolf thirsty for blood. His black leather jacket is also stained whith blood that sprinkled from Lungisani's face when he punched him.

"Uhmm...sir I don't know what you want but I have money...please tell me how much you want..." the panicking Lungisani pleads with a trembling voice as he is vissibly in pain but Ntokozo responds by throwing in another powerful punch on the face that sends Lungisani and his chair tumbling to the floor. He quickly picks him up to sit straight again and says, "That's exactly where your problem is with you rich people...you think you can buy your way through everything huh?" as he shouts on top of his voice. "No, no, no, your family fortunes won't get you out of this one Mbhele...you hear me? It won't."

"Alright then please tell me what you want with me...please..." the crying Lungisani begs as tears fall down his face. Ntokozo thinks for a second as he goes over by the window to look outside to the sun that is almost settling down as it nears 16:30 in the afternoon. He doesn't want to be here for too long...he has to get back home before his family worries about his whereabout.

"Well Mr Mbhele...like I said before, you are here because of your past sins. You are here to pay for them..." he says as he continues to look outside to the sun but the seemingly confused Lungisani asks,

"But I don't even know who you are sir...please tell me what you want so that I can give it to you..." as he tries to free his hands that are tied tight into the armchair. "Well okay then...I will ask you a qustion and how you answer it will dertemine what happens to you next, okay?" Ntokozo says with a low voice as he turns around and goes to his favourite table of torture that has all instruments of nightmare.

"You know Mbhele...I really should have been a doctor since I'm so good with these instruments..." he says as he picks up from the table what looks like a very sharp which terrifies Lungisani who has eyes popping out in terror.

"Now, what I want to ask you is this..." Ntokozo says as he comes closer to his target. "How many sins have you not paid for? Who have you ever wronged and got away with it?" He looks at a terrified Lungisani as though he is trying to read him. Lungisani himself has to think long and hard about how he answers because he has been told it will dertemine what happens to him next. Tears begin to fall from his face when he realises that from his eyes, Ntokozo is not bluffing. Once again he tries to move his hands but it is no use as they are tied tight to the chair. Screaming won't help, he knows that by now.

"But sir I really don't know what you mean...I don't know anyone I have hurt and..." the crying Lungisani pleads ingnorance as his voice trembles in fear but in anger Ntokozo cuts his right thigh with the sharp knife which goes through the light brown trousers deep into the skin, tearing it apart. Lungisani screams on top of his voice as blood spills all over the place and onto Ntokozo's hand as well. "Aaaah no sir please...please wait, aaah my thigh...please, please, please sir I'm begging you stop. I really don;t know what you are talking about...aaah please, sir...please...aaah..." he screams as he begs for his life.

Ntokozo who shows no remorse throws the knife away and looks at the helplessly beeding man with eyes of rage. "Alright then, tell me...how many women have you abused in your whole pathetic life and got away with it?" he asks with a low voice but when Lungisani looks up as though he is trying to recall he shouts, "Answer me you piece of sh*t...how many?" as he spits on him.

"Okay, okay, okay...Uhmm I don't know sir...please...I don't know..." Lungisani says as he starts to cry all over again which seems to annoy Ntokozo who shakes his head in disgust before saying, "Alright then, what about when you were in high school? Do you remember all the sh*t you did then huh? How many girls did you rape in high school and got away with it you piece of sh*t, tell me..." as his voice gets louder and louder with rage. Lungisani's eyes pop as he tries to recall. It is as though someone just transported him back in time as the images of hos young self play in his mind. But what terrifies him is the man standing right in frint of him waiting for an answer.

"Uhmm...sir...Uhmm...uhmm..." he stutters in in fear as tears cowntinue to flow from his eyes. "Sir please, I was young and stupid then...I don't remember the things I did in highschool. Please sir tell me what you want me to do okay? I will do it...but please I'm begging you don't kill me. I will give you all the money you want..."

Ntokozo looks at him and shakes his head in disgust as he seems lost for words. "One last question..." he says as he takes a deep sigh. "Do you remember Lungile Gunede...the girl you raped after your matric exam final paper? Do you remember yourself gloating to your friends who laughed at her because you thought you were the man? Do you remember that? Do you remember how your rich parents got you out of that trouble when Lungile pressed charges against you? You were the man, right? You could get away with everything huh? You thought this day wouldn't come, you piece of sh*t?"
Lungisani can't believe this as he tries to recall who Lungile was but by the expression in his face it seems like he remembers her. Ntokozo pulls a gun and points at him. "Oh so please I'm begging you...please don't kill me okay? I'm begging you...I was young and stupid...I regret that very much, please sir...please..." Lungisani begs for his life as he stares at the burrel of the gun in his face. Ntokozo thinks for a second as his eyes turn red with rage. He takes a deep breathe as he looks to the ceing of this collapsing building. In his mind is the picture of his sister and mother with pain in their eyes as he looks at this now grown Lungisani Mbhele who took away his sister's innocence. He takes another deep breathe before squizing the trigger to let fly two bullets that hit Lungisani's forehead as he falls back to the ground with his chair.

Chapter 12

War Looming

"We apologise for instruding like this but this is important, and we are glad that we finally get to see you as well Mr Gumede..." detective David Skhosana says with a calm voice as he and his partner Lindiwe Zulu sit down on the couch opposit Ntokozo who is sitting next to his sister at the Gumede home. This is after a few days since Ntokozo put two bullets in Lungisani Mbhele's head, and he must have known that at some point the police will knock on his door. His face though doesn't show any panic as he sits comfortably on the couch. Dora and Lungile on the other hand seem as little worried becaue they don't know why the police are here.

"So what is it this time, detectives? Have we murdered another person?" an anxious Dora asks nervously as she looks at her daughter on the right couch. David looks at his partner before saying, "Oh uhmm...no, no, no you didn't...but yes you are right, there has been another body." with a rather nervous and uncertain voice which seems to shock the Gumedes, including Ntokozo himself.

"What? Who died now?" a shocked Lungile shouts in disbelief as she looks at bother her mother and brother but Lindiwe interjects, "Uhmm...do you remember Lungisani Mbhele?" she asks calmly but with sharp eyes. "You opened a case of rape against him about 12 years ago...he was found dead last Saturday and his body dumped in a river in Richard's Bay. And just like the other bodies we have questioned you guys about, this one also was tortured before being shot in the head, which suggests to us that the killer is the same person. All these same murders seem to be about revenge, so naturally we'd come here to ask a few questions."

"Wait, so are you saying my daughter is now the number one suspect in this? This is absurd..." a worriedly-looking Dora says as she looks at Lungile and Ntokozo. "Well..like I said Mrs Gumede, it's only natural that we'd come and question your daughter here seeing that she had a history with Lungisani Mbhele who is now dead..." David says nervously as he clears hi throat. "Plus she is the only one so far who seems to have had a motive, because as I said these were revenge killings...not rendom."

"So what? Are you charging me with murder?" a shocked Lungile asks with a voice of panic. "Oh no, we don't have any evidence placing you at the crime scene at the moment. Like we say, you are the only who seem to have a motive in all this..." detective Lindiwe says as she looks at her partner who jumps in, "Yeah, that's why we want to ask you a few questions...all of you infact." he says as he pulls a small handbook from his jacket pocket. "Where were you on Saturday noon to later afternoon miss Gumede and can anyone collaborate your story?" he asks as he looks at his partner who also seems interested in the question.

"Well that's pretty much easy actually...I was here at home spending time with my family." Lungile says as she shrugs her shoulder while looking at her mother who nods but Lindiwe cuts in, "So you were home too Mrs Gumede?" she asks as she raises an eyebrow. "Oh yes ofcourse I was here home baking for my family. "Dora says with a very confident voice.

"Uhmm...what about you Mr Gumede? Were you home also?" David asks as he writes something down. "Oh no I wasn't home..." Ntokozo says calmly which makes the detectives interested as they raise eyebrows but makes his mother and sister a little nerveous as they look at each other. "I actually went to see someone about business and I only came back home a little late, like around 19:00, right mama?" Ntokozo says to which his mother nods in agreement. "Oh and that someone has a name perhaps?" Lindiwe asks curiously.

"Oh yes...his name is Eric Xaba, his offices are in Umhlanga..." Ntokozo says with a confident smile.
"And what business were you discussing with him again?" David asks as he writes something down but Ntokozo seems a little puzzled by this as he takes a deep sigh. "Well, uhmm...I'm not sure how that's got anything to do with your business here today but if you must know, I'm starting my data solutions business and Eric is helping me set it up" he says with an annoyed face as he shrugs his shoulders.
"Speaking of which, we can't seem to find any record of you in the last 12 years Mr Gumede? Why is that?" Linidiwe asks curiously whaich once again makes Lungile and Dora very anxious and worried but David adds, "Yeah, where were you and what were you doing the last 12 years? Nobody just disappears like that without a trace..." he asks as his hand itches to write something down. Now this is beginning to feel a little uncomfortable for Dora as she worries about what her son may tell these persistent detectives who may be looking for a way to link them with the murders.
"Well, uhmm...I actually travelled around the globe for different jobs..." Ntokozo says as he shrugs his shoulders but Lindiwe cuts in, "What kind of jobs exactly?" she asks curiously as she looks at her partner who writes something down. Ntokozo thinks for a second before saying, "Uhmm...I worked in a cruise ship for a few years and then it was jumping from one comany to another all over the globe...mainly for IT companies..." with a measured voice.
Now Lungile and Dora are anxiously looking at the detectives to see how they will react to what is being said to them while Ntokozo himself isn't showing any sign of panic at all. David and Lindiwe look at each as though they don't know what to think about what Ntokozo is saying to them. "Uhmm...ofcourse you know that we will need to have the references of those companies you worked for...you know, to verify the info you are giving us." David says as he

clears his throat while he is writing down. "Ofcourse officers, anything you need...even though I don't understand why you need this. I mean, it's not like I'm applying to work at the SAPS, right?" Ntokozo says with a smile that nobody in the room returns. "That is true Mr Gumede but the fact that since your return we have had bodies droping like flies in this area and four of them are linked to your sister raises levels of curiosity on our part." Lindiwe says as she shrugs her shoulders. "I mean, I'm sure your mother here told you about what happened to your sister during the period you were way and that couldn't have been easy for you, right?"
"Ofcourse it was not easy...it wouldn't be easy for you if it would have happened to your loved one, right?" Ntokozo says as he turns and looks at his sister who looks anxious but David interjects, "So you were really angry when you learnt what had happened, right?" he asks with a straight face. "Ofcourse I was angry...like I said, you would be as well detective if it was your loved one that had gone through that" the vissibly annoyed Ntokozo says with a rather firm voice. "So is it safe to say you wanted all of these men dead, right?" Lindiwe asks as her voice also becomes firm. But now this is making the environment a little tense as everyone looks a little unsettled. "Look, detective...am I under arrest? Am I a suspect or something?" Ntokozo asks calmy as he wears a straight face. David looks at his partner first before saying, "Oh uhmm...ofcourse not, but please we'd ask you to not leave the city without informing the police first as we may have more questions at a later stage" with a calm voice and a half smile.
"Uhmm...so its that all, officers?" a little annoyed Dora asks. "Oh uhmm...yes ofcourse that's all for now but like my partner said, we will come back if we have more questions to ask you." Lindiwe says as she and her partner stand up. "Ofcourse detectives, you are welcome anytime..." Lungile says as she also looks a little annoyed. The Gumedes watches on as the officers gets out of the house and

off through the small gate outside. They watch them through the window as they get into their car and drive away. At that point they all seem to breathe a little sigh of relief as if it was a close call.
"What the hell Ntokozo..." Lungile suddenly shouts as she goes back to sit on the couch. "What the hell happened to Lungisani? Oh my God Ntobeko...did you kill him?" She begins to panic as she covers her mouth with her hands but Ntokozo comes to sit next to him and says, "Why does it it matter who killed him sisi? That dog is dead, aren't you happy with that?" he says as tghough he is confused by his sister's outbursts.
"What the hell do you mean 'does it matter'? Ofcourse it does matter Ntokozo...damnit..." the visibly upset Lungile shouts at her brother. "The police suspect meas the a murderer, do you know what that means? It is ruining the business and this family's name. Do you even care about that Ntokozo, huh? Do you care?" but Dora quickly interjects, "Okay, okay, okay...calm down sweetheart, okay?" she says with a begging voice as she brushes her daughter's back before turning to her son, "Okay son, you know that we got to ask about this, alright? Because if you did it then it's better if you told us now than finding out later..." she says politely as she continues to brush Lungile's back. "Now that we know you are a government assassin, we can't avoid this topic forever..."
Ater thinking about it for a second, Ntokozo takes a deep breathe before saying, "Okay yes...yes I killed him." with a low voice which almost sends his mother and sister tumbling on the floor with shock. It's not even so much that they didn't suspect this but hearing it for the first time from Ntokozo himself is what shocks them because they still had some hope that it wasn't true.
"Oh Ntokozo...what have you done?" a defeated-looking Lungile asks with a shaky voice as she sinks on the couch but her mother interjects again, "So you killed all four of these men?" she asks as her eyes pop buy when she sees Ntokozo throwing her hands in the air

she covers her mouth in shock. She had never imagined her son turning out to be like this. Perhaps learning about how these men were killed is what's most shocking about this all. Lungile on the other hand is just struggling to process this information as tears begin to fall down her face in disbelief. It's hard to tell whether she's angry or hurt at this point.

"Look sis...honestly, would you have preffered that those dogs lived? Are you going to pretend that you are not happy that they are all dead?" Ntokozo asks as he raises his voice a little bit but his sister quickly interjects, "No, no, no Ntokozo...you did this in order to ease your conscience right? You were trying to right your wrongs...it had nothing to do with justice..." she shouts at her brother.

These words kind of cuts deep to Ntokozo as he looks down in shame. He knows that his sister is not lying about this so he takes a deep sigh before saying, "Okay look, you are right okay?" with a low voice. "Yes I did it to try and ease my guilt after what happened to you and the truth is I don't regret it one bit. I was wrong for abandoning you okay and there's nothing I can do that can ever change what happened to...I will always be haunted by guilt over that. You shouldnlt have gone through what you did alone sisi...I should have been there for you and I should have prevented it from happening. For that I am asking for your forgiveness...you too mama..."

This suddenly makes Lungile feel a little emotional as she wipes her tears. Part of her is feeling a bad for guilt tripping her brother, especially now that she knows where he was all this time. Dora herself is keeping quiet as her son and daughter talk things through, which is what she has always wanted them to do in order to move on from this chapter.

"Now what, Ntokozo?" Lungile asks with a low and somewhat sad voice. "The police suspect me because I'm the only one with the motive here but ofcourse they can't prove it because I wasn't involved. But what if they one day link the murders to you? You will go to jail, for life...do you realise that? The police are talking about a serial killer here and since those detectives have began to ask questions about you, soon you will be a person of interest to them." She begins to be emotional all over again but her mother once again pulls her to herself to comfort, making the moment in the room very sombre.

"Look guys, no one is going to jail over this okay?" Ntokozo says calmly but his mother cuts in, "What do you mean? I mean, this wasn't sanctioned by your...people, right? No one even knows who you work for, won't that be a problem." she asks as she looks very puzzled. Lungile herself is confused by all this.

"Look guys, my people are aware of this...don't worry about it okay?" Ntokozo says calmly. "I asked for a small favour and in return I have to deal with the drug issue in this area, and they want Jabulani Ngubeni."

This comes as an absolute shock to his family as they look at each other in wonder. "What? So it was you? It's you who killed Ngubeni's men? Oh my God Ntokozo..." Lungile shouts in disbelief as she looks at her mother who is just as shocked. "What happens when he finds out about this? And what about your girlfriend, Pearl? Have you told her that you are actually planning on killing his father? Are you okay with doing that job yourself?" She is juist in disbelief as her eyes pop out but Dora adds, "Yeah I mean, if you do that for them what do they want in return? What is this favour you asked from them?" she asks curiously as she dreads the response from her her son.

"Uhmm...the favour is that they cover for me on these hits I did. They won't be linked to me or any of us..." Ntokozo says calmly with an assuring voice but his sister interjects, "But can you trust these people to not sell you out on this if somehow something goes wrong?" she asks as she shrugs her shoulders. Dora seems to be worried about the same thing.

"No guys, they won't...I trust them okay?" Ntokozo says with an assuring smile. "Oh and who said I will kill Pearl's father? I'm gathering evidence against him and all his associates...and once I have what I need he will be arrested. In no time this area will be a drug free zone and no drug dealer will ever want to come and deal here. No child of this area will become a drug mule ever again...I'm here now."

These words seem to warm Dora and Lungile's hearts as they look at each othe and smile. Suddenly they see the Ntokozo they always knew who is considerate to other people but Dora's face suddenly changes as she looks at her son. "Uhmm...but son, are you sure you want to do this?" she asks with a low voice. "I mean, this will break Pearl's heart when she learns that you want to arrest her father. You love her, don't you?"

This makes Nokozo think for a second before saying, "Hey I thought you two didn't like this girl, what changed?" with a raised eyebrow. "Well that was then okay? This is now...I got to spend a little time with her and I realised that she really loves you and would do anything for your saftey..."Lungile says as she shrugs her shoulders but her mother quickly adds, "yeah she seems like a very nice girl Ntokozo and you also love her. Who knows? She may turn out to be nothing like her father afterall..." she says with a little smile which makes Ntokozo thinks for a second before saying, "Look guys, we will cross that bridge when we get there alright?" with a low and kinda worried voice.

"Excuse me you guys..." he says with a low voice as he gets up and heads upstairs to his room, leaving his mother and sister wondering what could have happened.

***

At the Ngubeni house things are sour between father and daughter even since Pearl came back home. All she ever does these days is thinking about Ntokozo so much that nothing else seems to matter to her anymore, not that her father is bothered by it. Jabulani is just happy that her daughter is back home to continue with running the family businesses that he hadn't notice how miserable she is. Perhaps he feels that she will get over it soon or will find a new man somewhere. Since Pearl came back she and her father have not spoken about the incident that made her run away in the first place and it doesn't look like she wants to know anything about it either.
"So after all this time, no one has found my drugs anywhere or who may have killed my men? This is making me look bad...do you understand that?" Ngubeni asks his men as they sit in the lounge where they are holding their meeting, unlike in previous times where they'd be in he garage. That might have been a mistake on Ngubeni's part because he hadn't realised that his daughter sitting up in the stairs listening to the conversation.
"Uhmm...the drugs haven't been found Bra J but I heard from a contact of mine at the police station that the cops are following leads somehwere..." one of Ngubeni's man says which makes his boss very interested. "Lead? Lead where? Who are the police suspecting?" Ngubeni asks as he puts his glass of whiskey down. "Uhmm...one guy from PMB who works for Kruger...he is on the police radar." the man says with a rather nervous voice but Ngubeni shakes his head and says, "Nah man...this doesn't make sense at all. Why would Kruger come after my territory? I mean, we are not friends sure, but we are respectful towards each other...so why start a war now?"
Ngubeni seems a little puzzled and in disbelief over this as he tries to wrap his head around it. His man shrugs his shoulders and says, "I don't know boss but that's the word from my contact at the moment. Maybe Kruger wants to expand his empire...he won't be

the first dealer in the world to be greedy and go after competition..." with a low voice.

"No man, I'n not convinced by this..." the disbelieving Ngubeni says as he picks up his glass again. "There must be another explanation...it could be that his man was hired by someone else, if indeed it was him. Our guys were killed by a professional, someone who knew not to leave any trace. My gut feeling tells me that this was a personal crusade, some Robi Hood of the area. I suspect it was someone from the community who wanted to get rid of drugs in the area..."

"But after all this time Bra J? I mean, who would in their right mind dare try to do that, knowing exactly who you are?" another man asks as he looks across the room where everyone nods in agreement.

"What about that Gumede guy? I mean, this hasn't happened to us in years but he comes back here and our men get killed? Is he not maybe trying to be like his father who was seen as the pillar of this community?" another man asks as she takes a sip of his glass, which makes Mgubeni raise an eyebrow as if this he ais really entertaining this theory. But Pearl sitting up in the stairs suddenly has her heart racing when she hears the name of the person she loves beung mentioned.

Ngubeni thinks for a second before saying, "Uhmm...I don't know hey, this has never crossed my mind." as he takes a deep sigh. "But ofcourse anythng is possible these and you are right in saying that we haven't had this problem in a very long time and suddenly this Gumede guy comes back home and we have two bodies? Who has his background after he left home?"

"Uhmm...that's just the thing Bra J, I have had my contact check him out like you requested and there are no hits..." one man says with a low voice but Ngubeni quickly cuts in, "What do you mean?" he asks cuwriously as he raises an eyebrow. "I mean, there's nothing on the man...no record of him for the past 12 years, it's like he never existed." the man responds which suddenly makes Ngubeni a little anxious, but he is not the only as Pearl upstairs begins to wonder a little bit.

"You see? That's the kind of thing that makes me anxious okay? It sounds like he is a ghost..." a curious Ngubeni says as he finishes off whatever was left in his glass. "Now this Gumede boy has become our primary person of interest. Like I said before that the killings on our men were carried out by a professional so we need to dig deep on Ntokozo Gumede's past...someone, somewhere knows something. I'm now even suspecting that he was getting close to my daughter because he wanted to get close to me or to maybe to get some information. Yes...this is a very possibility, Ntokozo is our guy..."

He now looks a little troubled but his men don't respond to what he is saying. Pearl on the other hand in a panic mode as she knows well how her father treats anyone whom he regards as an enemy. She doesn't know what to do but there must be a way to warn Ntokozo about this as she stands up and goes back to her room.

***

Back at the Gumede home Ntokozo is sitting under the tree feeling a little down after the visit by the police in the morning. He is a little worried about what his family is thinking after he confessed to them about killing those four men but he is also a little relieved because they now know who he is. Also on his mind is the question his family asked about Pearl and now that he had time to think about it he is feeling a little sad for having to turn in the father of the woman he loves.

"Hey big bro...are we disturbing you? We baked buscuits..." Lungile says as she and Dora bring buscuits and juice, which seems to brighten Ntokozo's eyes as he smiles widely to them. Without really giving him a chance to respond, the two sit down with the tray as Dora begins to pour juice for the three of them.

"So uhmm, are you okay?" Lungile asks with a low voice as she takes the glass of juice from her mother who quickly adds, "Yeah son, you look down since this morning so we thought that uhmm...we don't want you to be alone. We are a family and we will always look after each other..." with a nervous smile as she looks at her daughter who nods in agreement. This seems to warm Ntokozo's heart as he smiles to them before picking his glass. "Uhmm yeah guys I think I'm okay buy you know...after this morning I began to wonder about a lot of things you know. But I'm gonna be okay..." he says as he takes a sip.

"What kind of things were you wondering about?" Dora asks curiously. "I mean like...if dad was still around, how everything would be like. If maybe I hadn't joined the military, things would be very different from how they are now...don't you think?" Ntokozo says with a low voice as he looks away which makes Lungile kind of feel bad as she looks at her mother.

"Look brother, I'm so sorry that I blamed you for abandoning us...but you must never regret serving your country okay?" she says as she takes her brother's hand. "I think I resented you because I assumed the worst about your whereabouts. I thought you abandoned us and went to live a lavish lifestyle somewhere with family money. Dad used to try and avoid any topic that has you in it and we never understood why. But he'd always try and defend you if we spoke about you which was always strange. Now we know why he did that but that's something I'm still trying to process...it will take a little bit of time."

"Yeah your sister is right..." Dora adds, "We thought you had abandoned us and we really apologies for that son but never ever regret serving your country...it's the greatest honor. We just wished that your father could have said something because he saw the pains

that we had to go through, especially when we were beginning to accept the possibility you might be dead..."
These words make Ntokozo feel a little sad but also happy that they can now openly talk about this subject. "I know mom alright?" he says with a low voice. "But you know, dad just had a mind of his own and I'm pretty sure he did this to protect you guys. I don't think it was matter of not trusting you guys but he couldn't take any chances with your safety. Even he and I were always careful about how we communicated since he was my handler when I joined the special program. You know it's hard to trust people in this government sometimes it's hard to know who the real enemy is and who to trust..."
"But this new handler of yours...you trust him?" Lungile asks curiously. "I mean, he's not gonna turn on you especially about these murders, right?" She looks at her mother who also raises an eyebrow in wonder but Ntokozo responds, "You guys don't have to worry about that okay? I can trust my handler and besides, in this special program this is what we deal with all the time. Those scumbag are asscociated with corrupt cops, corrupt businessmen and politicians so no one will miss them when they are gone. Soon they will be linked to dodgy and corrupt activities no who knows them will want to be associated..."
"So their reletives won't want revenge?" Dora asks with anxious eyes.
"No mama they won't...you don't have to worry yourself about that." Ntokozo says with a smile of assurance which Dora returns as she stands up and says, "Okay then, let me go prepare lunch for my granddaughter, she will be back from school any moments now..." as she walks back into the house.
"Thank you mama..." Lungile shouts with a smile as she watches on her mother gets in the house. Her face then suddenly changes to being serious as she turns to Ntokozo, "Hey, here's another thing I wanted to say..." she says with a low voice. "Uhmm...I was just

thinking...I know you may think that I don't appreciate what you did to make those men pay for what they did to me, but I do." This comes as a bit of a surpise for Ntokozo who raises an eyebrow and says, "Oh...really? You know, I thought were angry about what I did. I thought you said it won't change anything...what has changed now?" in disbelief.

"No, look I was a little rattled at first because I didn't expect it from you but it doesn't mean I didn't want those men to pay for what they did." Lungile says as she looks a little embarrassed for saying that. "I know that you did it with good intentions and I'm now asking you big brother, please stop feeling guilty about what happened to me...it wasn't your fault. I'm asking you to please forgive yourself okay?"

These words are heart-warming to Ntokozo as he lets out a little smile but his sister continues, "But I do feel a little guilty..." she says with a low voice as she looks down but Ntokozo quickly jumps in, "About what sisi?" he asks curiously. Lungile thinks for a second before saying, "Uhmm...for turning you into this person who is thristy for blood?" as she looks down. "I really feel responsible for that Ntokozo...I do. When you first came back here I made you feel so guilty that you had to go do this for me. I didn't want you to become this person buthi(brother) and I can't imagine that you enoyed torturing those men, but guilt probably made you do it. It was my fault..."

This makes Ntokozo feel bad as he looks at his guilt-driven sister who is looking down. "Hey look at me..." he says with a smile, "Taking out trash is kinda what I do, okay? It wasn't you who made me do it. I just can't stand and watch when people take advantage of others, especially women. That is why I am also dealing with the drug dealers in this area...it has to stop..."

"Even if it's the father of your grilfriend?" Lungile asks politely as she lifts her head. Ntokozo thinks for a second and says, "Job is a job, I just hope that Pearl will forgive me one day." as he takes a deep sigh. "She knows that her father is hurting people and someone has to stop him. If it means that she and I never work out, then I guess we will never work out but I believe that she wants to do what's right.

People will surprise you sometimes hey...we never choose the families we are born to but we can always forge our own paths as he learn to separate wrong from right. Let's hope this is true of Pearl..." This just makes Lungile smile as she feels warm about it. "Well, think we need a bottle of wine...don't you think?" she says as she stands but Ntokozo just smiles and shakes his head in this belief as he looks at his watch while his sister goes into the house to fetch a bottle.

***

While Lungile is still inside the house a call comes through for Ntokzo:
Ntokozo: "Hello"
Caller: "Hey, it's me..."
Ntokozo: "Pearl? Hey uhmm...how are you?"
Pearl: "Uhmm...I'm okay, how are you?"
Ntokozo: "No, you are not okay...what's wrong?"
little silence
Pearl: "Uhmm...can you talk?"
Ntokozo: "Uhmm...I'm with my sister but she's inside the house right now. So yeah we can talk, what's up?"
another silence
Ntokozo: "Pearl?"
Pearl: "Uhmm...I need to tell you something okay?"
Ntokozo: "Okay?"
Pearl: "Uhmm...my dad is...uhmm...I think my dad is on to you..."
Ntokozo: "On to me about what?"
Pearl: "Oh come on Ntokozo...stop treating like a child okay?"

Ntokozo: "No seriously I don;t know what you are talking about."
Pearl: "Okay fine, you don't have to tell me but look...whatever you did, they are on to you."
Ntokozo: "Pearl you gonna have to be more specific than that okay?"
Pearl: "Uhmm...my dad suspects that you had something to do with his men's murder and he has asked his men to dig into you and watch your every move. If he finds out that you did he will kill you..."
Little silence
Ntokozo: "And you know this how?"
Pearl: "I overheard them speaking earlier today but my dad didn't notice that I was listening..."
silence
Pearl: "So did you have something to do with the death of those men Ntokozo? And please don;t lie to me okay?"
Ntokozo: "Can we meet? Do you think you can get out without anyone following you?"
Pearl: "I can try...where are we meeting?"
Ntokozo: "I will text you the details later okay?"
Pearl: "Okay..."
Ntokozo: "I gotta go...my sister is coming..."
Call dropped

Chapter 13

Gloves are off

"Did anyone follow you?" Ntokozo asks an anxious-looking Pearl as they sit in the car parked in the underground parking at the mall. "No..." Pearl says nervously but Ntokozo quickly interjects, "Are you sure?" he asks as he looks at her in the eyes. "Yes I'm sure..." Pearl says as she rolls her eyes, visibly annoyed. "Look, I'm sorry that couldn't come yesterday after we spoke on the phone...I couldn't get out of the house without being noticed."
"Yeah I get it...how did you get here?" Ntokozo asks curiously as he looks around the parking which is quiet since it's still in the morning. "Uhmm...I asked one of my friends to transport me. She picked me up at home, at the gate and dropped me here at the entrance and then left. So, incase anyone follows the car they will be chasing their tails because my friend has a few errands to run this morning." Pearl says with a smile as though she's proud of herself but Ntokozo interjects, "But what if your farher calls and want to know where you are?" he asks with a worried voice? "Well, we will cross the bridge when we get there okay? Now I'm here like you asked. So are you gonna tell me what's going on?" Pearl asks. Ntokozo thinks for a second before saying, "Uhmm...I wanted to know exctly what you heard your father saying yesterday." with a deep sigh but this seems to annoy Pearl a little bit as she suspects there's more to this than Ntokozo is letting up. "But I already told you over the phone yesterday Ntokozo, what more do you want to hear?" she asks as she throws her hands in the air. "Do you wanna hear that my father and his men think you are the one going around killing his people and threatening drug war? Is that what you want to hear?"

This leads to an awkward silence in the car as Ntokozo looks away but Pearl gently hold his chin and turns his head, "Hey, look at me. Please babe, just talk to me okay? You know that you can trust me..." she says softly with begging eyes as tough she is a teenager begging for love. Ntokozo slow looks at her in the eyes and notices panic and that makes him feel bad. "What's ging on with you? Is my father right? Did you kill his men? Because he believes that you did and he will kill you...he is a very dangerous man Ntokozo and I don't want to lose you over this. If you didn't do it then I will have to go speak to him about it and try to sort this out okay?" Pearl says anxiously as she desperately tries to read the man she loves.

"No, no, no...there's no need for that okay?" Ntokozo says as he quickly takes Pearl's hands. "Just...don't do that...uhmm...actually, because I did kill your father's men." he says with a low voice as though he is embarrassed by it but Pearl's eyes pop out in shock as she looks at him in disbelief. She is clearly caught of guard by this because she could not have guessed that the man she loves so much is capable of such.

"What?" she shouts in shock. "But why Ntokozo? Huh? Why would you do something like that? Do you know what you have done? My father will kill you for real...oh my God...my father will ki..." She begins to panic as tears start fall from her eyes but Ntokozo interjects, "Oh come on Pearl, you know why I did this, alright?" he says as he looks away. "Your father is busy destroying our community by getting kids hooked on drugs while he makes a lot of money from it. Not only that but he is killing people Pearl, killing people...Now people can't walk freely and safely on our streets. Someone has to put a stop to that Pearl okay? Someone has to..."
"Yes I know that Ntokozo okay? I know that...but why must you be the one who is a starring huh?" the visibly panicking Pearl shouts. "This is the job of the police, why are you getting involved? Do you want to get yourself killed? The drug business is very dangerous

Ntokozo, so please leave this to the police okay? Please I beg you babe..."

"Oh please Pearl, you and I both know that the police won't do sh*t alright?" Ntokozo says as he throws his hands in the air but Pearl quickly cuts in, "Oh and you think you can? Running around like a vigilante inflicting justice? Is that what you do now?" she says as she shakes her head in disbelief. "Well, atleast I'm doing something Pearl...what are you doing to do about this? You live with this man in the same house and that doesn't doesn't bother you?" Ntokozo asks as he raises his voice in frustration. "Oh or is it another case of blood being thicker than water, huh? So yopur father must go on and make other families father-less and son-less while you go on with your lavish lifestyle?"

These words seem to cut deep into Pearl's heart that she takes a deep sigh of shock, which makes Ntokozo wonder if that wasn't too harsh. This brings a little tension in the car as Pearl is in disbelief of what has been to said to her. "How can you say something like that too me Ntokozo? Huh?" she says with a low voice of dissapoinment. "Didn't I just risked everything to be here with you right now, huh? Didn't I warn you yesterday about what my father intends to do? Doesn't that tell you where my loyalties lie? The very fact that you are uestioning about that really hurts me Ntokozo. Did I choose to be the daughter of a monster? Was that a choice?"

Now this makes Ntokozo feel bad as he looks down in shame. The last thing he wanted was having this conversation with the woman he loves turn sour which is what his mother and sister warned him about. When he lifts his head and looks at Pearl he sees that her eyes are teary and red and he feels bad about it, but he doesn't seem to know what to say at this moment.

"Uhmm...look, Pearl, I really didn't mean like that but..." he says with a begging voice but Pearl cuts in, "Is there any other way you possibly could have meant this Ntokozo?" she says with a low voice as she wipes her eyes. "Here I am risking my life to warn you of an impending danger but what do you do? If my father found out about this he will disown me and I will be tossed to the streets cause I have no one else and yet you are questioning my authority. On top of all that, I have been straight up with you as far as my family dealings are concerned while you didn't even bother to tell me that you were killing my dad's men. So since we are talking about trust, is it safe to say you have been using me to get close to my dad? So is it safe to you never loved me at all?"

"Oh come on Pearl, you know very well that I love you alright? You know I wasn't..." Ntokozo says as he attempts to make a counter argument but Pearl once again cuts in, "So then how come you never told me about your plan huh? That you are going after my father? So your plan is to kill my father yet you claim to be loving me Ntokozo? Huh? Please explain that to me..."

"Pearl, someone has to stop what your father is doing okay?" Ntokozo says with a low voice as he tries to take Pearl's hands but she pulls away. "And I was not going to kill him but your father has to be put away Pearl and you know it...what he is doing in our neigherbood is not good. I really need your help to do this before he makes another family grieve for a loved one."

"What? Are you crazy Ntokozo? Are you asking me to help you put my father away? As in arrested? Are you even hearing yourself Ntokozo?" Pearl asks as her eyes pop out in disbelief. "Look Pearl, too many families are hurting because of your father okay and they can't even go to the police because your father owns the police." Ntokozo says as he shrugs his shoulders while raising his voice a little bit. "Families can't get closure Pearl because they don't know what happened with thier loved ones, but you do okay? You can help put an end to this and so that those families can get closure. This has gone on long enough and I want to put an end to it."

"But what I don't get is why you have to be the one doing this Ntokozo okay? Why it has to be you?" Pearl says with an anxious voice as she shakes her head. She is heartbroken as she like she is being pressed to choose between two people that she loves very much. She wipes her eyes and looks at the man who is asking him to do something like this and she just can't believe it.

"So...are you going to help me?" Ntokozo asks with begging eyes as he once again tries to take Pearl's hands. She doesn't pull away this time but she looks away in disbelief. "Do you know what you are asking me to do Ntokozo?" she asks as she continues to look on her side of the window. "Yes babe, I know what I'm asking you and believe me I wish there was another away but there isn't. Your father has to be stopped and the safest way is that he gets locked up intead of him being shot and killed by other drug dealers or the powerful people connected to him. We can nolonger turn a blind eye to this Pearl, something has to be done. Once he is gone, you can work on cleaning your family name which can only boost your family business..."

Pearl sits quiet as she listens to what is being said to her. She shakes her head in disbelief which throws Ntokozo off a little beit as he doesn't what she is thinking. "Look, let me go think about this Ntokozo...this is too much okay? I will be in touch..." Pearl says with a somewhat discouraged voice as she slowly opens the door but Ntokozo calls out, "No please wait Pearl..." he says but to deaf ears as Pearl gets off the car and walks towards the Mall entrance, leaving him banging his head against yhe steering wheel.

***

Few days later, it is Dora's birthday and Lungile has invited her friends to celebrate the day with her family. She has also invited her boyfriend Thulani with the hope that he and Ntokozo can have a formal sit down and get to know each other, much to the discomfort of both men. Now that Thulani is aware of Ntokozo's history he is not sure how to handle this-whether to try and impress his girlfriend's protective brother or just be himself. Ntokozo on the other hand had invited his friend Sthembiso because he did not want to be the only man in the house full of women, not knowing that his sister invited the boyfriend. He would have loved for Pearl to be here but he also knows that it would have made things a little awkward because she doesn't know Lungile and her friends that well.

Lungile and her friends are just catching up since they haven't been able to see each other lately with all the chaos that's been going on in the family. Everyone can use a breather to just to chill and relax by the pool on a sunny Saturday noon while Dora has also invited a few friends from the neighbourhood to celebrate with her, and they are inside the house. Ntokozo, Sthembiso and Thulani are chilling on the other side of the pool with the meat on a braai stand and a coolerbox full of ciders and beers.

"So man, how is the life of a doctor?" Sthembiso on a camp chair asks the nervously looking Thulani who has a cider in his hand. Ntokozo is turning the meat on the braai stand and seemingly trying to read his sister's boyfriend. "It's busy man, I hardly get time to relax and chill like this...but, I really love what I do so I guess I can't complain." Thulani says as he takes a sip to calm his nerves. "And you? What do you again?" he asks as he puts his cider down.

"Oh uhmm...I'm an engineer at Transnet. Well, my job is not as fancy as yours ofcourse but like you, I really love what I do. I guess I can't complain either." Sthembiso says with a smile as he also takes a sip of his beer.

"Oh come on man, what's not fancy about being an engineer? Transnet even..." Thulani says with a smile but Sthembiso just shrugs hs shoulders and smiles to the question. "So Ntokozo, what are your plans now that you are back? Joining family business?" Thulani asks his girlfriend's brother nervously as he tries to break the ice between them. "Oh no man I'm not joining the family business...I'm actually in the process of launching my own company." Ntokozo says as he comes back to sit down next to Sthembiso. "Oh wow, that's great man, what's it about?" Sthembiso asks as he picks up his cider again seeing that the ice has been broken.

"It's data analysis company. It will focus on many aspects, be it markets, health, politics, science and even sports." Ntokozo says as he picks up his beer and takes a sip. "Wow man that is great, goodluck on this journey..." Thulani says as he lifts his cider up but Sthembiso adds, "will you focus on public or private sector?" he asks curiously as he takes a sip.

"Oh uhmm...both bro..." Ntokozo says as takes another sip. "I am willing to work with anyone who is looking to use our services." He stands and goes to check out the meat on the braai stand. "Well man, you are going to be rich. Everything is about data these days." Sthembiso says as he also lifts his beer up to Ntokozo who smiles in gratitude. "Damnit, I forgot my phone in the car, let me quickly go grab it." he says as he stands and qickly rushes by the gate where his car is parked in the driveway, leaving that awkward moment between Thula in the possible futire brother in-law.

"So man, while there's just the two of us here I just wanted to say that uhmm...I know that uhmm..since you are now back you'd like to ensure that your family is safe from any form of hurm..." Thulani says with a low and nervous voice. "I haven't been coming over to your home because I didn't want to come across as disrespecting you as an eldest and only Gumede son."

"What's going on Thulani? Say what's on your mind man..." Ntokozo says with a straight face as he comes back to sit down which makes Thulani all the more nervous as he finishes off whatever was left on his bottle before saying, "Uhmm...look man, I know that you have already done a background check on me to see if I'm not a danger to your sister, but I can assure you, I am not..." as he clears his throat. "I love Lungile Ntokozo and I would never do anything to put her life in danger. I know what happened tp her and I can assure you that I will never do something like that or even lay a finger on her..."

This makes Ntokozo think for a second as he looks at this guy in the eyes. "Look man I know alright?" he says as he takes a deep sigh.

"Yes I did check you out a while ago but hey man, which brother wouldn't? And it wasn't even about you but I was feeling guilty for having not been there for her when she went through all that and I promised myself that I'd never ever allow something like that to happen to her."

"Don't worry about it, we are straight..." Thulani says with a smile.

"It is understandable man, I would have done the same if I was in your position and I think it is a good thing. It puts my mind at ease to know that you are here to protect your family." He quickly opens another cider for himself because he feels things are getting a little too sentimental for his liking but Ntokozo just smiles without saying anything.

"Oh uhmm...another thing man..." Thulani continues, "I know that things have been hectic in your family lately and it might not be the perfect of times for me and Lungile, but with your blessing I would really love to ask your sister to marry me." Well, it would be an understatement to say Ntokozo was caught off guard with that as he almost drops the bottle in his hand, which makes Thulani feels a little embarrassed. He doesn't know how this will come out but he is sensing that maybe the timing wasn't right at all as he looks down. Ntokozo doesn't seem to know what to say as he tries hard to keep a straight face.

"Oh wow man...uhmm that's, uhmm...are you sure about this? Did you think this through?" a shocked Ntokozo as he stands up to go and remove some meat from the stand. "Yeah man, I'm sure. Look I really love your sister and she is the woman I want to spend the rest of my life with." Thulani says nervously as he takes a sip of his cider. "Uhmm...well man, look all I can say is that goodluck to both of you and I trust that you will look after myself right?" Ntokozo says with a half smile as he looks over where Lungile and her friends are sitting on the other side of the pool. "Thanks a lot man, it really means a lot to me. I promise that I will look after your sister very well..." the relieved-looking Thulani says as he once again lifts up his bottle in gratitude.

***

Over to the other side of the pool Lungile has a big table set up that has a big cake on it and few bottles of champaigns. There are also coloured balloons decorating the wall that the table is leaning on and girls are just waiting for waiting for Ntokozo to finish with the braaing of meat since everything else has already been prepared. "So you really brought your boyfriend? You want him and your brother to be friends now?" Lindiwe asks as she rolls her eyes at Lungile who lets out a little smile before saying, "Ofcourse not friend but, I was hoping they can get to know each other a little bit..." as she shrugs her shoulders but Nompumelelo jumps in, "Is there something you wanna tell us friend? Are they soon to become brothers in-law or something?" she asks curiously as she takes a sip of her wine. "Oh come on bebe, ofcourse not, even though that's actually not such a bad idea hey..." Lungile says naughtily with a tongue out, which makes her friends laugh.
"Anyways, what's the story with the cases? Any progress with that?" Nompumelo probes. "Uhmm...oh that?" Lungile says with a sigh, "No the police haven't been back since the last time they questioned me about death of that scambag, not that I was ever worried about that anyways. For the record though, I'm happy he is dead..."

This last bit makes her friends look at each as they can see that this topic is making her angry. "Well, that's actually a relief my friend because that whole thing doesn't you even though, you know those men all got what they deserved." Lindiwe says with a smile as she takes a sip of her wine but this makes Lungile feel a little bad because she knows that she is not being compeletely honest with her friends. But ofcourse she can't go around telling her friends that her brother has murdered many people but her friends can see that she is becoming a little uncomfortable about something, even though they may ignore it.

"Anyways so what's going on between your brother and that drug dealer girl?" Nompumelolo asks as she takes a sip a vissbly uncomfortable Lungile cuts in, "Oh come on Mpumi, do you really have to call her that?" she asks as she rolls her eyes but Lindiwe also cuts in, "Oh wow, what has changed? Didn't you hate her a little while ago?" she asks as she raises an eyebrow.

"Okay look, I think I have had an opportunity to know her when she was here and we talked..." Lungile says as she shrugs her shoulders. "I don't think she's anything like her father okay? There's nothing she can do about it...nobody chooses the family they are born into, you know that guys..." This seems to come as a surprise to her friends who look at each other. "Oh so then if she ain't like her father why doesn't she turn him over to the police?" a visibly confused Nompumelelo asks as she looks at Lindiwe who also interested to to know but Lungile once again interjects, "Come on guys you well know as I do that Bra Ja controls the police. What good would that have done, huh?" she says as she shrugs her shoulders.

"Okay friend, it's well and good that you are now suddenly Pearl's biggest fan or maybe she's your future sister in-law but the truth is that the apple don't fall far from the tree okay?" Lindiwe says as she rolls her eyes and Nompumelelo seems to be in agreement with her she nods but Lungile doesn't seem to be comfortable with this topic. "Look guys I know why you are concerned okay? That's how me and my mom felt about her in the begining..." she says with a low voice but Nompumelelo quickly interjects, "Whoa wait, even your mom is now her fan? Friend clearly something you are not telling us, what is it?" she asks curiously. "Yeah friend, is there something you wanna tell us? Why this change of heart about this girl? We k now that her family deals with drugs and we know how many bodies have dropped to the floor because of them. There are families in this community that have suffered because their kids became drugs eddicts as result of that family. So what is this? What's going on?" Lindiwe adds as she also looks confused and curious.

Lungile needs to think carefully about ths because she knows there are things she can't tell her friends, but she has now put herself in a corner.

"Look guys, I know all that you are telling me is true okay?" she says with a low voice as she looks across the pool where her brother is. "I know what that family has done but from what I can gather is that Pearl has nothing to do with it. That is the reason she ran and came to stay with us for a little while. She and her father don't get along at all."

"Well, then if that's the case why is she back there in that house friend?" a visibly annoyed Nompumelelo asks as she throws her hands in the air but Lindiwe adds, "Yeah, doesn't she have relatives she can go to? Better yet, why doesn't she rent an apartment if she can't stand her father?" she asks as she looks at Nompumelelo who once again cuts in, "Look friend, all we are saying is that you and your family better be careful okay? You know very well how this drug business is like and if this girl starts to get close to your family, especially your brother it may not end well. We just want you to be careful friend, okay?" she says with a low voice.

This makes Lungile think for a second because not so long ago these are the words she and her mother used to tell Ntokozo. Part of her fears that her friends may be right because now that Ntokozo has made his intentions clear that she wants to arrest Pearl father, things may get a little tense. But also, part of her wants to believe that Pearl is not as bad as she may have initially thought of her.

While she is thinking about this she is interrupted by her brother across the pool who indicates with his hands that the meat is ready. "Okay guys let me go call mom and her friends, the meat is ready..." she says with a low voice as she stands up and gets in the house.

***

Meanwhile at the police station detectives Lindiwe Zulu and her partner David Skhosana are under the pressure they have never felt before since they can't seem to make a breakthrough in the case of the mysterious murderes that have happened over the last few weeks and their commissioner is not happy since he himself is getting pressure from those above him. The people that Ntokozo killed are from rich and well known families and they are demanding answers. It is becoming hard to know if commissioner Ncube is clean or not but he is close to Judas Masondo whose son Philani was killed by Ntokozo.

"Guys do you know the pressure I'm getting from above concerning this case? And I had told people that you two are the best men I have on this and now you are making me to look bad, do you realise that?" a visibly frustrated Ncube says angrily to his super team as they sit in his office. He looks very intimidating when he is upset about something.

"Yes sir we know, but we are really trying hard to get some solid leads but so far we are hitting a brick wall..." a nervously looking David says as he looks at his partner who nods in agreement. "What about that family? The Gumede family...aren't yo making any headways with that? Didin't you say all things seem to be pointing to them? Why haven't you made arrests? People are expecting arrests, do you guys get that?" Ncube says as he raises his voice a little bit.

"Yes sir we know but we can't just make arrests without anything thing that can hold..." Lindiwe says nervously with a low voice.

"While we may say that Lungile Gumede seems to have a motive there's no evidence that puts her on the scene of the crime. All her alibis check out. We don't even have a murder weapon, making this even more diffcult for us." She looks at her partner who nods in agreement but the commissioner interqjects, "Have you asked around the area where these bodies were found? Are you telling me that no one has seen anything? No one at all? Come on guys..." he says with a low voice as he looks discouraged.

"No sir, no one at all..." David says with a low vouce as he looks discouraged but once again Ncube interjects, "You know what this tells me? These killings were done by a professional okay? But now our question should be, who and why?" he says with as he looks to the ceiling to think. "Who would pay a professional killer for these guys? Did you do a background check on the victims...people they were connected to? The businesses they were in and all of that? Something is obviously missing in all of this..."

"Uhmm...actually yes sir we did..." David says nervously as he looks at his partner who nods. "Strangely all of them seem to be connected some dodgy individuals. Philani Masondo for example, he handled money for a lot of people if I were to guess, I'd say he was laundering cash for dodgy people. As it turns out, he had a gambling problem. His father as you may know is connected to influential people including politcians and business people. He was also involved in some controvertial tender deals that saw him isolated by some of his friends who didn't want to be fingered in any wrong doing."

Ncube listens carefully without interrupting but Lindiwe interjects, "Oh and Mr Akhona Velenkosini Lukhele is just as dodgy..." she says with a sigh as she looks at David who agrees with a nod. "According to what we pcan gather so far is that he runs a trafficking ring with some foreign nationals...Nigerian to be specific. They traffic women in and outside the country and that's with the help of castom officials at the border."

"Goddamnit, is anyone running an investigation on that one?" a shocked Ncube who has his hands over his head asks in disbelief.

"Yes sir, uhmm...crime intelligence is heading that one because apparently it also involves some people in high places. So we have decided to not get in their way as far as that one is concerned, unless ofcourse sir you want us to look into it. Our focus has been on these murders that we suspected are connected to maybe one killer...but we just don't have any evidence to link them in anyway other than that Gumede family. But even that, it's only just the motive...other than that there's nothing."

"What about the third victim?" Ncube asks curiously as he raises an eyebrow. "Oh uhmm...Lungisani Mbhele?" David says as he jumps in. "Well, just like the other two he is not clean. He is a businessman involved in logistics, exports and imports business but he has dealings with some dodgy people as well. He was once arrested when he was found with about R4m cash in the boot of his car, but ofcourse he got away with it. One of his business associates was arrested for bein in possesion of illegal goods that were sneaked into the country through the harbour, but nothing could be linked to Mbhele, officially that is."

Well, this makes the commissioner to think for as second as he gets off his chair and goes to stand by the window. He seems to be really troubled by these revelations his detectives are revealing. "So what are we saying here detectives?" he asks with a low voice as he comes backs to sit down on his swinging chair. "Are these murders connected or what?"

"Well sir, that was actually our initial thought, that they were connected..." David says as he looks at his partner who nods in agreement. "I mean, how these murders happened it suggestsed that they were revenge killings from the same killer, and at that point Miss Lungile Gumede was the only one who had a link with all the victims and she had a motive. But even with that, there's no evidence putting her on the scene of the crimes so that was a dead end. We checked the family background, nothing outsatnding comes out of it. They are clean...so we are back to square one..."

"So what are you saying exactly detective?" Ncube asks with a worried face as he swings on his chair but Lindiwe jumps in, "What we are saying sir is that we are ruling the Gumedes out of this." she says with a low voice. "We are saying these killings may not be connected after all. All of the victims had shaddy dealings with dodgy individuals, that is where our focus should be. We will investigate all their associates and see what comes of it."

"But do you realise that we don't have that much time detective Zulu, huh? People want answers and they want them now..." the frustrated commissioner says with a sigh. "Yes sir we are aware of that sir but we can't cut corners with these things...we have to make sure that we do proper investigation before we start naming suspects." David says nervously but his partner jumps in, "And sir if we are going to investigate influential individuals connected to these victims we may need clearance from you..." she says with a raise eyebrow but Ncube cuts in, "No, no, no...just go as far as you can go okay? But if evidence leads to any powerful individuals like politicians you come back to me immediately, are we clear on that?" he says with a rather firm voice.

"Yes sir..." Lindiwe and David say simulteniously. "Alright then, you are dismissed..."Ncube says with a low voice and the detectives look at each other before they stand up and leave the commissioner's office.

Chapter 14

Cut off the head

On a Monday after Dora's weekend birthday party at the Gumede home, Ntokozo finds himself face to face with Judas Masondo at one of the restaurants at the Gateway Mall. Ntokozo must have known that Judas will be by himself this morning in what looks like a quick breakfast before he heads to the office, which is not far away from the mall.

Unexpectedly, Ntokozo comes in this relevantly quiet restaurent and finds Judas sitting in a far corner table all by himself having eggs, sausages and toasted brown bread breakfast. He is wearing a black suit which suggests that he either didn't have time to eat at home this morning or he is waiting for a business associate to join him. "Excuse me, incase you hadn't noticed I am having breakfast quietly, and expecting someone to join me shortly. I'm sure you can see there are many other available in this restaurent." a confused Judas says to Ntokozo with a calm voice as he looks around to see if anyone is watching them.

"Oh but what if I am the person you have been waiting for Mr Masondo?" Ntokozo who is also wearing a grey suit and white shirt says with a sarcastic smile which makes Judas a little curious as he raises an eyebrow. "Except that you are not who I am expecting, is it? So who are you and how do you know my name?" he asks with a low voice as he once again looks around.

"So you don't like your wife's cooking Mr Masondo? Is that why you are having breakfast in a mall instead of your wife's kitchen? Or maybe there's 6rouble in paradise?" Ntokozo asks, once again sarcastically much to Judas annoyance as he puts his folk down. "Well since you who I am you will know that this is a bad idea right? Now who are you and what f*ck do you want?" he asks as he raises

his voice a little bit but soon remembers that he is in a restaurent and has caught one table's attention. "Oh relax Judas Masondo, this is a cartesy call..."Ntokozo says as he leans back on his chair. He seems very relaxed as though he has everything figured out.
"Now look here...it's either you tell me who you are and what the hell do you want or, get the f*ck out of here before something really bad happens to you." the vissibly annoyed Judas says as he once again looks around the restaurant because he is beginning to feel a little uncomfortable with this little invasion.
"Oh I almost forgot, that's what you rich people do hey...you love making threats don't you?" Ntokozo says as his face suddenly changes to being a little serious. "Now tell me, shouldn't a person like you be having bodyguards to avoid things like this from happening? Well, considering your corrupt nature, you must have some enemies right? Someone can blow your brains out on this table and walk away and that would be the end of your pathetic little life Judas Masondo, don't you think? But I do hope hope that at home you have that famiky secured because you are out here having eggs and beacon, they could be dead..."
Now those last words have Judas' heart racing as it dawns on him that this isn't a joke. He looks around again but notices that Ntokozo is by himself as everyone else in other tables are eating their food oblivious to what's going on here. He doesn't carry a gun so he begins to wonder if this is the end of his life because when he looks around the restaurant he doesn't see any security.
"What the hell is going on here? Who are you and what do you want?" he whispers in panic as he begins to breathe a little heavily, but Ntokozo reaches out in his jacket's pocket and pulls out a phone, much to Judas' relief who was certain that he was reaching for a gun. "Now I want you to take a look at that Mr Masondo..." Ntokozo says calmly wth a low voice as he gives Judas the phone. "What you are watching there is a live feed, okay? That's your wife

and daughters right there having breakfast in the kitchen...wow you really have a beautiful family. You really do, how old are your daughters?"
Now Judas knows this is for real as he begins to sweat under color with panic. "Oh sh*t no man...that's my family. Please, please, please...don't hurt them I beg you. I have money, I will give anything you wany man...please I beg you, please don't hurt my family..." he begs in whisper as he begins yo sweat in fear of his loved ones.
Luckily no one in this restarent seems to be noticing what's happening.
"You know what? That's what your son said also when he begged for his life...he offered money." Ntokozo says as his face changes to being a little disgusted at the man sitting across him. "So this thing runs in the family huh? You do things because you always think your money will make everything go away right? Is that how you Masondos do things? Throw money at every problem?"
"Oh so you killed my son? It was you who killed my son...why?" Judas who is tryinhg hard to contain his emotions says with a low voice as he looks at the man threatening him in the eyes but Ntokozo cuts in, "Hey, hey, hey...look...my men are at your house right now as you can see there. They are waiting for my orders to put a bullet in your wife and daughters..." he whipsers as his eyes begin to turn red with rage but the panicking Judas cuts in, "Please don't harm my family...I'm begging you" he begs in a whisper of panic. "I still don't even know who you are or who sent you, or what you want...but please don't harm my family. I'm sure we can come to some kind of agreement you and I."
"Oh some agreement, huh?" Ntokozo says with another sarcastic smile as he leans back on his chair. "Alright, now listen here and listen very carefully. I know who you are Mr Judas Masondo...you are a criminal pretending to be a businessman. You and your son laundered money for corrupt poiticians and dangerous individuals

didn't you? Law enforcement authorities are on you and all your business dealings and it doesn't look good for certain people. Well, now that your activities are out there in the open, the people I work for want you gone before you draw all attention to them."

"Uhmm...what do you mean by that?" Judas asks with a shaking voice as he looks around the tables. "It means you will leave now and go home...you and your family will pack up and leave the country in the next 3 hours." Ntokozo says with a straight face but Judas protests, "Leave home? But I uhmm...I can't...we can't just up and leave, please. Kids have school and I have some business to..." he says nervously but once again Ntokozo cuts in, "Well, that's not my problem now is it? What I know is that if you don't and I find you at your home or anywhere in the country I will kill you and your whole family. So you will be out of this country in 3 hours, you hear me?" he says with a firm voice.

"3 hours?" Judas exclaims, "But that's not even enough time to get ourselves organises and I would still need to book a..." He doesn't finish as Ntokozo interrupts, "Well luckily I did for you scambag..." he says as he pulls about 4 plane tickets and hands them over to the shocked Judas who takes and looks at them in disbelief.

"So now, all you have to do is pack and I don't think that should take more than an hour right? Unless ofcourse there's something else that's more important than your family that you have to take care of..." Ntokozo says as he raises an eyebrow but Judas is still in shock to respond as his eyes pop out. "Now Judas don't make qme kill you and your entire family when you can actually get away with it, you hear me? My man will be watching you to ensure you get on that plane in 3 hours time, so don't give them a reason to kill you and your family because they will. Your only chance of staying alive is to get on that plane."

"Singapore?" Judas asks in shock as he looks at the plane tickets. "Well, yeah...appatently it's a very beautiful country and you are

going to love it." Ntokozo says as he shrugs his shoulders. "You have a few businesses across assia so it won't be hard for you to access resources right?"
Judas is still in shock as he struggles to respond to this but Ntokozo continues, "I suggest that you leave now Masondo because that plane leaves in 3 hours and it is the only chance that will ensure you and your family are not dead by 13h:00 this afternoon." he says, to which Judas quickly gets up and walks out of the reastaurent without even paying the bill leaving Ntokozo stunned as he shakes his head before pulling out a few notes from his wallet to settle the bill.

***

Later on at the Gumede home everything looks normal as Ntokozo is sitting in the lounge with his family. He didn't tell them about the little encounter he had with Judas Masondo because he doesn't think they need to know about such things. As they watch TV there's a door bell ring, making everyone wonder who might that be. Perhaps for Ntokozo it's little unsettling after the visit to the restaurant earlier this morning. He knows for certain that Judas and his family indeed did board the plane at noon but now he wonders if he didn't alert anyone. "I will get it..." he says as he gets up and heads towards the door, much to everyone's anxioiusness.
He picks through the door and is surprised to see that it's Pearl who is standing on the other side. He quickly opens the door. "Uhmm Pearl? What are you doing here?" he asks anxiously as he looks outside to see if she is with anyone. "Uhmm hey...can I come in?" Pearl says with a nervous smile as she looks at the man she loves in the eyes.
"Oh uhmm...yeah ofcourse I'm sorry, please come in." a little confused Ntokozo says as gets out of the way so that Pearl can come in. He leads her to the lounge where everyone is. "Uhmm...Good

afternoon everyone..." Pearl says again with a nervous voice as she looks at Lungile and Dora who are also confused about what might be going on, seeing that Pearl is carrying a back pack. "Uhmm...we will give you guys some space to talk..." Dora relunctantly says as she attempts to get up but Pearl calls out, "Oh no please ma, that's not necesary because I would like to say something to the family..." she says nervously which makes Ntokozo wonder as he raises an eyebrow.

"Oh uhmm...alright then. Sweetheart, can you please excuse us for a minute?" Dora says as she smiles at Lungile's adaughter Mbali who quickly gets up and goes upstairs to allow the adults to have a conversation. Ntokozo and Pearl sit down next to each other while Dora and Lungile also sit next to each other as they wait anxiously to hear what's going on.

"Uhmm...ma, I'm so sorry to show at your home unannounced like this..." Pearl says with a low and nervous voice, "But I'm asuming that you know that Ntokozo has informed you about asking me to help him turn my father in? Well, if he didn't..." she says as she tuns and looks at Ntokozo, "I thought about it and yes I am willing to help you do this, whatever you need..."

This comes as a shock to everyone in the room as it is so unexpected. Lungile and Dora look at each other in disbelief because they know what this could mean for everyone.

"Uhmm...Pearl, are you, uhmm...are you sure about this? This is a really big decision and you know what it could mean for you..." the disbelieving Ntokozo asks with nervous voice as he looks at his family. Pearl thinks forever a second before saying, "Look you guys, I know that my father is a really bad man and for too long I have watched on and kept quiet when he did bad things in this community, but enough is enough now." as she looks a little emotional about all this.

"Uhmm...Pearl mntanami(my child) this is a big decision, but why? Why did you change your mind? Why now?" a shocked Dora asks as she looks at her daughter who is lost for words. "Uhmm...ma, I know that it's hard to believe okay but I'm really done with that man." Pearl says with atrembling voice. "But it's not just that he...uhmm...Uhmm...too much blood has been spilt here because of him."
"But Pearl do you realise that this means your father will disown you right? I mean if he doesn't do something worse even..." Lungile says as she raises an eyebrow but Ntokozo looks at her as if to say *'Really? Did you have to put it like that?'* but Pearl lets out a little smile and says, "Yeah I am aware of what my father will do Lungi..." as she looks down in shame but Dora cuts in, "So is it safe that this has something to do with mu son? Are you doing this for him?" she asks curiously, to which once again Ntokozo feels a little embarrassed about because he thinks his mom is asking something inaprorpiate. "Uhmm...mama, uhmm...part of it yes..." Pearl says with a little blush as she looks at Ntokozo. "Uhmm...mama, I love your son, I really do. From the very moment I laid my eyes on him I know that he is the man I really wanna be with, but father threatens that so I can't let that happen. I know that once I do this I will have to go far away and will never have a chance to be with your son, but atleast I'll kow that you guys are safe from my dad and his men. I thought long and hard about this guys so you don't have to worry about it. If I had t choose between my dad and Ntokozo and his family, it wasn't really a difficult dicision to make..."
Ntokozo is in disbelief and lost for words as he looks at this woman sitting next to him. "Oh wow Pearl..." Lungile says in disbelief. "Honestly I never thought I'd ever hear you say this. I judged you a lot because I thought you were exactly like your father, and now to hear you say this is so heart warming. That you'd give up your own father just for us..."

Suddenly everyone is a little emotional in this room as Lungile wipes a tear threatening to fall down her face. "Uhmm...my child I really don't know what to say..." says with a low voice as she looks a little embarrassed by all this. "To hear you willing to disown your father, who is your only family...for this family? Uhmm...my child, I was wrong about you and I don't think you have to go away. You can come and live here with us, this is your home now and the man you love is here in this house, right?"

This catches Ntokozo by surprise as he looks at his mother...this is the last think he thought he'd ever hear from her, but Lungile adds, "Yes my mom is right...you can come live here with us. You love Ntokozo and he loves yu back and since you are doing this, why should you go away and never see him again? We will figure it out as a family..."

Now these words are so heart warming for heart-warming for Pearl who lets out a little smile of joy but quickly snaps out of it as she says, "But the thing my dad or his men will come here if I stay here..." with a sad face. "The point of me going away is so that I don't bring war at your door-step. I want to make sure that you guys are safe from harm and that can't happen if I'm here with you."

"Look, we will deal with that together as well, right?" Ntokozo says with a nervous smile as he looks at his sister who says, "Yes, yes, yes...we shall deal with it together, as a family. You are family now." with a smile of assurance but Ntokozo jumps back in, "But now we just have to figure out how to do this right, okay? I think I may have a plan but it hasn't come together just yet but it will soon." he says but Pearl interjects, "Maybe this will help..." she says as she pulls a laptop from her backpack. "Uhmm...this laptop has my father's info, all of it: bank accounts, contacts, addresses where he keeps drugs, peole he works with and everything else..."

"Oh my god Pearl, how did you uhmm..." the speechless Ntokozo says as his eyes pop out in excitement but Pearl cuts in, "Don't worry it's not my dad's laptop, it's mine..." she says with a smile. "I coppied everything from his laptop...it has a lousy password. Some of the stuff is in flash drives in my bag, just incase. My dad won't notice anytghing that is off...atleast not until the police show up at his door. So will this help?"

"Ofcourse it will...I really don't know how to thank you for this babe..." Ntokozo says as he opens the laptop to look at some of the files but Pearl suddenly stands up. "Whoa, whoa, whoa...where are you going?" Ntokozo asks in panic as he closes the laptop. "Oh uhmm, I got to go back home before my dad's men notice that I am not in the house." Pearl says with a nervous voice but Dora interjects, "But won't that be dangerous for you after you brought this here?" she asks as she looks at Ntokozo who nods in agreement with the question. "Yes she is right Pearl..." Lungile adds with a worried face.

"Guys it will be dangerous the day it all goes down...that day I can't be at home. But if I don't come back today home today my father will come here guns blazzing before you have had any chance to go through those files. Just keep me informed when they are about to arrest him so that I will be out of the house..." Pearl says as she goes oiut the door leaving everyone stunned.

***

Few days later, Ntokozo finds himself in one of Ngubeni's depot where his drugs arive in trucks and stored up in containers. This looks like a very busy place and even though it's night, if he could guess, there's probably about 10 men or more who are security for those ofloading the drugs and storing them in a container. Since this is a solo mission to take down a drug operation, he has no back up here. In order to avoid detection Ntokozo decided to dress in all black and will use a semi automatic assault riffle with a silencer to eliminate threats and his targets. He is carrying a backpack full of exposives and ammunition, clearly today he is upping the ante a little bit.

He was lucky that this whole depot doesn't seem to have an alarm, which allowed him to cut through the fence undetected. As he sneaks behind two men who are having a smoke behind one of the containers he needs to be careful that he is not blown before he has accomplishes this mission because that will kind of complicate things for him.

It is super dark out here they can't see him, so he has a perfect aim at his targets. He takes a deep breathe as he looks through his night vision scope. His finger is on a trigger. As he breathes out the night cold air he squeezes the trigger and lets fly to bullets that hit the two men who go down in silence. He pauses for a second to see if they are moving but they are not...it was a perfect shot. He moves to the front of the container and luckily for him, it is opened. He doesn't want to use flashlight to look what's inside the container because he may be discovred. He then pulls out from his backpack what looks like C4 explosives with a transmitter or timer on it and put it inside the container.

It's time to move quickly before the two dead bodies are discovered by the other security guards. He c arfully moves to the back of this small building that looks like a toilet and hides behind a tank. From where he is he can see two men in overrolls moving packages that definately look like bricks of cocain from a truck to one of the containers. There is one security guard on the roof of that container so he has to be careful. He thinks for a second as though he is trying to calculate. He pulls out the magazine from his riffle to make the round count and then puts it back.

He quickly takes out the man on the roof who falls down to the ground which draws the attention of the two men who wants to see what just happened, but Ntokozo takes them out too before they could alert anyone else. He then quickly moves towards the truck

and fires through the windshield at the two men sitting upfront tallying the body count to 7.
There is still a few security personnel that are not accounted for yet so he will come back to the container after. He uses the truck as shield so that he can see who else is out there. There is a small vehicle that is parked a little far from the truck and there are about 3 security guards there talking and having a smoke. They have their guns in holsters so he quickly rush to them and fire shots that take all of them down. He is really pilling up these numbers as he changes the magazine. He quickly goes back to the container and once again puts explosives inside it before picking up the few bricks on the floor that the men he killed dropped. He put them inside the container before closing it.
Now he moves toward the gate where the rest of the security team is but he must be careful that they don't see him, so he uses the fence for cover. There's a fuel tank closer to the gate so he rushes towards it to use it as cover. He thinks for a second before pulling out another explosives and puts it under the tank. He quickly checks out his watch before setting his sights on the guards again.
These 4 guards also have their guns down and unaware of a threat behind them so Ntokozo quickly moves in and fires shots on them...they all go down. He then runs outside the gate and walks about 90 metres to his car that is parked under a tree in the dark bush. He gets inside and immediately makes a call.

phone rings
Man: "Hello..."
Ntokozo: "It's me...it's done. Now you can send your people..."
Man: "Okay good...you did great. This will certainly draw him and his associates out"
Ntokozo: "Thanks...That's the plan...did you get my mail?"
Man: "Oh yes man I did...how did you get those files?"

Ntokozo: "Don't worry about it man...the good thing is that you have them now."

Man: "It's the daughter isn't it? Man, is she going to be a problem?"

Ntokozo: "I said don't worry about it man, okay? She is not going to be a problem."

little silence

Man: "Does she know about you...who you work for?"

Ntokozo: "No...All she knows is that I'm taking the evidence to the police. I had to tell something. She ain't stupid."

Man: "I know man okay? I just wanted to make sure because you know...since you are attachd to this girl they if you are made they may use her to extract information."

silence

Ntokozo: "You don't worry about that man okay? She doesn't know anything."

Man: "And your family?"

Silence

Ntokozo: "Yeah they know some but not all. It's my family man, they had to know."

Man: "alright then..."

Ntokozo: "So you are watching Ngubeni's house, right?"

Man: "Don't worry man we are watching it and all the activities coming in and out of there. The sky is up running."

Ntokozo: "Good..."

Man: "We are watching your back too, you know, incase Ngubeni comes in there guns blazzing..."

Ntokozo: "So when are you moving in on him?"

Man: "Whenever you give us the go-ahead, but hey man I know that you want us to only arrest him but if he and his men engage us we will be forced to bring up the heat."

Silence

Ntokozo: "Understood..."

Man: "Okay...'keep in touch."
Call dropped
Ntokozo puts the phone down and then pulls out from his backpack what looks like a remote detonator before looking at his watch again. He takes a deep breathe and closes his eyes before pushing the botton leading to a have series of explosions at the depot. The yellow flashes and a billow of smoke can be seen for about a mile or two as the blast sound threatens to turn ears deaf for a second. Ntokozo drives off as he watches the smoke reaches the heavens and covers the night skies.

***

A couple of days later the explosion at the depot is all over the news and it's been since that night. Everything about the drugs is now out in the open and this spells bad news for Ngubeni who is sitting with very unhappy guests who have to find out what happened that night. He is usually confident and intimidating when he is with his own men but today it looks like there are other people who can intimidate him as well.
"So Ngubeni are you going to explain yourself or we must watch more news to learn how much you f*cked up?" one unhappy colored guy asks as he takes a sip of whiskey. This gentleman is with two other people, a Pakistani national and an indian guy. They also look very unhappy as they fix their eyes on the shaken Ngubeni. There is so much teansion in this lounge that every word you utter must be thoroughly thoutght of. "Uhmm...yes, yes, yes...I'm sorry about that Mr Abrahams, I think I can try to explain things..." a stuttering Ngubeni says with a nervous voice as he uickly turns the news off.
"You are going to try? To try? How about explaining to the rest of us what the f*ck happened that night? Huh?" the Pakistani guy shouts at him in anger. "I'm sorry Mr Imram, I can explain..." the terrified Ngubeni says with a trembling voice but Imram cuts in, "I

don't need your sorry goddamnit, I need you to explain yourself to us." he shouts even higher. "I want to know where is my f*cking money since I have already delivered 300kg of cocain to you and I want it now. Do you realise what you have done? Now that this whole thing is all over the news, do you know what's going to happen now?"

"Uhmm...Mr Imram, the thing is, the money was also burnt in one of the containers before it could be moved..." Ngubeni stutters in fear but once again Imram cuts in, "How the f*ck is that my problem, huh?" I delivered the coke and I want my money...I don't care how you get it but I want it. I don't care if the drugs burnt down or the police took whatever was left. I delivered them to your depot like we have always arranged."

"Look here Ngubeni...the people I trepresent also have already paid you in advance, in anticipation of this delivery. They want their product now or you pay back the money immediately, and after that our dealings with you are done." the Indian guy who has been sitting quietly says but Ngubeni pleads, "Oh come on Mr Naidoo don't say that okay? Why do we have to cut ties now?" he says with a nervous smile as he begins to sweat a little. "Look...just give me a little bit of time to sort this out I'm sure I can be able to deliver in the next couple of weeks or so. Please give me sometimes guys..."

"Couple of weeks? What the hell are you smoking Ngubeni?" Imram shouts as he puts his whiskey glass down. "Do you think we have a couple of weeks to joke around? No...what you will do is that you will go get my money now or things will really get bad for you. My people don't have time to play games with you Ngubeni...you understand that?"

"How much was in that container?" Abrahams asks curiously with calm voice. "Uhmm...about R350m give or take..." Ngubeni says with a low voice as though he is embarrassed but Abrahams cuts in, "R350m? What the hell Ngubeni? Who the hell keeps so much koney in one place, huh?" he asks as his eyes pop out in shock but Ngubeni jumps in again, "No it's actually was a consolidated money collected from different sites. I was going to move it yesterday to where it was going to be cleaned before I can access it. This is how we have always done it guys, but this was not expected at all..."he says as he looks down in shame.

This leads to a very uncomfortable and awkward silence as Ngubeni's guests look at each other in disbelief. "Ngubeni, do you realise that if all of this leads to you, you are on your own?" Abrahams asks politely. "No one is coming back to get you. The people I work with can't be seen to be associated with something like this, so if your name comes up and peole start scrutinizing your associates, you know what that means."

Now this is beginning to terrify Ngubeni as he wipes the sweat from his forehead. "Look Abrahams there's no need for this okay? I will fix this situation as soon as possible, you can trust me..." he says nervously but Naidoo jumps in, "You better have this handled Ngubeni and very fast..." he says with an angry face. "You must deliver the product in the next 3 days or pay back my f*cking money, otheriwse you know what's gonna be. This is not the business for ametures, you know that. We have mouths to feed out there on the streets and you are making a whole lots of us look bad Ngubeni."

"Yes, I want my money in 3 days Mr Ngubeni, otherwise things will get ugly, I can promise you that." Imram adds as he is fuming before Abrahams intejects, "Well, you know what to do Ngubeni. Clean this sh*t up or it will be you who will be cleaned," he says as the three gentlemen stand up and walk out of the lounge with Ngubeni following to escourtg them to their cars.

He watches on as the men get into 3 separate cars and drive off outside the gate, before calling his men back inside the house. Needless to say that he is fuming over this visit, no doubt Ngubeni

will get it out on his men who look nervous already as they all sit down on the edge of their seats.
"Now who amongst you want to tell me what the hell happened the other day, huh? Who the f*cked my drugs and my money?" Ngubeni asks with a rather measured voice as he tries to control his temper. He goes straight to the side table and pours himself a double and downs it all in one go. This spells trouble for his men who look at each. "Well? someone please speak up because I need answers right now. Who the f*ck did this, huh? Who the f*ck did this?" he shouts at his men as he throws the glass to the wall and it shames into pieces leading to everyone diving for cover.
Suddenly he takes a deep breathe to calm himself as he looks to the ceiling. "Uhmm...Bra J we supsect that it is the same person who has been killing our guys..." one of the guys says but Ngubeni cuts in, "I know that it is the same person but I'm asking who?" he says with a low voice as he closes his eyes as though he is praying.
"Uhmm...I'm sorry boss we still don't know yet..." another man says as he looks don in shame. "Well then you better found out soon because if you don't we will all be dead men in 3 days time. Imram wants his money and or his drugs back but all of it burnt down at the depot and ypu idiots don;t even know who did it." He goes back to the side table to pour himself another double and his men can only hope that he doesn't smash another glass on the wall as they all look a little anxious. "Maybe in the meantime we can move some funds around from the other offshore accounts to buy ourselves time." Ngubeni says calmly.
He pulls his phone from the jacket pocket and fidles with it but suddenlt his eyes pop out in shock. "No f*cking way..." he shouts in disbelief. "What is it boss?" on of the men asks in confusion as he looks at the others. "What the f*ck happened to my money? All my accounts are empty...where is my money?" Ngubeni shouts as he throws the phone to the man who asked.

Everyone suddenly gathers around the phone to see what's going on and everyone is shocked and confused. "What happened to my money? Who has access to these accounts?" a disbelieving Ngubeni asks in panic. "No one boss...you are the only one who has access, not even your daughter does." one of the men says nervously not knowing what will happen after. They are all scared at this point because everybody kn ows that no one can mess with Ngubeni's money and get away with it.
"Peal...Pearl..." Ngubeni shouts as he looks upstairs. "Pearl...where the hell is she? Go upstairs and call my daughter to come down right now..." he orders one of his men who quckly goes upstairs to Pearl's bedroom. A moment later the man comes down and says, "Boss, she isn't here..." much to Ngubeni's fury as he as he shouts, "Damnit..." on top of his voice. He takes a second to think and then says "You...go to Criston street and get the guns, we are going hunting. And you...get me a few extra men if you can get them. I think it's time I remind people that you don't mess with Jabulani Ngubeni." he orders his men who all quickly move out of the house.

Chapter 15

Showdown

"So what happened last night Pearl? I mean we didn't get to talk about it because you looked quite frightened? Is everything okay?" anxious Ntokozo asks a nervous looking Pearl as they sit on the breakfast table on a Monday morning. Everyone is present for breakfast except for Mbali who has gone to school. "Yeah child, what happened at home? Did you and your father fight again?" Dora probes with a concerned face as she looks at Lungile who is just as curious because Pearl knocked at the Gumede door very late last night and unexpectedly. They didn't want to put pressure on her since she looked shaken.

"Uhmm...I'm sorry guys that I had to show up like that unannounced but I had to come over here..." Pearl says with a nervous voice as she puts her fork down but Dora quickly interjects, "No, no, no mntanami(my child)...you don't have to apologies. I told you that we are family and you can come over here anytime alright? So, what happened?" she asks curiously as she takes a sip of her orange juice.

"So, uhmm...first of all...what's on the news about the depot on fire, was that you?" Pearl asks as she turns her attention on Ntokozo who seems to be caught off guard by that question as he looks at his mother and sister. It's not like he can hide any of this from her...she already knows most of it. "Uhmm...Pearl you know what was in those containers, so I couldn't just let..." he says with a low voice but Pearl cuts in, "No it's okay, you did great." she says, much to everyone's surprise in the table. They could have been expecting a different response to this but she keeps proving them wrong.

"Look, I know that you did what you had to do alright?" Pearl continues. "But unfortunately you made some people very happy and they were at my home yesterday. They came to see my dad demanding their drugs or their money or they will kill him. There were three guys...colored guy named Abrahams if I remember well...there was an indian guy called Naidoo and some Pakistani national."

This suddenly brings an akward moment in the room as Lungile and Dora look at each other and feel sorry for Pearl. "Uhmm...I'm sorry for this Pearl. I know that he's your father and it was never our intention to..." Lungile says but Pearl quickly cuts in, "No Lungi, you did nothing wrong okay? You have nothing to apologies for. My dad got himself in this mess and too many people have suffered because of him." she says with a low voice as she looks down as though she is ashamed. "But they didn't harm him, right?" Ntokozo asks anxiously as he looks at his mother.

"No, no, no...they didn't." Pearl says with a sigh. "But they said they want their money and drugs in 3 days or they will kill him. Those people don't look like they joke a lot." She suddenly looks a little anxious. "Uhmm...the people you have mentioned I think I have heard about Naidoo, very well known and dangerous drug dealer in Chartsworth but I haven't heard of Abrahams. We can assume though that they are all drug dealers, right?" Ntokozo says as he shrugs his shoulders. He feels bad because he knows he has just lied to Pearl and that what he has told is half truth but it has to be this way.

"Yeah definately and if they are threatening Pearl's father it means they have something big to lose..." Lungile says as she shrugs her shoulder and her mother nods in agreement.

This conversation is interrupted by a phone call that Ntokozo receives. He looks at his phone and says, "Excuse me guys, I got to take this." as he moves to the lounge where the people in the dinning room can't hear.

Ntokozo: "Hey man..."

Man: "Dude there is movement okay? Ngubeni and his men have left the house...we are tracng them and I think they are coming your way."
Ntokozo: "Alright? And where are you?"
Man: "Don't worry there are men coming your way now and others are following Ngubeni and his men."
Ntokozo: "So what? Do I engage when they come here?"
Man: "No...I don't think that's a good idea alright? Just try and stall him untill we are in position..."
Ntokozo: "Alright then...see you soon."
Call dropped

***

Ntokozo comes back to the kitchen and everyone can see that he is troubled by something. "Mntanami(my child), what's wrong?" Dora asks with a worried face but Ntokozo doesn't seem to know how to answer that. "Ntokozo, yini(what)? What's going on?" Pearl also asks as she looks at Lungile who is just ask curious.
"Uhmm...your father and his men are coming here." Ntokozo says with a low and seemingly worried voice. "What? How do you know?" a shocked Pearl asks as her eyes pop out in disbelief. "Doesn't matter but I suggest that you guys go upstairs okay? I will handle this..." Ntokozo says as he looks at everyone on the table but Pearl quickly intejects, "No ways, I'm not going anywhere okay?" she says. "You guys can go upstairs but I'm going to stay here with Ntokozo." she says as she turns to Dora and Lungile. Ntokozo realises it's pointless to argue with her.
"Look, I don't think that's a good idea Pearl okay? Just come with us, let Ntokozo handle this please." Lungile pleads as panic sets in.
"Look guys, my father is not going to come here guns blazing because he knows I'm here. And when he sees me he is not going to shoot anyone okay so please, just relax okay? He will want to talk."

"In that case then we are all staying..." Lungile says with a firm voice which is almost irritating Ntokozo as he looks at her. "But why do you guys complicate this, huh?" he says as he throws his hands in the air in frustration but his mother interjects, "No we are not complicating anything okay? If you two stay down here then we are all staying, okay?" she says as she suddenly moves to the lounge, much to Ntokozo's annoyance. Suddenly everyone moves to the lounge to wait for the apparent storm that is coming.

The next 15 minutes seem like eternity and the anxious wait for the family as they await their unknown fate. Ntokozo in particular seems so worried about his mother and sister because he had promised to protect them from any harm. He can only hope that Ngubeni is not going to come in here guns blazing and start shooting all over the place. He is also worried about Pearl because after what she did, who knows what her father would do. He is a ruthless man who loves money and power and how that he took that away from him, he may get out of control in search of revenge. A moment later the family can hear the sound of cars pulling out of the driveway because Ntokozo deliberately left the gate opened. He stands and goes to the window to see who it might be. There are 2 cars in the driveway and out comes 3 men from the front car and another 3 from the car that is behind...Ngubeni was in the second car.

The 6 men carrying heavy weapons and led by Ngubeni approach the door but surprisingly Ntokozo is calm about it as he opens the door before they could knock. "Gentlemen..." he says calmly with a straight face which seems to throw Ngubeni off a little bit because he probably was expecting to be met with a terrified face. Now this doesn't tell him much about what Ntokozo could or could not know so he thinks for a second before saying, "Gumede..." with a straight face himself. "Mr Gumede...how can I help you?" Ntokozo

says calmly as he stands at the door unsighting Ngubeni from seeing who is inside.
"May we come inside, so that we can talk?" Ngubeni pleads calmly, which also surpises Ntokozo a little probably because he also was expecting hostility. "Wow, I have never heard of talks that involved machine guns, not even during CODESA . Are you sure it will be just talk?" Ntokozo asks as he mantains a straight face.
"Well that's the plan Gumede, unless you have something else in mind..." Ngubeni says calmly with a straight face which makes Ntokozo thinks for a se =cond as he looks at him in the eyes to try and read him. He takes a deep sigh before moving out of the way for Ngubeni and his men to come in, which seems to terrify Dora and Lungile as they look at Pearl who seems to be infuriated by her father than she is scared. "Oh you see? What's the poit of fighting Gumede when all I have come for is right here..." Ngubeni says with a sarcastic smile when his eyes are met with Pearl's who is sitting next to Lungile in the lounge.
"Sanibonani endlini(hello everyone)" Ngubeni says with another sarcastic smile as he comes to sit down on the lone couch while his 5 men stand behind him with guns, but no one greets back.
"Uhmm...ndodakazi(daughter) I'm here to fetch you, so please grab your things so that we can go home. You know that you are the only familiy I have. I have missed you so much." Ngubeni says as he looks at Pearl.
Ntokozo who left the door opened comes and sits down next to Pearl who can't even stand to look at her father. "Uhmm...Mrs Gumede I want to thank you for looking after my daughter here but as you may know, she is the only family I have now, so I have come to take her home." Ngubeni says but before Dora could repsond Pearl quickly interjects, "No dad, I'm not coming with you..." she says as she looks away from him but this comes as unexpected to Ngubeni who raises an eyebrow. "Sweetheart what do you mean?

But it's time to go home now okay? This isn't your home..." he says as he lets out a little smile.

"Dad I said no...I'm not going to that house with you." Pearl says as she raises her voice a little bit when she turns to look at her father but Ngubeni smiles and shakes his head in disbelief. "Uhmm Ntokozo, this is what I meant when I said 'unless you have something else in mind'..." Ngubeni says as his face suddenly changes to being serious. "Now this will be the right time to talk some sense into her okay? Because I have come here in peace and I would love to leave this place in peace but your friend here is making this difficult for me."

"Dad please leave him out of this okay? He or his family have got nothing to do with this dicision to not go back home with you..." Pearl says with defiance as she looks at Dora and Lungile who are now beginning to look terrified. "Dad I can't stand and watch you hurting people anymore and making the lives of other families a nightmare. No dad...I can't be part of that anymore so if you want to kill me then go ahead and kill me but I'm done with you. You can disown me if you want but I can't be that naive little girl that turns a blind eye to every evil thing you do okay? So please just leave us alone and we will leave you alone."

Ngubeni shakes his head one more time in disbelief of what he is hearing. "So you are really insistant on testing me huh?" he says with a low voice as he looks down for a second. "And stop being silly, you are my daughter...I love you, why would I wanna kill you. I just want us to go home and sort out whatever our differences are like adults." As the moment becomes tense Ntokoz is becoming anxious as he keeps looking towards the door. "But as for you..." Ngubeni continues as he looks at Ntokozo with sharp eyes of hate. "I knew from the moment you made your way into my daughter's life that you will be trouble. Ever since she met you she has become so defiant and challenges me all the tme...which is something she never used to do that. My Pearl was always a very sweet girl that focused on growing the family business...she and I made a promises that we will always stand side by side as we grew the Ngubeni empire. But now she doesn't listen."

"Dad, leave him alone...he has got nothing to do with this..." Pearl says as she raises her voice a little but her father interjects, "Shut up...I'm not talking to you, I'm talking to him..." he shouts which terrifies Dora and Lungile who had never actually seen Ngubeni's outbursts before. They had always heard stories but today they get to see it for the first time and it is terrifying.

Ngubeni pulls out a gun from his back and points it at Ntokozo who doesn't move an inch but looks at the burrel like he has accepted his fate. "Oh no please Mr Ngubeni, I'm begging you okay? Please don't kill my son..." Dora shouts as she begs for her son's life. "Oh but that's not really up to me Mrs Gumede, is it?" Ngubeni says with a straight face as he fixes his eyes on Ntokozo. "You tell my daughter to come with me now or your son's brain will be all over this coffee table...you hear me? So what is it gonna be Mrs Gumede? I don't wanna kill anyone but then again, that's up to you."

"Dad please don't this okay?" Pearl says with a begginbg voice as she lets out a tear for the man she loves but Ngubeni interjects, "Oh better yet...Pearl, if you don't get up and leave with me now you will be mopping the brains of this family you have now adopted...is that what you want?" he says with a straight face and suddenly Dora and Lungile have guns pointed at them by the 5 men behind Ngubeni's couch.

As the Gumede family stares at death in the face they hear shouts, "Police...Police...Police...No body moves." as about a dozen law enforcement officers storm the house with guns pointed at Ngubeni and his men. Even though he is a hardcore gangster he knows that they are outnumbered by the officers but perhaps what goes through his mind is that he doesn;t want his daughter caught in the crossfire when everyone starts shooting. So he and his men drop their weapons to the floor as the officers quickly come in to put handcuffs on them, much to Ntokozo and his family's relief.

Pearl watches on with a broken heart as she sees police take her father away into one of the cars. Few tears drop as her father turns around to look at her in what seems like the very last time before one of the officers shoves his head inside the car. She immediately clings on to Ntokozo for comfort as the cars drive off the gate.

Chapter 16

Start over

"So uhmm...how are you feeling today? I know that you said are not ready to talk about all that has happened but just know that I and everyone in the family is here for you okay? No pressure..." Ntokozo says with a polite voice to Pearl that he finds sitting under the tree on the Gumede lawn. It's been about two weeks or so since Pearl's father Jabulani Ngubeni was arrested by law enforcement right at this home and its a very emotional period for the only child. She's been living at the Gumede home simce then while trying to sort herself out and the Gumedes have welcomed her with open arms as one of their own.

Lungile has already updated her boyfriend and friends about what had happened recently and while Thulani felt maybe it's not a good time for him to propose to Pearl considering what had happened, Mpumi and Lindiwe aren't happy about Pearl living at the Gumede house and Lungile has been trying in vain to convince her friends that she's not all that bad.

After the arrest of Ngubeni all his powerful and well-known associates seems to have distanced themselves from him and no one is taking his calls, but then again this is exactly what Abrahams told him would happen if any of this led to him. But perhaps what hurts Ngubeni even more is the fact that his own daughter, the only family he has does not take his calls, let alone coming to visit him in a cell. Ofcourse there's still a very long way to go before this goes to trial and a person like Ngubeni can never be ruled out of getting out of this situation, perhaps something that terrifies Pearl more because her father is not someone you can double-cross and get away with it. At the Ngubeni home they have been trying to deal with the trauma following what had happened two weeks ago. They had never had people storming the house with guns before so staring at death in the face couldn't have been easy for any of them, well...maybe except Ntokozo who has been in these kinds of situations before many times. His situation with his handler is not yet clear-whether he still works for them or not.

In the end, detectives David Skhosana and Lindiwe Zulu can't seem to piece the puzzles together in the case they are dealing with as they seem to hit the brick wall at every turn, but police commissioner Ncube is the one more confused after he learned that Judas Masondo left the country without saying a word. Ngubeni's associate Imram had to quickly leave the country after Ngubeni's arrest before his name is drawn into this saga while Naidoo went dark until this storm has settled. Well, Abrahams has made his position clear. In the end no one knows what had happened to that depot but all evidence lead Ngubeni and him alone.

"Arg no I'm really sorry about that if I have been a bad company to you guys the lastg couple of weeks. It's a huge adjustment for me and there's a lot to process right now..." Pearl says with a low voice but Ntokozo interjects, "Come on, there's no need for you to apologies okay? It is understandable and I'm sorry that it had to end the way it did." he says softly as he takes her hand.

"Nah it's okay...it had to end the way it did Ntokozo..." Pearl says with a smile of assurance so to ease Ntokozo's guilt. "I won't lie it was hard for me to see my father being handcuffed in front of me knowing that I had a hand in that but I don;t regret it. If anything, I wish there was a way of making up to all those families that he ruined. I know that this community painted me in the same brush as him and it would take a lot for anyone to accept me agian, but I believe that selling all the family businesses will give an opportunity to start afresh somewhere. It was not an easy decision ofcourse but a neccesary one."

"I hear you..." Ntokozo says with a somewhat dissapointed voice as though he is embarrassed. "So uhmm...are there any buyers yet? I mean for any of these businesses-the butchery; Car Wash and Hardware store?" he asks curiously as he takes a sip of his beer that he brought with him.

"Oh yeah actually I forgot to tell you guys...I got the buyer the other day." Pearl says as her eyes brighten up with excitement. "Oh really?" Ntokozo says as she raises an eyebrow of curiosity. "Yeah, yeah, yeah I did hey..." Pearl says with a smile. "You remember when I had to go to the mall last week? Yeah I had to meet this businessman who represented a consortium. They were looking for businesses in townships that they can revamp and upgrade so they made me an offer. My lawyer is currently going through the offer and I am expecting that we will close the deal soon."

"Oh wow this is really great news babe, I'm really happy for you, you know that?" an excited Ntokozo says with a smile. "Thank you my love...It was notg easy for me I won't lie. I thought I'd grow with these businesses and lift the Ngubeni name you know..." Pearl says as she becomes sad a little bit. "But considering what has happened the past few months, this can only be good for me. It will give me time to figure out what I want to do next and how. Oh and I had a good look at the house you got for me, it is really beautiful. I think it is what I really need right now to recharge. But I wish you guys could have let me pay you for it, you know..."

"Oh come on it was a gift okay? It is something the family wanted to do for you..." Ntokozo says with a blushing smile. "Besides, it's not like you will be gone forever right? I mean, this is just for until the dust settle this side and then you can come back and stay with us. This is what me, mother and my sister want. We want you here because this is your home now." He seems pleased as he says that. "Your family is too kind and I really appreciate you guys very much." Pearl says with a smile as she invites Ntokozo for a kiss, which he accepts as they have that moment they have been longing for, for a little while now.

"Alright then, now please tell me something okay?" Pearl says as they break the kiss. "So the whole thing about the arrest of my father, how did you do it Ntokozo? I mean, I have been trying to play that over and over in my head...you know someone in the police service?"

Now Ntokozo can't say that he didn't expect this question to come at some point but he had never given it much of a thought about how he'll respond. He thinks for a second before saying, "Uhmm...tell you what, when you come back home I will tell you all about it okay?" with a smile that makes Pearl to think for a second as she raise an eyebrow. She wants to say something but then she decides against it as she lets out a little smile and shakes her head. Ntokozo is relieved to be off the hook when he sees his sister coming towards them from the house. Much needed change of topic this.

"Hey guys...uhmm, Ntokozo mama needs you in the house right now." Lungile says with a smile and Ntokozo quickly stands up and rush into the house, leaving the girls alone to have a moment.

"Uhmm...so are you better now?" Lungile asks with a low voice as she sits down. "Uhmm...yeah I think I'm readjusting to the new reality hey..." Pearl says with a smile. "That's good but you know...honestly I wish you didn't have to have to go away for a little while. I think I was getting to having a sister around and now it's back to square one?" Lungile says as she looks a little sad over this but Pearl takes her hand and says, "Arg sis, it's gonna be okay. I mean, who said you can't visit for a weekend or week or even months? Hahah...I mean, whenever you want you can just show up and I will be happy to have you."

"I will definately take you up on that offer hey..." a comforted Lungile says with a smile as she squeezes Pearl's hands. "But seriously

I do understand why things have to be this way for now and I know that soon you will come back here, home. And I know that you are my brother's girl but you will always be my sister..."

These words warm Pearl's heart as she becomes a little emotional about it. "You don't understand how much these words mean to me sisi. I mean, I also have longed for a sister and now here you are and I promise to never let you and your family down. I will never hurt your brother in any way." she says as she tries hard to hold back a tear from fallimng down. "Speaking of vows...when are you two making vows to each other? Hahaha..." Lungile asks as she bursts out laughing but this makes Pearl blush as she says, "Oh come on now Lungi, really? hahaha..." as she laughs back.

"Okay then, okay let's go inside...mama has prepared lunch for us." Lungile says as she takes Pearl by the hand and they walk into the house holding each other like sisters, something you wouldn't have thought will happen not so long ago.

The End

About the Author

Bongani Mpanza is an author, a musician, a song writer and a singer.

Milton Keynes UK
Ingram Content Group UK Ltd.
UKHW010616250624
444652UK00001B/86